BLOOD FOR BLOOD

The "repairman" pulled a badge from under his shirt and flashed it at the stunned colonel.

He grinned, "Major Bobby Samuels, C.I.D. investigator, Military Police. You are under arrest, Colonel, for rape and carnal knowledge under section 120 of the UCMJ, and before you say another word, I want you to clearly understand your rights under the Uniform Code of Military Justice."

The colonel started to speak and Major Samuels's hand lashed out, slapping the older officer across the cheek as he held his finger up to his smiling lips in a shushing gesture, saying, "Shhh. I don't want to violate your rights."

The colonel whimpered and Bobby's hand lashed out again, smacking the colonel once more across the face, and he again made a shushing gesture, saying, "I told you to be quiet, you disgusting pile of dog vomit. Just stand there and bleed, Colonel, but no more whimpering. You are already an unconscionable disgrace to the uniform and the entire officers corps—don't whine and cry like a baby, too. Just bleed."

CRIMINAL INVESTIGATION DETACHMENT

DON BENDELL

BERKLEY BOOKS, NEW YORK

THE BERKLEY PUBLISHING GROUP
Published by the Penguin Group
Penguin Group (USA) Inc.
375 Hudson Street, New York, New York 10014, USA
Penguin Group (Canada), 90 Eglinton Avenue East, Suite 700, Toronto, Ontario M4P 2Y3, Canada
(a division of Pearson Penguin Canada Inc.)
Penguin Books Ltd., 80 Strand, London WC2R 0RL, England
Penguin Group Ireland, 25 St. Stephen's Green, Dublin 2, Ireland (a division of Penguin Books Ltd.)
Penguin Group (Australia), 250 Camberwell Road, Camberwell, Victoria 3124, Australia
(a division of Pearson Australia Group Pty. Ltd.)
Penguin Books India Pvt. Ltd., 11 Community Centre, Panchsheel Park, New Delhi—110 017, India
Penguin Group (NZ), Cnr. Airborne and Rosedale Roads, Albany, Auckland 1310, New Zealand
(a division of Pearson New Zealand Ltd.)
Penguin Books (South Africa) (Pty.) Ltd., 24 Sturdee Avenue, Rosebank, Johannesburg 2196,
South Africa

Penguin Books Ltd., Registered Offices: 80 Strand, London WC2R 0RL, England

This is a work of fiction. Names, characters, places, and incidents either are the product of the author's imagination or are used fictitiously, and any resemblance to actual persons, living or dead, business establishments, events, or locales is entirely coincidental. The publisher does not have any control over and does not assume any responsibility for author or third-party websites or their content.

CRIMINAL INVESTIGATION DETACHMENT

A Berkley Book / published by arrangement with the author

PRINTING HISTORY
Berkley mass-market edition / January 2006

Copyright © 2006 by Don Bendell Inc.
Cover illustration by Ben Perini.
Cover design by Steve Ferlauto.
Interior text design by Kristin del Rosario.

ISBN: 0-425-20738-2

BERKLEY®
Berkley Books are published by The Berkley Publishing Group,
a division of Penguin Group (USA) Inc.,
375 Hudson Street, New York, New York 10014.
BERKLEY is a registered trademark of Penguin Group (USA) Inc.
The "B" design is a trademark belonging to Penguin Group (USA) Inc.

PRINTED IN THE UNITED STATES OF AMERICA

10 9 8 7 6 5 4 3 2 1

Today, the first day I began writing this, it is less than two weeks to our presidential election of 2004; my second youngest son, Brent, is awaiting the birth of his daughter any moment, and is in Phase 3 of training at Fort Bragg, North Carolina, earning his green beret; my youngest son, Joshua, just told me he, too, is joining the U.S. Army and wants to also earn his green beret; I just watched *Stolen Honor—Wounds that Never Heal* and am humbled and angered; we have Green Berets deployed all over the world in the War on Terrorism; my friend Jimmy Dean, a fixture for decades in the Special Forces Association, retired recently; Colonel Aaron Banks, our very first commander of Special Forces, passed on to Higher Headquarters not long ago; and my friend Colonel Roger Donlon, first recipient of the Medal of Honor in Vietnam, was made Honorary Colonel of the Regiment in the Special Forces Association.

Only three out of one hundred earn their green beret and flash, and it is one of the proudest accomplishments of my life. This book is dedicated to all those silent professionals of the U.S. Army Special Forces who have worn or are now wearing that honorable forest green "Badge of Distinction," the Green Beret.

I must note, wearing my own green beret, I was present at Fort Bragg on March 3, 2005, when Brent was awarded his green beret; he has been assigned to the 1st Special Forces Group and leaves for Iraq as this book is released. Joshua is now in training to earn his green beret. President George W. Bush was reelected and is serving his second term.

I want to say a special thank-you to a former Green Beret Sergeant Major, a fellow "Dak Peker," ODA-242-Co B-5th SFGA-1st SF. For your advice on certain aspects in this book and your service to our nation, to my friend Bill "BOOM" Roderick. "Thanks, Bro."

"A soldier of the Great War, known unto God."

—RUDYARD KIPLING, 1917

SABOTEUR

Baghdad

Security was tight in the Green Zone and there were "night eyes" watching all around, but the Saboteur was very accomplished and nobody would ever suspect him. His trained hands moved quickly and efficiently as he opened the military HUMVEE door, hopped in, and inserted the one-pound block of C4 under the passenger seat. He placed the small battery next to it and attached the positive wire to the wire on one side of the plastic alligator clip. He then carefully hooked the negative wire to the negative pole and to the negative jaw on the clip. The little wooden plug was then very carefully held between the two jaws of the alligator clip, while using his right hand, he carefully took the piece of army trip wire attached to the wooden plug and wrapped it around the inside passenger door handle of the military HUMMER.

When the door opened, the wooden plug would be pulled out of the alligator clip and the metal contacts would touch, completing the circuit and detonating the electronic blasting cap stuck into the block of plastic explosive, and boom. He looked at his expedient little system, backed away from the door, nodded at a passing PFC, and walked off into the night.

One of the MPs watching from their high building perch said, "Who was that?"

"Just a soldier putting something in his vehicle," his sidekick said.

The Saboteur returned to his barracks and rummaged in his rucksack. It was already packed. Tomorrow he would be in Basrah, while pieces of an infidel captain and his driver would be put into body bags by fellow soldiers, tears streaming down their cheeks, suppressed sobs bursting out from time to time. He grinned at the thought.

The muscular young man changed into shower clogs and wrapped a towel around his waist. Grabbing his shaving kit, he headed for the shower room. The Saboteur looked at his handsome face in the mirror. The pale blue eyes, the short red hair, the slight scar over the left eyebrow, and the broad shoulders. A blond-haired corporal walked into the shower room and nodded.

The Saboteur grinned at him in the mirror. "What d'ya say, man?"

He grinned at his own face in the mirror. Nobody could ever guess he was a personal assassin sent into the midst of U.S. military ranks by his first cousin, the Director, Osama bin Laden.

The blond left the room, and the Saboteur went into a toilet stall and locked the door. He pulled his cloth prayer mat out from under his wraparound towel and laid it on the floor. Now nude, he knelt on it facing toward Mecca and began to pray.

This was the hardest thing for him, making opportunities to pray several times day without getting caught. Other than that, he felt very superior to the infidels and could easily outfox them. To him, they were all stupid and should be destroyed. He even felt that way when he lived in Athens and attended the Ohio State University, and when he attended high school in Canton, Ohio.

He remembered riding by the Pro Football Hall of Fame, one of America's premier pieces of architecture and a shrine to something that occupied so much of American males' energy and time. He was laughing at them about the time wasted watching others "do," and he thought to himself, "What fools!" knowing he would go to Paradise one day with many virgins to serve him at his pleasure, especially after he started to rid the world of unbelievers.

He had been doing so ever since the War in Iraq began, and so far, the U.S. Army had never suspected that the terrorist was one of their very own, almost. The Saboteur figured they did not have anybody good enough to ever figure it out.

ABUSE OF POWER

Fort Benning

Adolpho Luis Rodriguez was graying along the temples, so he had started using black hair dye on the short stubble covering his weathered head, and he took Viagra regularly, although he felt a bit upset to his stomach afterward. To him, it was well worth it, especially now.

She whimpered beneath him, so he grabbed her throat and chuckled cruelly, as her face started turning red.

"Make you wanna cum?" he said. "You always love it rough, don't ya, Baby Girl?"

Karen Gramby had been raped before, when she was in ninth grade, and she immediately developed a weight problem. Although she knew it was not her fault, there was something in her that made her blame herself. Psychologically, she felt that if she was heavier and appeared less "attractive sexually," it would deter any future such betrayal. Now she was once again sprawled on the leather sofa in Rodriguez's office, with him sweating and pumping furiously between her legs, sometimes choking her, pinching her nipples until they were bruised, and occasionally slapping her.

She whimpered, "Please stop, sir? Please?"

He grabbed her hair, jerking her head back, and clenched his teeth, getting more excited seeing her fear.

"Shut up, little bitch," he said. "You know you always love it like this!"

"No!" she finally screamed bravely. "You keep raping me! I hate you! I hate you! You're older than my father!"

She might just as well have poured a bucket of ice water on him. He immediately withdrew and raged around his office totally naked. He came back to her and pointed. His face was crimson.

"Young lady, you have wanted this every time. You like it rough," he raged. "You always show me that, and you better not ever report it! Nobody will ever believe you, and I will court-martial your ass! Understand?"

He pulled on his BDU trousers, and then his OD T-shirt, and finally his BDU jacket. She looked at the crossed cannons on one lapel and the eagle on the other. Now, in the uniform of a full bird colonel, he was much more intimidating to the young specialist 4th class.

Adolpho was quite simply a classic "power rapist." He honestly thought this young lady and the other ones he had violated enjoyed the rough sex. Karen was a little overweight but had a beautiful face and was his adjutant's secretary. In fact, he would frequently walk out to the adjoining office to ask the S-1 a question just so he could lust after Karen.

Adolpho raped his first victim shortly after graduating from artillery OCS at Fort Sill, Oklahoma. The young second lieutenant went home on leave and ran into a girl from high school who had snubbed him way back when, but was now entranced by the uniform and maturity she saw. When she tried to report the date rape by the new Tac Officer to his company commander, the first sergeant intervened, wanting to protect the image of his boss, his company, and the army. He simply frightened her away with ominous warnings about repercussions if she pursued the matter any further.

As Adolpho rose in rank, so did his protectors, as he had E-9s protecting him the past several years, instead of E-8s. None of them were bad guys. They were just conditioned to be very loyal to their commander, no matter how much he was despised, and he indeed was.

The chain of command and unspoken loyalty system worked well for him, until the next E-9, Command Sergeant Major Darryl Shanahan, came along into the picture. He was the proud papa of three teenaged daughters, Brandi, Brenna, and Brooke, and they were very close.

Karen had seen him interacting with his daughters at a unit family day picnic, and she felt she could trust him. She was correct. The daughters were twenty, nineteen, and eighteen years old respectively. That day at the picnic, she witnessed two separate incidents. Many army gatherings had a tendency to get "gross," and the picnic was no exception. Four letter words were flying around Shanahan's daughters and he paid no attention, but one E-4 had too much to drink and made some very lewd and suggestive remarks to the eighteen-year-old daughter, Brooke. The good sergeant major overheard, and the spec-4's heels may or may not have touched the ground when Top's right hand closed around his bicep and whisked him off to the side. Nobody could hear the tongue lashing, but he was standing at attention during it, and afterward he walked over to Brooke and stood at attention again, apologizing profusely and vowing never to disrespect her again.

The second incident involved Brenna, the nineteen-year-old daughter. A fun softball game was being played, a

"Battle of the Sexes" if you will, between the men and women. Each of the bases was nailed down by two long spikes that were hammered into the ground at opposite corners. Brenna hit a single and was on first. Brandi was up next and hit a triple. Brenna was almost to second base, but the toes of her right foot caught in the dirt, and she came down right on top of the head of one of those two spikes, sticking up an inch out of the ground, on her kneecap. She suffered a hairline fracture, and the pain was excruciating.

Although she was nineteen, the first words out of her mouth crying were "Daddy! Daddy!"

The sergeant major was standing there listening to some polite complaints from the wives of two of his first sergeants. He heard his daughter scream, looked, dropped his paper plate full of food and plastic glass full of beer, and ran. He ran up to his daughter, quickly checked her, and picked her up and carried her to the aid station, very tenderly talking, smiling, and joking with his sobbing daughter, trying to alleviate her shock and pain.

Karen was so impressed. She knew she could speak to this man.

After tying his boots, the sleazebag colonel walked over to the sobbing young lady and grabbed her left nipple, pinching it until she screamed.

He undid his fly and grabbed her hair, pulling her face forward, saying, "I didn't cum yet. Baby. Gimme some head."

Small explosions suddenly went off, and both looked up as bullets tore through the grating in the air-conditioning ductwork overhead. They saw a hand smash at the louvered air vent, and it gave way and came down with a man's body. He hit the floor and landed on his feet and hands, standing quickly, a civilian air-conditioning repairman with a Glock Model 17 nine-millimeter semiautomatic cocked and pointed straight at the colonel's midsection.

The field grade snapped, "Who the hell are you? What's the meaning of this?"

The repairman pulled a badge from under his shirt and flashed it.

He grinned. "Major Bobby Samuels, sir. C.I.D. investigator, Military Police. You are under arrest, Colonel, for rape and carnal knowledge under section 120 of the UCMJ, and before you say another word, I want you to clearly understand your rights under the Uniform Code of Military Justice."

The colonel started to speak, and Major Samuels's hand lashed out, slapping the older officer across the cheek, as he held his finger up to his smiling lips in a shushing gesture, saying, "Shhh. I don't want to violate your rights. Sergeant Welch!"

The colonel whimpered and Bobby's hand lashed out again, smacking the colonel once more across the face, and he again made a shushing gesture, saying, "I told you to be quiet, you disgusting pile of dog vomit. Just stand there and bleed, Colonel, but no more whimpering. You are already an unconscionable disgrace to the uniform and the entire officers corps—don't whine and cry like a baby, too. Just bleed."

A young black female MP staff sergeant appeared in the doorway, OD army blanket folded under her arm. She looked to Karen on the sofa and smiled softly. Staff Sergeant Welch rushed to the young soldier and wrapped the blanket protectively around her, and only then did Major Samuels look her way and also smile softly.

His hazel eyes now pierced through the colonel like laser beams, and the handsome army detective said, "Under Article 31-Bravo of the Uniform Code of Military Justice, you have the right to remain silent, do not have to answer any questions, and or make any statement. You have the right to consult with a JAG officer, a military lawyer, at no cost to you, or to speak with a civilian lawyer at no cost to the government of the United States, or both. And you have the right to have either or both present during questioning. If you decide to make any statements or answer any questions, they may be used as evidence against you in any court-martial, nonjudicial proceeding, administrative proceeding, or civilian court."

Four other MPs entered the room, and two now cuffed and searched the commander.

Bobby went on. "Colonel Rodriguez, do you clearly understand your rights under Article 31-B of the UCMJ, as I have explained them to you?"

There was a small trickle of blood now coming from his left nostril and another at the corner of his mouth. Tears welled up in his eyes, and he remembered his mother growing up always crying, it seemed, at his father's constant controlling outbursts and tantrums. He could not believe he was about to cry and fought hard to hold the tears back. He would use anger like he always had before to replace the self-pity.

"He hit me right before you walked in here!" he raged.

"No, he did not!"

All eyes turned to Karen, sitting up quickly from Sergeant Welch's caring caress. "I hit him when I was trying to fight back. I will be happy to testify as such under oath in the old bastard's court-martial, Major. Thank you, sir. God bless you. God bless all of you."

She started sobbing uncontrollably.

Samuels smiled and looked at the others. "Get his dishonorable face away from me quickly."

"Yes, sir," two MPs said simultaneously, and they roughly removed the now sobbing colonel.

Sergeant Welch followed, gently guiding Karen, who

was now going to go to Martin Army Hospital there at Fort Benning, where more evidence would be gathered with a "rape kit."

Bobby Samuels stopped them at the door.

He carefully and lightly touched her shoulder, and softly said, "Specialist Gramby, Karen, I want you to know that you did absolutely nothing wrong to deserve this. It is totally his fault, and we will see that he pays for it. He is not what army officers represent. Sometimes one falls through the cracks, Karen, but now we have nailed him."

"I know, Major," she said, "I love the army. I was just so scared. Thank you again, sir. God bless you."

Alone in the office, preparatory to gathering evidence, Bobby sat on the highly polished walnut desk and picked up the phone. He pulled a piece of paper from his pocket and dialed.

Seconds later, Bobby smiled, saying, "Hello, ma'am, this is Major Samuels, from PMO, the Provost Marshal's Office. May I speak to Command Sergeant Major Shanahan, please? Thank you, ma'am."

After a short pause, Samuels said, "Top, this is Major Samuels. We just nailed the sick bastard. No, it will stick. When I came in here two days ago as an air-conditioning repairman, I planted three video cameras in his office. We have him on videotape clearly raping her today."

After listening, he went on. "Roger that. I think she would love having your wife come to the hospital. She is on the way right now. I want to thank you very much, Top, for doing the right thing."

There was another pause, "Hell no, Sergeant Major, you were not disloyal. You were totally loyal to one of your young troops, who is one scared young lady right now. You were also loyal to your command and the army. He is a total disgrace to the uniform."

Bobby chuckled. "No, Top, sorry, they won't let me cut

them off. Violates his rights, besides making it awful hard to walk. I have to collect evidence and go do a bunch of paperwork, so I better hop off here. Thanks again for the heads-up. Hope the new CO you get will be a lot better."

3

HOME

D C

Bobby had been staying in a BOQ near the main officers club while he was at Fort Benning for this case. The paperwork took him long into the evening, so he stopped at the O-Club for a Wild Turkey and Coke and a large steak. At the bachelor officers quarters, he took a long hot shower, which was now the perfect thing to prepare him for sleep, something he usually dreaded. Bobby would spend the next day with JAG officers, going over his case preparation, and in a few days would catch a flight back to DC, home for now. He would have to return to Fort Benning, Georgia, to testify in the eventual general court-martial, if Colonel Rodriguez did not eat a bullet first.

Finally at home in Alexandria, Virginia, outside DC, Bobby hopped the blue line metro and hopped off, so to speak, at the Pentagon exit. Twenty minutes later, he entered the door marked "USACDIC—CRIMINAL INVESTIGATIONS," having just walked the maze of corridors inside the Pentagon. His particular floor was full of classy-looking walnut-paneled hallways, with narrow columns every so often. He entered a sterile office, plopped down in a plain black executive chair, and lazily punched in on the computer and started to check his e-mails.

A minute later, a tall, leggy female captain walked in the door and set a cup of coffee down in front of him, sipping from her own cup. She did not wear much makeup, but nature had already seen to it that such a tactic was unnecessary. Even the green uniform could not hide the curves of Captain Bo Devore's body. Bobby looked at the jump wings proudly displayed on her left breast area, and noticed that they almost faced the ceiling instead of the wall. She had long, naturally curly hair that would be described as auburn with strong red highlights, and very green tinted hazel eyes.

He looked at her and simply grinned, unspeaking, and sipped from the cup. She followed suit, a flirtatious smile on her flawless face. This went on for a couple of minutes.

"Captain," he said.

"Major," she responded.

"How did your case go at Fort Rucker?" he asked.

"Got to play hooker for a while," she responded. "That was fun. I think it is the dream of every female cop. Anyway, we broke up the prostitution ring before it really got up and going."

"It's amazing how some of the better scroungers get greedy and step over that line."

"I know," she said. "To me, scrounging is just part of being a good soldier. Your unit needs something, and you get it to accomplish the mission. You're not stealing, because it all belongs to the army, as long as you don't keep another unit from functioning."

"I agree, Bo, totally."

"I think," she went on, "that some of these guys get

caught up in their own ability, go over the line, and start outright stealing, pimping, or whatever to make money."

"I think it is more than making money," he added. "I believe they get off on being able to do it."

"You're right."

"Hey, you want lunch today?"

She smiled and nodded.

"Great, what do you want for lunch?"

"I don't care, Bobby. Let's just get away from downtown," she replied.

They left the Pentagon and hopped on the metro heading out to a stop in Alexandria. They went to a small restaurant not far from their stop and ate a leisurely lunch discussing each other other's cases and busts. An hour later, they headed back, Bobby feeling strange the whole way. He was really glad she was back, and he had wondered about her the whole time they were apart. On the other hand, Bo Devore scared him, and he did not understand why.

She felt the same way, but she did not worry about him at all. She never worried about Bobby coming out on top in a job, gunfight, arrest, or anything he was up against. She knew he would win.

Taking the blue line metro to the Pentagon, Bobby thought back to Arianna, his late wife.

They had eaten a similar lunch, and he asked her honest feelings about something, and Arianna, answered, then half-jokingly asked the question "When are you going to make an honest woman of me?"

Little did she know that Bobby had already made very elaborate plans in that regard for the very next day. At the time, the young Green Beret captain was a cadre member of the HALO committee. High altitude/low opening, after all these years, since the sixties, in fact, was still a major means of infiltrating Special Forces personnel behind enemy lines, by having them free-fall from great heights, usually wearing oxygen masks, and then deploy their parachutes when they were very low. Hitting their target, they would cache the chute and move on to the objective.

In fact, after the War in Iraq began, one scene in particular became humorous to a number of Special Forces personnel. The news media kept replaying a scene along the Tigris River in Baghdad where numerous Iraqi insurgents kept firing bullets into the water along the river's edge. Several Iraqis said they saw two American pilots parachuting into the river during the darkness, because their jet had been shot down. None of the news personnel could find any reports, however, of any American aircraft being shot down. The Iraqis who said they spotted the pilots were finally discredited by their own people, but in actuality, they were the ones who were in the know. They did see two Americans parachute into the river. The men they saw were two members of a team Bobby had originally commanded in Delta Force. They had done top secret HALO/SCUBA infiltration wearing specially made parachutes, which sank after impact with the water. Then, wearing rebreathing apparatuses, they swam upriver almost a mile to meet with their insurgent contacts, and then carry out some direct action missions, including several assassinations of high-ranking Ba'ath party officials close to Saddam Hussein.

On the day of the proposal, Bobby invited Arianna to Normandy Drop Zone at Fort Bragg to watch what he termed a "Hollywood jump" by his unit. A lot of times on Saturday mornings, the commanding general of Special Forces Command held Hollywood jumps for guys needing jump pay, or just wanting to jump. These were always helicopter jumps, and guys would pool money together, and the man who landed closest to the parachute turn in point won each week. They would use the standard T-1-steerable, MC1A parachutes that SF static line jumpers

used. The jumps were almost always held at St. Mere
Eglise Drop Zone, but this one was at the biggest, sandiest,
and best, Normandy. There was also no helicopters around.
Bobby had gone separately to Pope Air Force Base and
simply told Arianna what time she had to be there.

Arianna sat in the small bleachers at the end of the drop
zone, near the parachute turn-in truck and trailer, and
watched in fixed fascination as the AC-130 Hercules four-
engine aircraft appeared in the distance very high up in the
sky, thousands of feet up, in fact. When they were almost
overhead, Bobby and his team exited the plane, and she
saw red smoke coming from the heels of two of the
jumpers. At the time, she did not know it, but Bobby was
last man out and would be last to deploy.

The two wearing smoke grenades got in tracking posi-
tions facing away from each other and made a giant red
heart in the sky with their smoke, crossing within meters
of each other at the bottom of the heart. Such an amazing
coincidence made Arianna feel chills down her spine; then
she worried a little that it could be an omen that Bobby
would be killed. She shook that off and laughed at herself.
After a few minutes, all the chutes deployed, the last two
being the rectangular wing-type parachutes of Captain
Will Potter, Bobby's best friend and a member of the U.S.
Army Golden Knights parachute team, and then Bobby.
Both men had flags which streamed behind them and were
apparently attached to the back of the risers on their
parafoils, the rectangular, more contemporary parachutes
they used.

As they got closer to the ground, Arianna could see that
Will's flag was the American flag, and her heart fluttered
again. Suddenly, she heard loud music from the back of the
bleachers and turned to see the clerk-typist for the
HALO/SCUBA Committee, Specialist Inga Johnson, play-

ing it. Arianna waved and Inga waved back, smiling broadly.

The song was one of her favorites. Although she loved all the contemporary music of the 1980s, Arianna was head over heels in love with the love songs of earlier eras, not the fast songs, just the love songs of Elvis Presley, and the song playing was Elvis singing, "It's Now or Never."

She also recognized an official Golden Knight jumpsuit and wondered if Will had come out to jump with Bobby and his team that day.

Bobby's flag was yellow with black lettering on it, but she could not make it out. She heard a colonel from JFK Center looking through binoculars and chuckling, so she figured it must be some joke.

As the jumpers got lower though, the message became quite clear. Bobby, now the last one in the air, had a flag whipping softly behind his risers which read: "ARIANNA, PLEASE MARRY ME?"

They all landed within fifty feet of the bleachers in a semicircle, and Bobby landed thirty feet to her front. The young beauty, tears streaming down her cheeks, was now on her feet, heart pounding, and a smile beaming on her beautiful countenance, and the strains of Elvis in her ears. Knowing the military had proper protocol and procedures for everything, and she could not compromise such things lest Bobby get in trouble, she stayed in the front row of the bleachers, transfixed. The whole team stripped out of their jumpsuits and were all wearing dress greens underneath; they pulled out their berets from inside their jackets. Three riggers ran out to grab their jump helmets and parachutes, while they assembled behind Bobby, on line, and marched forward, until the captain was directly in front of her. They halted, stood at attention, and all saluted together, then came to parade rest, as Bobby dropped to one knee. A beautiful, flawless one-carat diamond engagement ring appeared in his hand, and he smiled up into her bright blue eyes, curly auburn hair framing such a beautiful sight.

He said simply, "Arianna, I love you and always will. Will you marry me?"

Sobbing with joy, she leapt into his arms, screaming, "Yes, Bobby, yes!" and she gave him a kiss that he was teased about for months after.

Bobby looked over at the auburn hair on the back of and sides of Bo's head, and he almost had to stifle a sob. Man, does her hair remind me of Arianna, he thought. Then he thought Bo reminded him of a lot of the good things he loved about his wife. He thought to himself that he was really glad she was a coworker, as he was never planning on falling in love again, and he would not let himself fall for a coworker.

In fact, he would not let himself fall for any women again. Love hurt too much.

They both had a lot of catching up to do on unsolved cases, and paperwork, so they returned to DA (Department of the Army, the Pentagon) and went to their respective offices.

The next several days were uneventful. Then on Friday, Bobby got a call from Veronica Caruso.

A female specialist, Jennifer Berken, walked down the hallway and looked in his door, saying, "Major Samuels, you have a call on line one, sir, from Ms. Caruso, you know, that national news anchor?"

Bobby replied, "Thank you, but she's not an anchor, yet. She is a reporter/producer," and he looked at the ceiling, grinning, after the soldier disappeared.

He reached for the phone, whispering to himself, "Out of the frying pan and into the fire."

"Hi, Ronnie, how are you?"

A very low, sexy voice on the other end of the line cooed, "You tell me, Bobby Samuels: How am I?"

Bobby said, "Beautiful."

"Thank you," she said. "I cannot wait until you see the tan I got all over down in Cancun last week. I've missed you."

"You had a nice story on the homeless two weeks ago," he replied.

"Thanks," she said, privately bristling.

He had not replied, "I missed you, too." It was very important for Veronica to hear such things, especially from men she was playing.

In fact, she played all men. That was simply part of being her.

Bobby did not want to be alone with her anywhere and "see her whole tan," so he asked to meet her in the National Mall.

Bobby watched tourists and droves of government workers heading home and wondered how different things would be if that fourth passenger jet had hit the White House back in September of 2001. He thought of that jet going down into the field in Pennsylvania and how sometimes the actions of one or two people can significantly change the course of world history.

Veronica Caruso looked the way she always did when Bobby saw her. She looked like a woman who never had to work out, apply makeup, or brush her hair. She had an air, a classy look, as if she were of aristocracy, but that look was belied by an impish smile. Her eyes were the bluest he had ever seen on any person, and her waist-length hair looked like it had been dipped in honey, and the honey was melting off of it in bright sunlight. Seeing her striding down the sidewalk in a blue pin-striped business suit, slit up the front of the skirt, she looked like she could be a corporate attorney or a very high-priced call girl.

A big smile crossed her face as she looked upon the tall military cop, and she seemed totally oblivious to every man who passed by her and stared after her the same way they would if a '63 Corvette Split-Window coupe drove by them on the street. They just had to watch it go by and wish, try to visualize, what was under the hood, and wonder what the ride would be like.

She walked up to him and did not wait for any body language signals. She planted one on his lips, then grabbed his upper arm and spun him toward the tall Washington Monument looming above a short distance away.

"I missed you," she cooed. "Where are we going to have a private talk?"

He'd had his "private talk" about cases, with Bo earlier in the day, and had tons of desire, but common sense, too, and had no wish to be alone with Veronica. He knew better. He also knew how easily she could dissuade him. She was the ultimate seductress, and it seemed to be a part of being Ronnie, her nickname since elementary school, when she used to make boys get into fights over her.

"I thought we could walk through the National Mall and talk," he said.

She pouted in a flirting way. "But I thought we could go somewhere more private, Bobby. I have really missed you. Why here?"

"I headed this way so I could meet you at a mutually convenient place, Ronnie," he replied. "Besides, I cannot be alone with you, sweetheart."

"Why?"

Bobby grinned, saying, "Ronnie, I think there is a very strong possibility that you could be the anti-Christ, or at the very least a major demon."

Her laughter was evil enough as she slapped his arm.

They soon were sitting on a bench looking at the back

of the Smithsonian National Museum of Natural History, the Washington Memorial two stone's throws away.

Veronica said, "Why didn't you call me when you got back to DC?"

"I just got back."

"Oh" she cooed. "Well, I'm glad you're back. I heard you nailed a rapist at Fort Benning."

"Ronnie, Ronnie, Ronnie! I haven't read anything about anybody being charged with rape at Benning."

Bobby had taken a vow, just to himself privately. Veronica was extremely sexual, very beautiful, lots of fun, an engaging conversationalist, and the best manipulator he had ever known; the perfect combination of femininity, sexuality, intelligence, and self-serving actions that could spell doom and gloom for any man, all while he was smiling. So Bobby vowed she would be repaid, and he would at some point use her; but in the meantime, he would follow some silver screen philosophy he had latched onto from Brando's Don Corleone in *The Godfather:* "Keep your friends close, but your enemies even closer."

Besides the very strong sexual attraction to her, this was something Bobby kept ever-present in his mind around Ronnie, lest he fall into the old same trap. She was, as mentioned, indeed the seductress, and she had certainly woven her spell on him. He had trusted her before, but she had stuck a knife in his back, a long, sharp, nasty, wicked, rusty knife.

She worked for a large TV station then, a network affiliate, and Bobby was a Gulf War hero, a Green Beret captain, with impressive "tossed salad" on his chest. He had been with the famous Delta Force. He had been a cadre member on the HALO Committee at Fort Bragg. He had served on Green Beret A-teams, or ODAs (Operational Detachment-A).

He was hurting when they met, and Veronica was incredibly beautiful and sexy, and she knew how to use that to her own advantage. She and Bobby flirted, then dated, and soon knew each other in the most intimate ways. It was in those quiet moments after intimacy, holding and touching, that Bobby finally let his guard down a little. It was then that he opened up to her. He felt strange speaking to a lover about his wife, the woman he had loved, more than life itself, but Ronnie had reassured him. She liked it that a man could love so deeply, and his wife was gone, she was dead, and no threat to her.

She knew, from his confidences, that his wife loved Elvis love songs, so one night they were at her penthouse, and ever the manipulator, she tuned her stereo to an all-Elvis radio station. The music played softly while he made love to her. Afterward, he stroked her long tresses, while they talked quietly. Then, inevitably, the song came on; Elvis singing "It's Now or Never." Finally, he let himself go and cried in her arms. She simply held him and let him cry. Bobby was embarrassed.

He talked about his decision to leave the army at the height of his career. He was a young SF captain with a good record and had the world by the tail. He quit. And then, he returned.

Over time, Ronnie pressed for more information, with Bobby not knowing that it was for her planned blockbuster story.

She had indeed betrayed him, but this was not new to Veronica. Daddy was a liberal New England congressman for years, and had come from "old money." They had a vacation home and frequently went sailing in the Hamptons. A good portion of Veronica's formative years were spent shopping with "Mummy," or spending time at the Club, which was really not one, but three, high-prestige country clubs. Her mother was actually called Buffy, and fit in perfectly in that world. She also had frequent affairs, and at her knee, Ronnie learned how to play men perfectly.

She had worked Bobby very carefully and finally got the full story out of him.

Arianna and Bobby had been married one year, almost to the day, when she gave him the good news. She was pregnant. It was going to be a boy, and the couple was delighted. They were one of those couples that everyone spoke about. You know, how much in love they were, how devoted they were to each other.

Bobby had been sent with an A-team on an MTT (a mobile training team) in northern Europe, and they had HALOed (military free fall) into a remote DZ (drop zone). Scarcely an hour had passed when the team commo (commications) sergeant walked up the captain and handed him a satellite telephone. Bobby was told he was being replaced, and that another captain was en route on a Blackhawk to rendezvous with the team. He was given coordinates for the planned LZ. If this had been a real mission, the Blackhawk would have compromised it, so he knew something was up.

The next several days were a blur and still foggy in his memory. He was flown to Ramstein AFB, just outside Landstuhl, Germany, where he met with his battalion commander and an SF chaplain. He was taken into an office and the "Old Man" (commanding officer), after much shuffling and discomfort, told Bobby that his wife was driving home from a shopping mall in Fayettteville, North Carolina, on Highway 401 and was hit head-on by a twenty-eight-year-old son of a tobacco-farmer-turned-developer, who had a 2.1 blood alcohol level. Both were killed instantly. Bobby Samuels was beyond devastated.

Bobby left the army, almost immediately, and surrendered what was becoming a colorful and success-filled career. He had a new goal in life. He would become a civilian police officer in a major metropolitan city, and he would write more DUIs and DWAIs than any officer on the force.

He could think of few places more metropolitan and populated with automobile-driving candidates for the drunk tank than Los Angeles, California, so there he went. He was indeed soon busting drunks right and left.

There was one problem, however. Bobby Samuels was a highly trained Special Forces and special ops officer. He was overtrained for writing DUIs. He naturally gravitated to investigations and then homicide. He even sought and received counseling from the LAPD to help him deal with the loss of Arianna.

Then, his life made another major turn. Bobby had a small bachelor apartment a stone's throw from the ocean at Playa Del Ray. He awakened one morning after an all-night homicide investigation in downtown LA. He had left the TV on to NBC, and he heard voices from the sweet blackness of sleep, which registered in his brain. Katie Couric and Matt Lauer were talking about a plane crashing into the World Trade Center Tower One. He jumped out of bed, ran into the bathroom to splash cold water on his face, and returned to the TV in time to see the second plane hit Tower Two. Like the rest of the nation, Bobby sat trans-fixed and horrified for several hours.

Like other special operations veterans watching that morning, when the second jet slammed into the WTC, Bobby said aloud, "Osama bin Laden."

On September 18, 2001, Bobby Samuels called Colonel Carl Eastwood at the Officers Personnel Office in the Pentagon, or OPO. This was the man at DA that Bobby had earlier made friends with, and who had helped plan out his previous career, before he left active duty. At that time, Eastwood was a major, but now after other assignments like Command and Staff College at Carlysle Barracks,

Pennsylvania, he had returned to Department of the Army with more experience under his belt, and more contacts.

Bobby said, "Colonel Eastwood, I am a warrior. We have been attacked. I want to come back into the service, but I am a cop now and want a branch transfer to the MPs."

The colonel said, "You are an LA homicide detective, and you want to be a military cop?"

"Colonel, we are at war now. We have not struck back yet, but we will. I am a cop, sir, an okay one, I think," Bobby responded. "I want to make a contribution."

"You already have, son," the colonel advised. "You gave to this country in spades. Why come back now?"

Bobby said, "I am an American fighting man, sir. We have been attacked."

The colonel said, "I will make it happen, Captain Samuels, as quickly as I can."

There was a branch course to take, a refresher course, trips to Fort Gordon and Fort Benning, Georgia, and because of his unusual military and civilian credentials, Bobby Samuels ended up in Washington, DC, with the C.I.D., Criminal Investigation Detachment, and a gold oak leaf on his lapel. He had been on the list for major when he got out earlier. He was, in a few year's time, the army's top investigator, specializing in two things, working undercover and solving the impossible cases, because of his Special Forces mentality, an innate ability to "think outside the box."

Veronica knew he was the nation's best army detective, so she wanted a background story on why a highly decorated, very successful Green Beret officer would give up his career to become a cop, and what would make him reenter the service as a military policeman.

Yes, she seduced him, but she reasoned, Bobby was a man any woman would desire. Yes, she feigned emotion beyond lust, to get him to open up to her for her story, and it worked. Yes, she used all the contacts she had been building in the Pentagon and around Washington to put her feature story on Bobby together. No, she did not really care, though, because her story got her from an affiliate anchor position to a major network newsmagazine. From there, she manipulated, politicked, and worked her way into doing feature stories for one of the major network's evening news. She was a well-known rising reporter for one of the top four networks.

They talked until it was time for dinner, both manipulating their words, careful not to divulge more than they wanted.

Finally, she said, "Remember where we ate on our first date?"

Bobby smiled, "Still my favorite restaurant."

"Mine, too," she said. "And I work for a big network which has more money than Saudi Aabia, so let me buy you din-din, for old time's sake?"

"Okay," he said.

Bobby led her to the nearest thoroughfare and hailed a cab, then held the door for her, as she climbed in the backseat.

"Old Ebbit Grille," he said.

The driver, a dark-complected man with a nice smile and a thick Ethiopian accent said, "Sure thing, okay, sir."

They zigzagged through the horrendous downtown DC traffic for a short time, turning on 15th Street, and both were soon glancing down now blocked-off Pennsylvania Avenue, and they could see the fence and front lawn of the White House, but the old building was mainly obscured from view by the U.S. Treasury Building on the corner. A half a block down from Pennsylvania Avenue, on 15th Street, the cab whipped an illegal U-turn in the middle of the street and pulled them up in front of Old Ebbit Grille.

Bobby grabbed the brass handle of the door on the right, and Ronnie led the way inside the storied business. Bobby asked if she wanted to go downstairs into the bar first, or into the bar by the dining room, but she was ready for a table. Bypassing the line of ten who did not have reservations, the couple walked up to the young hostess, a shapely college-aged woman with perfect teeth.

"Samuels, party of two," Bobby said, as he moved his hand around the dark wooden lectern she stood behind, as if she was preparing to give a speech.

The young lady covertly took the rolled-up bill from his hand, and said, "Nice to see you again, Mr. Samuels. We have a table ready for you."

Ronnie grinned at the moans of two different men in line waiting for a table.

Another young lady, with long brown hair, led them beyond the maître d' station with a series of small two-person tables on their right and a long, green upholstered bench running along the wall. On the other side of that wall was a noisy bar, crowded with singles or tourists hoping to catch a glimpse of maybe Barbra Steisand eating Old Ebbit's famous oysters, a senator with a page or a call girl, or just any government official. This had been an unspoken pastime there since the mid-1800s. After all, the White House was just around the corner, and this was one of the main in-places for those in the know who made their daily moves inside the Beltway, and it had been for decades.

On the left of the aisle were four-person booths, with green leather upholstery, and Bobby and Ronnie were seated in the fourth one down. A long walnut wooden planter divided the room from another row of booths. Atop the planter were two giant silver vases, filled with dozens of flowers of varying colors, and several five-foot-tall candelabras, each with four globed lights, containing what looked like candles but were actually gas flames. Ronnie already knew Bobby, being ex–Special Forces and a cop to boot, would be totally uncomfortable with his back toward the door, so she slid into the side of the booth that had her facing the restaurant's rear.

Bobby looked around the packed restaurant and up at the walls, containing many large panels with a very large oil painting within each. Three of the many paintings were nudes, and there were patriotic scenes of DC sites such as the White House, the Lincoln Memorial, and so on. Bobby noticed that there were also three gas lamps sticking out from the walls, similar to the upright ones in the center of the long planter, something he had not really paid attention to before.

Ronnie said, "I didn't see you call on your cell phone and make reservations. How did you pull that off, Robert?"

He smiled, saying, "Didn't say a word. Just looked at the young hostess when we came in and licked my eyebrows."

Instead of laughing, she leaned forward, a seductive look on her face, and said softly, "As I recall, Major Samuels, you actually can lick your eyebrows."

Bobby flushed bright red.

A fortyish-looking goateed man in a burgundy apron appeared before them and said, "Hi, my name is John, and I will be your server this evening. Would you like to start with drinks or appetizers?"

Bobby smiled at Ronnie with his best "I remember" look and said, "Hi, John. We'd like a bottle of Sauternes Château Villa Franche 6 and two glasses."

"Certainly, sir," John said, with a small bow, secretly taking a quick, admiring glance at Veronica's ample boobs.

He was back in moments, it seemed, with the bottle, and poured a small amount into a stem before Major Samuels. Bobby swirled it around in the crystal in front of his eyes, took a small taste, swirled it around in his mouth, and swallowed, winking at Ronnie.

John simply asked, "Shall I pour?"

Bobby winked and nodded in approval. The couple smiled at each other like actual lovebirds, while John poured the wine into each stem.

"Thank you," she said.

John said, "Would you like a recommendation tonight, Major?"

Bobby was surprised. John apparently remembered when Bobby came in wearing dress greens one winter night, escorting the provost marshal.

Bobby said, "John, with a memory like yours, how could I refuse?"

John blushed, saying, "Sir, you don't see too many MPs wearing a Special Forces combat patch on their right sleeve, as well as a Silver Star with Oak Leaf Cluster, Bronze Star, and a Purple Heart with Oak Leaf Cluster."

Bobby said, "Guess the tip just went up. First, who did you serve with, John?"

John said, "I did four years, mainly with the Third Infantry Regiment."

Bobby said, "The Old Guard. Thank you for your service, John. Did you guard anything exciting or unusual, like the Tomb of the Unknown Soldier?"

John said, "Mainly drop jobs, er, excuse me, I'm sorry, funerals at Arlington. But a few presidential events. It was fun, but you are the one who should be thanked. Thank you, sir."

Bobby grinned when John slipped with "drop jobs," a slang term used privately by Old Guard soldiers, referring to the many military funerals they performed.

"Veronica," Bobby said, "would you like to hear John's recommendation?"

Ronnie smiled seductively, saying, "How can I refuse when he is so attentive. Obviously, he knows what is happening. Besides I love just about everything on the menu."

John smiled, "Today, I suggest the parmesan-crusted trout, flash-fried with hollandaise sauce, roasted red potatoes, and green bean shiitake sauté."

Bobby looked at Ronnie, and she gave him an approving nod.

"Two, please," he said.

A short while later, the couple looked longingly at the dishes being set before them.

"So," Ronnie said, her fork dipping into the flakes of trout, "I hear you are leaving for Iraq to solve a big case. What is it?"

Bobby chuckled, sarcastically replying, "They want me to find Saddam Hussein. Hey, maybe he is hiding in a spider hole and has a long gray beard full of lice and creepy crawlers. Where in the hell do you get your intel from, honey?"

Ronnie replied, "Ooh damn! If I ate here every day, I would be a blimp. John was right."

Bobby said, "Even if you did, you would still be beautiful. The food is great. Please, enjoy."

"Bobby Samuels, don't be coy with me. When do you leave?" she asked.

The tall detective stopped chewing and swallowed his food. He looked into her eyes.

"Am I a man who keeps his word?"

"Yes, absolutely," she said unhesitatingly.

Bobby looked her deep in the eyes still, saying, "Nobody has breathed a word to me about going to Iraq."

"My source has never been wrong," she said.

"Do I lie?"

"No, Bobby. I was just saying my source has never been wrong, so far."

"They are now," he replied.

For dessert, he had a warm pear ginger cake with vanilla ice cream and caramel sauce, and Veronica cooed over a chocolate banana bread pudding with vanilla ice cream and caramel sauce.

Bobby opened his eyes, blinking against the morning sun streaking through the windows, and he stared at a large, firm, very well-rounded woman's breast six inches away from his eyes.

He sat up with a start and looked at Ronnie's still gorgeous naked body next to him. Still asleep, she was doing a cross between purring and snoring. Not knowing how he got there or even what happened, he carefully got out of bed and realized he was in her Crystal City penthouse apartment.

Bobby tiptoed to the bathroom and relieved his bladder for what seemed like six hours. He had a horrible taste in his mouth, headache, and knew he would throw up if he even smelled food. He was startled as he noticed a large hickey just under his left ear, and then another one on his right hip. He found a bottle of Aleve and took two even though the directions said to take only one.

Bobby crept into the room and retrieved his clothes, dressing on his way toward the door. Outside in the early morning light, he spotted a pretty red rosebush and pinched one stem off, carefully ran back inside, and quietly set it on his pillow. He would have time to take the metro all the way across DC to his apartment in Alexandria, Virginia, shave, shower, change, and take the blue line back toward town getting off at the Pentagon. He tried to sleep on the metro, but he was haunted by wanting to know what had happened the night before. He remembered the warm pear ginger and that was the last thing. He suddenly wondered if Ronnie had drugged him, and he laughed aloud at himself. Bobby also wondered if he had been a good lover or a drunken slob. He was also mad at himself for even sleeping with her.

The next morning, Bobby was only halfway through his first cup of coffee, when he was summoned to a briefing room. Two white-gloved MPs in Class-A's stood at parade rest on either side of the double doors, and there was a wooden easel by the MP on the right with a yellow and white placard on it, which read "TOP SECRET" in large letters, with the standard verbiage about need-to-know, automatic downgrades, etc. Above the placard was a small, thin black-lettered white placard, which simply read "BRIEFING."

At a whispered command or signal he could not detect, the two MPs came to Attention, and Bobby quickly said, "As you were, gentlemen."

He entered the briefing room and sat at a large mahogany table with leather-backed chairs all around it. At the end of the room was a large whiteboard, with the American flag on one side, the MIA/POW flag on the other side, as well as several red flags with stars on them, one with four stars. Two Old Guard PFCs stood on either side of a white linen-covered long table with two large coffeepots, an assortment of cups, and a tray covered with pastries.

A full bird colonel in dress greens came in first.

Bobby jumped to attention and the colonel said, "As you were."

Samuels extended his hand, saying, "Major Bobby Samuels, sir. Pleased to meet you, Colonel Dweib."

Bobby Samuels could hardly contain himself at the name. He might not have paid attention, except that the man's demeanor was almost laughable. He had AG brass on, Adjutant General Corps, and he was very obviously filled with himself and anal retentive.

Dweib said, "Major, your shoes are not polished, and you need a shave."

Bobby was wearing a blue shirt, maroon tie, navy blue blazer, tan slacks, and brown deck shoes. He also had not shaved that morning.

Bobby thought it was a joke at first, then realized the colonel was serious, and responded, "Colonel, I am a detective, a C.I.D. investigator."

Dweib countered, "That matters not one whit. First and foremost, we are officers, and our appearance must be of the highest standards at all times."

Bobby rose and said, "Colonel, with all due respect, you are not my CO, and I am in uniform. When I first went to Fort Bragg, I saw my first two C.I.D officers years ago. An old Special Forces sergeant major said to all of us, 'Boys, there's a couple a C.I.D. guys.'

"I said, 'How do you know, Top?' and he said, 'Cheap ass suits, whitewall haircuts, white socks, and spit-shined low quarters. You kin spot 'em every time.' "

Samuels went on, "Colonel Dweib, you are a full bird who made it to the Pentagon, because you are obviously a man of great intellect, so I don't need to tell you how important it is for me to never look that obvious to any suspects."

The high-ranking nerd stood up a little straighter, saying, "Exactly! I totally agree with you, Major Samuels."

Fifteen minutes later, it dawned on Bobby that he was drinking a cup of hot tea and eating a glazed donut with the commanding general of U.S. forces in Iraq, Jonathan L. Perry, sitting to his right and enjoying the same snack, while a measly lieutenant general with only three stars sat on his left, also enjoying the exact same snack. The eight in the room were intently watching the PowerPoint presentation going on to their front, presented by a J2 (Department of the Army Command Staff intelligence officer) full bird (a colonel), and it was clear to Bobby he was headed to Iraq. Looking around the room, he also came to the realization that Colonel Dweib was sucking hind tit as far as rank went in that room.

Samuels thought to himself, "No wonder the guy was posturing. It was because he was so scared."

Bobby thought for another second, and grinned to himself, thinking, "And he is simply a jerk."

Shifting his eyes back to the screen, Bobby was looking at photograph after photograph of blown-up vehicles, blown-up buildings, and dead or wounded soldiers.

The briefing ended, and the four-button general turned to Bobby saying, "In short, Major Samuels, I have men and vehicles being blown up and sabotaged in several locations in Iraq, and we are talking about locations where I have been assured that security was not breached. Somehow, the enemy is infiltrating our secure locations over there and causing problems, but our security is very tight. Nobody at any of those locations has been able to come up with any clues on how the terrorists are accomplishing this. We are stumped, but this has got to stop. I am counting on you to solve it and stop the bastards, Major."

"Yes, sir," Bobby said. "I will. But, General, if I may, you said you were assured that security was not breached, but you are the boss, a four-star general. Sir, you know some, in fact most, commanders are not going to admit to you if their security was breached."

"Excellent point, son," the general replied, "but I did not get four stars by keeping my nose up people's asses. I have ways of checking on people and things. It is as I explained."

"Yes, sir," Bobby responded. "I will saddle up immediately."

The general said, "Ladies and gentlemen, leave us and close the door."

The staff officers present left the room, taking the two PFCs with them.

The general leaned forward. "Major Samuels, you know what is at stake here?"

"I think so, sir."

The general said, "I have given orders; anything you need, just ask and it will be there, but we must nail these bastards, and the secretary and the President would prefer that CNN, CBS, NBC, and the like do not find out we have had such a security lapse."

"Sir," Bobby said, "my concern is the morale of our troops, which affects keeping them alive. I will accomplish my mission, and I will not carry handcuffs with me for any terrorists I apprehend."

"My boy." The general smiled grimly. "You read between the lines quite well. What do you need right off the bat?"

Bobby said, "All the spot reports and after-action reports relating to the incidents, sir. I also want a Glock 17, a stainless-steel Ruger .44 magnum Super Blackhawk with ten-and-a-half-inch barrel, and an M4. What is my chain of command over there, sir?"

"Well, a couple of those weapons aren't exactly army issue, but whatever you want is yours. Just tell my aide. The chain of command is simple. You report to and answer to nobody but me. Anybody gives you any shit, they will get my boot right up their ass."

"Thank you, sir," Bobby said. "I need a couple weeks buried in my office with those reports, before I even pack my ruck."

The general stood, and Bobby jumped up to attention.

The old man said, "At ease," while offering his hand. "The reports will be in your office within the hour. Find those terrorist sons of bitches and blow their asses away, son, but make sure CNN or one of those networks is not lurking around with a damned camera."

Bobby grinned, "Wilco, sir."

How did Ronnie find this out before he did? he wondered. She certainly had the contacts, he admitted.

Bobby headed home to start getting ready. He was at a market about two blocks from his place when he ran into Spook Johnson. Spook was a retired Special Forces sergeant major who was African-American, and gave himself the nickname Spook because he was an outstanding intel sergeant for years before he became a team sergeant and later sergeant major. The man had a perpetual smile, physically had to look down at most people he spoke to, and was so large and muscular that whatever he grabbed ahold of moved. Spook had earned a Distinguished Service Cross, when a Medal of Honor recommendation was downgraded, had a Silver Star, six Purple Hearts, and three Bronze Stars. He was a Vietnam veteran, having served there for four years, as well as serving in Laos in Operation White Star, Det-A in Bad Toelz, Germany, chasing Che Guevara in South America with the 8th Group, running a Hatchet Force for CCN out of Danang in MAC-V/SOG, and all in all, was pretty doggone legendary among Green Berets and other Specops types.

Spook was with his lovely Korean wife and introduced her to Bobby then told her to take the van home. He would be home later.

"Come on, son," Spook beamed, "I am buying you a couple of beers!"

Bobby Samuels first met Spook when the man was one of his instructors in Delta Force. They just hit it off immediately. Maybe birds-of-a-feather syndrome, and more importantly, Spook had been mentored by Bobby's late father. He and Bobby had gotten drunk together several times, and that was now worrying Bobby. He kind of cringed when he heard Spook say, "a couple of beers."

Bobby could not remember when he had only had "a couple of beers," but he had been thinking what a few drinks would make him feel right now. After the accident, the drinks had anesthetized the pain, so he drank often and alone. It also helped with things bothering him lately, like not remembering half the evening with Ronnie.

Major Bobby Samuels heard noises, which seemed magnified by the throbbing headache. His mouth felt like he had filled it with cotton balls soaked in spoiled sweet-and-sour sauce, and then the balls had been dried out. His tongue felt like it had a coating of fur on it, and his stomach was queasy. His mind categorized the children's voices. They were African-American. His eyes opened, but he did not move. He was lying on a couch and was covered with an afghan. He moved his eyes all around the room.

He got up and stumbled around until he found a bathroom and went in. Bobby Samuels was starting to get tired of waking up, then looking in strange mirrors in the morning, with no memory of the night before, and then seeing strange things. This hit him in the gut, as he peeled the bandage off his left shoulder and viewed his deltoid muscle, looking in shock at the long incision, running parallel to the floor that he now wanted to fall onto and cry, he was so frustrated. What had happened? He strained to figure out how he'd got here. He got a flash of a smoke-filled noisy bar, with cigarette fumes burning his eyes. That was all he remembered.

The incision on the shoulder had been stitched, expertly, and was covered with a sick orange-yellow-looking dried antiseptic. He counted and there were thirteen stitches in his bulging deltoid muscle, and it hurt like a toothache right then.

Now Bobby paid closer attention to his face, as he heard heavy footsteps heading his way, followed by the footfalls of little ones, who were giggling and chuckling.

Bobby Samuels thought Darth Vader or his alter ego James Earl Jones was outside the bathroom when Spook's deep, booming voice came through the door: "Hey, Bobby, good morning! Ya want some LRRPs or C-Rations, or maybe ham, eggs, biscuits, and hot coffee?"

"The latter please, Spook!"

His own echoing voice in the hard-tiled box of a bathroom made Bobby grab his temples and massage them in circles. While he cleaned up a little and inspected the cut in his hairline, he soon started smelling the fragrances of a family kitchen in the early morning.

Bobby thought about his father and about Spook having a friendship with both, but he did not even know the half of it.

Bobby's dad was one of the men who'd started the Special Forces Decade Association, which became the Special Forces Association. A Green Beret command sergeant major, he did it all, saw it all, lived it all, and was it all. Command Sergeant Major Theodore Roosevelt "Honey" Samuels was standing there at the ceremony when then President John F. Kennedy created the green beret as the official headgear of Special Forces, a "badge of distinction," a "symbol of courage." Up until then, most in SF were considered the miscreant castoffs from other airborne units, the mavericks, the rebels who would not conform and refused to think inside the lines and march in lockstep with the commanding officer. In actuality, it was an apt description.

Ted Samuels received his nickname when he was on an

RT, a recon team, with the Top Secret MAC-V/SOG unit. Wearing "sterilized" uniforms and equipment, RTs from FOB 4 (forward operating base 4) in Danang would operate primarily in North Vietnam and northern Laos, along the border of the northern II Corps and all of the I (eye) Corps zones. They had a variety of missions, from following POWs being taken up the Ho Chi Minh Trail, to prisoner "Snatch Missions," to gathering intel, and many other direct action and top level reconnaissance missions.

On one such snatch mission, Ted was with his teammate, Sergeant First Class Lou Mollelo, and four Montagnard tough guys. The NVA, specifically sappers, had invaded the Top Secret compound in Danang, tossing satchel charges into billets and killing some of America's best fighters, even pursuing some onto Marble Mountain and killing them there. The well-planned and well-executed sneak attack struck at the very heart of Special Forces, who provided 99 percent of the American manpower for the classified project.

Everybody in the 5th Special Forces Group serving all over Vietnam took that attack as a personal failure, and all wanted revenge in spades for months.

Ted's team had captured an NVA trail watcher just north of the DMZ, and Lou had the man blindfolded, gagged, and handcuffed, while the six waited for an old black banana-looking helicopter to fly in and extract the team up through the triple-canopy jungle on a McGuire rig, a special harness for pulling soldiers up into a helicopter.

They thought they'd gotten in and almost out without notice, but a team of four, two North Vietnamese sappers and two Chicom Special Forces "advisors," had been watching the trail watcher, as it was a major trail junction and two prisoner snatches had occurred there before. They had silently trailed the RT, and were now closing in.

ETA on the extraction was ten minutes, and the team

members were relaxing when suddenly Ted saw the four Yards bring their AK-47s to bear. Whenever the Montagnards suddenly got on guard, Ted knew the enemy was closing in. They had a sixth sense about it. He gave a hand signal, and all six dropped silently into the vegetation. Ted and Lou both screwed silencers onto the end of the .22 pistols they carried for just such an emergency. Lou gave hand signals to the Yards to hold their fire.

As the black-pajamaed warriors appeared quietly out of the jungle mist, the six good guys tensed up waiting. The patrol was spread out about ten meters apart, and they actually passed right by the RT. As the last man went by, Lou was aiming when Ted suddenly came up out of the jungle floor and thrust a large KA-BAR knife into the belly of the last man, slicing diagonally, and the man's intestines spilled out onto the green. His mouth opened in contorted agony, but no sounds came forth. Lou understood why when he saw the wide gash all the way across the throat, where Ted's knife had also passed.

Before the man even fell, Ted had dropped back down into the greenery, only to appear seconds later out of the foliage and start the same maneuver on the second-to-last man. But this one charged forward as Ted lunged, and the blade of the knife went deep into the man's genitals, sticking into the pelvic bone. Ted clasped his hand over the man's mouth, as he twisted and yanked hard on the knife trying to dislodge it. He did so while the Chinese soldier bit hard on Ted's palm, and Ted shoved the knife up under the chin and straight into the man's brain. He died instantly. Ted and Lou then quietly trotted after the rest of the patrol, taking the rest out with head shots.

On the chopper on the way back to Danang, Lou said, "You looked like a friggin' honey badger, man, coming up outta that green shit and stickin' that gook in the nuts."

Ted laughed and said, "Honey badger?"

Lou said, "Yeah, man. Meanest animal in the world. Lays in the tall grass in Africa and waits on elephants or Cape buffalo to come by. It jumps up and bites their crotch out and then moves off and watches them bleed to death and die in agony."

For a month, everybody at FOB 4 called Ted "Honey Badger," and it eventually it was shortened to "Honey."

On the very next mission, Lou took a direct hit in the left ear from a Chicom SKS, dying instantly, and was replaced by a big, black, well-built, gung-ho E-6 named Spook Johnson. Honey took him in like a younger brother and kept him alive, saving his life several times, as well as teaching Spook the ways of war. After six months, Honey was medevaced for shrapnel to both legs from an RPG that hit a treetop by him while he was being extracted on a Stabo rig (another harness device used to extract with a helicopter).

Spook took over a Hatchet Force then and got many teams out of trouble in the nick of time.

Bobby was never aware of how close Spook and his father had been, but he saw a big, knowing grin when he told Ted about developing a friendship with the older man when they served in "The Stockade," headquarters for Delta Force.

Honey died a year before Arianna, when an old piece of shrapnel worked its way loose from his upper thigh and eventually cut into his femoral artery. His leg swelled quickly, and he bled to death internally in the ambulance.

It was a very sad day for the Special Forces community, and sadder yet for Bobby.

Bobby got back off the toilet and now noticed a large bruise on his right rib cage. He touched it and winced.

After breakfast, the uncountable brood of Johnson kids and grandkids were sent out into the backyard to play while Bobby, Spook, and Kyung drank large mugs of coffee.

"Feel better?" Spook asked.

Bobby did not want to answer, but he sheepishly said, "What happened?"

Spook said, "You don't remember, son?"

The familial term from Spook felt strangely comfortable, but answering the question surely did not.

Bobby just shook his head.

Spook chuckled. "Just like your ole man."

Bobby looked up, shocked, saying, "I never saw my dad taking a drink my whole life."

Spook said, "That is because he made up for it in his early years. He even tried to get me to go to an AA meeting with him when he visited me the year before he died."

Booby smiled a strange smile and said, "That trip to Washington. I thought he was going to see the Capitol, White House, and monuments, and Mom wanted to see the cherry blossoms."

Spook laughed. "She did love the cherry blossoms in the spring. Why would your dad just want to look at buildings he'd been inside of for important meetings?"

Bobby shook his head. His dad was a man of very few words, but little did Bobby know how few.

Spook said, "How much you remember?"

Bobby sighed and said, "Running into you two at the store."

Spook roared with laughter. "You don't even remember the stitches or the knife fight?"

"Knife fight?" Bobby said startled. "That is how I got cut?"

"I'll say, young man," Spook replied. "That big guy pulled it out of nowhere and sliced you, and what did you do? Stuck your fingers in your own blood, tasted it, and laughed."

"I did?"

Spook said, "Yes, sir. Then you stared at the big guy and

said, 'Now I got a hard-on. I'm gonna stick that knife up your fat ass.' "

"My lord," the MP answered, looking over, red-faced, at Kyung.

He went on, "What happened then?"

Spook started laughing loudly. "I thought you were going to. You disarmed the guy quicker than greased shit, then threw it straight up and stuck it into the big beam over the bar. It is probably still there, if the cops didn't take it."

"Cops?" Bobby said, getting very sad. "I guess my career with the MP Corps, even as an army officer, is over."

"Why the hell would you say that, son?"

"The police, a bar fight, I'm a cop myself, let alone an officer and a gentleman," Bobby said. "I'm dead, Spook."

Spook laughed again.

Bobby said, "What's funny about that?"

The big retiree replied, "I picked you up over my shoulder and ran out of there after you knocked the guy and his partner out. We were pulling out of there when the cops came."

Bobby said, "I do remember we drove there, but I would never drive even if I was flat-out drunk, and I would never let anybody else I was with drive."

Touching the goose egg on his left cheekbone, Spook sarcastically said, "No shit, Sherlock!"

Bobby said, "I did that? Oh, I am so sorry."

Spook chuckled again. "Don't be. I deserved it. I tried to drive and should not have. You punched me when I even tried to argue. We took a cab."

Kyung put her hand on Bobby's shoulder, saying, "Thank you, Bobby. You save him, maybe innocent peoples, too."

Spook poured more coffee.

Bobby dropped his head. "I'm still dead. What about the emergency room report on my stitches and the knife fight?"

Spook said, "What report?"

"Huh?"

Spook laughed again. "You never went to the ER. The ER came to you."

Kyung laughed now.

Bobby said, "What?"

Spook said, "Bac-si Riviera. Remember the SF medic that served with your dad and me in Nam?"

Bobby, now smiling, nodded.

"He came over here and stitched you up. Even was gonna give you a tetanus shot, but stopped when I told him you were active duty. He knew your shots would all be current."

Bobby then worried some more. "My car. The police will have checked it, since we left it."

Spook laughed again. "Son, you grew up the son of an SF sergeant major. I am one, too, remember? I took Bac-si, and he drove it back here. It is in my garage."

"Thank you, Spook, so much," Bobby said. "I cannot thank you enough. Hey, for you to call a guy big, that says something. How big was he?"

"Not just him," Spook responded. "His buddy, too. They claimed to be on the early training roster for the Washington Redskins. Don't know if that was true, but they sure had the size for it."

"Why did we get in a fight?" Bobby asked.

"The bar TV had a news story about the President, and one of them popped off. You got very pissed, declared he was your commander in chief, and the war began."

"Did they get hurt?"

Spook said, "You knocked them both out cold and bruised them up pretty good. They probably got treated and released, but I guarantee they did go to the emergency room."

Bobby said, "Good."

Kyung started chuckling, finding that, of all things, very amusing.

"Hey, thinking of old teammates," Bobby said, "do you ever hear from Boom Kittinger?"

Spook replied, "Sure, all the time. He's made a career of retiring and unretiring. Still does special jobs for the government when they need him."

"Good," Bobby replied. "I think I'm going to need him on this current case."

"Still the best in the world," Spook added.

4

DIFFERENT MO

Fallujah

Second Lieutenant Franklin Nightkiller Hogan, better known as "L. T. Cherokee" was from Asheville, North Carolina, and was one of the few true, "real" Cherokees around. So many claimed Cherokee blood, more than that of any other American Nation, but had not an ounce. L.T. was a warrior though and proud of it. His great-great-grandfather had survived the Trail of Tears. His grandfather earned a Bronze Star and Purple Heart at Inchon in the Korean War. His uncle and father had each earned the Silver Star and two Purple Hearts in Vietnam. His dad was in I Corps with Marine Force Recon, and his uncle was a grunt in II Corps, humping the Central Highlands with the 1st Brigade of the 4th Infantry Division, operating out of Dak To north of Kontum. L.T. rode shotgun in the Humvee.

The driver was Specialist Fourth Class Willis Reed from Scranton, Pennsylvania, a young man who was offered a full-ride scholarship in football to both Boston College and Texas A and M. He first wanted to serve. His mother's older sister was a secretary on the one hundredth floor of World Trade Center Tower One, and she never made it out alive.

The passenger in the back was the Saboteur.

The HUMVEE slowed down for a military roadblock and had been directed into a second lane for military vehicles, when the Saboteur decided that this would be the place to detonate the device. As the HUMMER passed between two lanes of tanks and armored personnel carriers, the Saboteur looked about quickly. There was nobody in sight, so he quickly pulled out his .45 automatic and shot both driver and passenger in the back of the head. He went headfirst out the door of the military vehicle, and his foot released the pressure on the release trigger he had set up to detonate the IED under the driver's seat. At the same time, he spotted Marine Lance Corporal John Toomey, who had just exited one of the APCs (armored personnel carriers) to his front. Toomey saw the man execute the two Americans. The Saboteur had replaced the pressure-release detonator fuse with the fuse from a smoke grenade, so he had a second or so for the vehicle to roll before it exploded. In the meantime, he came up from a shoulder roll into a kneeling position, jerking a taped HE (high explosive) fragmentation grenade from his webbing, flipping the ring with his right thumb, and tossing it straight at the shocked Marine, who was bringing his rifle to bear. Toomey had no chance. The grenade exploded on the skin of the APC and tore his head off almost completely.

Quickly, the spy turned his own .45 downward and shot himself through the left thigh, being careful to miss bone and artery alike. The bullet, however, nicked the sciatic nerve wrapping from the front to the back of his thigh, and sent excruciating pain down his leg, behind the knee and calf, and up into his tailbone. He screamed in agony. Still thinking and manipulating, the Saboteur gritted his teeth and opened fire, on full automatic, with his CAR-15 rifle. He also tossed another high explosive grenade out past the armored vehicles in the direction he was firing.

It had the desired effect he was after, as a thunderous staccato of automatic weapons fire cracked all about him from American soldiers, the automatic response from nerve-riddled fighting men. Now feeling he had adequately covered his tracks, he set his rifle down and quickly wrapped his thigh with a field protective bandage. He then lit up a cigarette, slammed another magazine into his weapon, and wasted more ammunition, smiling at what he perceived to be the stupidity of his fellow American soldiers.

The next time, he decided, he would take an entire military headquarters building. He would use a longer fuse on the IED and figure a way to bail out before the vehicle hit the building. As always, if he did get killed, he would end up in Paradise with his promised virgins, but he was in no hurry to be a martyr.

This explosion had really been a test run, with the spy knowing he would get bumps and bruises jumping from the vehicle, but not realizing he would have to wound himself to better cover his tracks. It was one of those split-second decisions that separate a martyr from a living, breathing terrorist, still a threat to civilized society. Allah would be most pleased. More infidels would be sent to hell, and more importantly, the al Qaeda leadership would be quite happy, especially the Director.

The Saboteur had the same mind-set as many members of al Qaeda. They were playing catch-up with the West. Their countries were all hundreds of years behind the U.S., Israel, even Europe. They hated all nonbelievers of Islam. Dominators of the world? It had not happened as promised. Jihad was something drummed into the head of the Saboteur from early childhood, but he was different from most of the terrorists, because he grew up in the United States of America.

As the firing wound down, the Saboteur felt the presence of soldiers coming around, and he saw a medic coming toward him.

He had started to slip into unconsciousness, a smile on his face, as he heard the medic say, "Quick! Over here, guys! It is one of those imbedded reporters, and he's alive!"

Buck Sergeant Samuel Ajamo felt himself being lifted on a stretcher, and he was placed in a Blackhawk helicopter. He heard a young lieutenant yelling that he was going to get a Bronze Star for his courage under fire and, of course, his Purple Heart, and he grinned to himself as the chopper lifted off.

He thought to himself, "What would the ignorant infidel think if he knew my real name is Usama Ibn Ajam-Vash?"

Usama was born in Timken Mercy Hospital in Canton, Ohio, but by then his father had changed his own last name to Ajamo, which a friend told him could be mistaken for Italian or Spanish. Very sensitive to being from Iran, he always referred to himself as "a Persian" when people asked about his origins, always adding, "You know, like the rugs."

His forward-looking mullah had sent him to America for such a mission as his only son was on now: jihad by stealth and strategy. His mullah was also his father, and Usama's grandfather.

Usama's father was to prepare his son for jihad and was to prepare him for service in the military of the infidels, so he could destroy from within. He was to blend in as much as possible to American society so suspicion would not be raised, even allowing his wife to be uncovered around men so as not to arouse awareness. Usama's father was also to teach the boy the ways of the Quran, inside and out, and the teachings of the Enlightened Holy One, as well as good sprinklings of hateful jihad-spouting philosophy from his favorite mullah, Gramps.

His mother, a strawberry blond, blue-eyed woman from Cherry Hill, South Carolina, could not quite bring herself to marry a black man to rebel against her southern Baptist upbringing and her overbearing "mother" and "poppa." When she met Muhammad, she knew he could serve the same purpose, since anybody who was dark-skinned, even well tanned, would bring her scorn and adequately push the buttons of her folks. She could, at the same time, allow herself the opportunity to live out her own *Lawrence of Arabia* fantasy, which was a real-life dream that lasted long enough to just get past denial. Papa Ajamo was not exactly Omar Sharif.

Her mother and father had gone berserk one time because she had met two new girls in her class and invited them to her house. They were both Indians of the Lumbee tribe and had moved there from Pembroke, North Carolina, about an hour away. Usama's grandmother would not let the poor kids in the house, and they went home crying. Usama's mom was devastated and angry.

The mother raged, "I swanee, girl. You invited them Croitans into my home. I don't think so."

"What are croitans, Mommy?" she asked.

"Well, now you ask after the damage is done. Croitans are half Indian and half nigger. They come from Lumberton, Pembroke, all those towns," the racist old biddy said, "and young lady, you can just cut you a shiner until yer tears run out. Ain't no croitans or any other niggers steppin' across my threshold. Why, they're like dirt under mah feet."

Not only was the young lady upset by racism, but years

later, by anti-feminism as well. By the time Usama was in fourth grade, she remembered she was an American woman, and got very inspired by hearing Gloria Gaynor singing "I Will Survive." She told Usama's dad, after one of his beatings, that she was done with the marriage and was a modern-day woman, American born and raised, and would take care of herself and her son quite well without his help.

He shot her. Simple as that. Daddy had a snub-nosed Smith & Wesson Model 10, .38 special. She put her foot down, stood her ground, and stuck out her jaw defiantly, for the first time in her marriage, and she felt good about it. She felt empowered. Then she saw him produce the cocked weapon, which he grabbed from his nightstand and pointed at her. Her sense of empowerment disappeared immediately. She screamed briefly, the noise drowned out by the sound of a single gunshot.

The body ended up crammed under a log in a swamp on the highway to Myrtle Beach. It rotted there, while Usama and others wondered about her whereabouts. His father would not allow him to grieve, and reminded him women were basically chattel.

Then, in seventh grade, a life-changing incident occurred at school. Usama carried his prayer mat in his backpack into the dark auditorium every day after lunch, so he could privately set it down, kneel down facing toward Mecca, and pray, as he was instructed by his father.

Mr. Gergen was a very slight, effeminate math teacher, who also was always planning new school plays, which he wanted to produce and direct. He caught Usama, aka Sam, praying, and was very shocked to find out that he was a Muslim. He said he was going to report the double life of the young man to the principal. Usama grabbed the microphone from a podium on the stage, ran up behind Mr. Gergen, and swung as hard as he could. He kept swinging until the teacher's head was a bloody, pulpy mess. He then dragged Gergen's body behind one of the big stage curtains. He wiped the microphone off and got out of the auditorium undetected.

The body was discovered that night by the janitor, who became the prime suspect for a long time. It was finally revealed that one of the women teachers had seen Gergen coming out of a gay bar in downtown Akron, the next city to the north. The detective in charge finally concluded that Gergen had had a fight with a gay lover and the man had beaten him to death. Why he decided that is hard to know, but it was clear he was not much of an investigator. Nobody, for example, even checked the angle of the swing, which would have determined the shortness of the seventh-grade killer, compared to an unseen, homicidal, angry or jealous gay lover. The murder was never solved, and young Usama felt a sort of elation at his conquest of the adult, even if he had been effeminate.

His father wanted him to keep progressing and become a more efficient killer. There was little time for play for young Usama. His life was geared toward one thing only: jihad against the infidels, especially Americans and Israelis.

As a testament to Usama keeping his eye on the brass ring, his father had him join the Boy Scouts, and his scoutmaster was Jewish. Even worse, as far as Papa was concerned, was that David Stienmetz was in actuality Jewish by birth, but during his college days he'd become a Hebraic Christian or Messianic Jew. In other words, influenced by his college sweetheart, he attended church and one day accepted Jesus Christ as his Personal Savior, did the full-immersion baptism, the whole works.

In fact, it became a standing joke whenever anyone brought religion up in a conversation and asked David about his.

His automatic response was always "I'm a completed Jew."

People would say, "What?" "Huh?" or something similar, and Steinmetz always got a chuckle out of it.

He would usually say, "Well, we are God's chosen people, but are not completed Jews until we develop a personal relationship with Jesus Christ as our Savior. Then, we become completed Jews."

Regardless, Usama's dad kept him focused on the long-term, saying, "You must think of jihad, not the enemies who surround you each day. You are a weapon that must not be fired yet, so pay them no mind."

Usama learned many skills in the Boy Scouts and earned his Eagle Award, putting him in the company of most astronauts and presidents. The testament to Usama's restraint was the fact that he never killed his scoutmaster, who attended Shabbat services, celebrated Hanukkah, Yom Kippur, and other Jewish holidays, but also studied the New Testament in services that were conducted on Saturday mornings, almost like being in a synagogue. If ever there was a target of hatred for Usama, it was David, but the young man was a model Boy Scout, albeit somewhat weird to most of the boys.

His father also enrolled him in martial arts classes all through middle and high school. Yes, Usama was exposed to many teachings contradictory to what he was being taught at home, but he always began his studies with others viewing them as fools, as he did all "unbelievers." He was indeed brainwashed by early elementary school. So indoctrinated was Usama Ibn Ajam-Vash that he knew deep down inside that his father probably killed his mother, yet he was unfazed by it, feeling she had become argumentative and rebellious and probably deserved whatever she got.

Sam Ajamo was a very good wide receiver all through high school. He actually learned to be a good team player and enjoyed himself. His father told him, if he was to be proficient, he had to be a part of the team. If he was standoffish, like he sometimes was in Boy Scouts, it just would not work.

He lived in Canton, Ohio, and the Pro Football Hall of Fame was there. It was football country. In nearby Massilon, one of the state powerhouses in high school football for decades, footballs were given to newborn boys in the hospital.

Canton McKinley was Usama's school, and it, too, was a perennial powerhouse in Ohio, as was Niles McKinley, and both were frequent rivals of Massilon. Massilon was a small-town suburb of Canton, joined primarily by Lincoln Way, a major thoroughfare with the usual assortment of small businesses, car dealerships, and restaurants.

It was Friday night, and the stadium was packed, the crowd was electric, and the adrenaline was running high. Canton McKinley was playing Massilon and both teams were undefeated. The game had been a defensive struggle, and the score was tied 13 to 13 late in the fourth quarter.

Massilon had possession, and instead of panicking like most high school coaches, their coach moved the chains, trying to eat up the clock. They played smash-mouth football, which was the most popular type of football in northeast Ohio anyway, and Massilon made it all the way to McKinley's twenty-three-yard line before stalling on fourth and five. The coach sent in his kicker, a junior who had been a soccer star all through his middle school, freshman, and sophomore years. The kid was not very well liked, but he could kick, and so he did. The ball split the upright, and the visiting Massilon fans went nuts as their team went up by three points.

Sam watched nervously from the sidelines as Massilon

kicked off. The second-string tailback for McKinley, whose dad had moved him to Canton just so he could play football and get scouted by colleges, was a speedster, running a 4.42 forty, and he could cut on a dime and give you nine cents change.

Not afraid to take chances, he took the kickoff on the run at the McKinley seventeen-yard line and simply went straight up the middle as fast as he could, juking one tackler and finally going down at the thirty-four-yard line.

The offense went out on the field knowing that to tie, they would have to march a half a field to get into field-goal range, but they didn't even think of ties. They were going to march fifty-six yards with a minute eighteen showing on the clock. They only had one time-out remaining.

Sam knew he would get called on with down-and-out's, so he could catch quick passes and step out of bounds to stop the clock as they tried to move the chains down the field. The corner covering him was a good-looking popular senior named Justin Hichcock, who planned on going to the pros, but he also had some dirty tactics taught him by his overeager beer-bellied father now in the stands, screaming for his son to level the speedy wideout.

First down, the ball was hiked, and Sam sprinted down the right side near the hash marks, planted his left foot at ten paces, and finally looked back as he turned sharp right. The ball was already in the air, and hit him just as he took his fourth step. He cut back upfield at the sideline, as the corner had slipped when Sam made his cut and was several steps off. Sam made four more yards and stepped out of bounds, just milliseconds before Justin tried to cut him in half with a spear into the side with the crown of his helmet.

Sam knew that Massilon was tough but did not coach its players to tackle with the head down, telling them instead to hit with the helmet slightly up, to avoid compression fractures of the spine, just like McKinley and most schools coached. Daddy had taught Justin to spear on most tackles with no concern for his son's safety.

The helmet nailed Sam beneath the floating ribs on his left side, just underneath his flak jacket, and he moaned with the immediate bruising. He kept himself, as he had been trained by his father, from making any comments to the player, or letting him know he was hurt.

The crowd cheered as the chains were moved and McKinley had a first down on the forty-eight-yard line, almost at the midfield stripe. There was still plenty of time.

On the next play, Sam ran the same down-and-out pattern, but the quarterback's primary receiver was the tailback swinging out of the backfield toward the left sideline. They made five yards on the play and still had plenty of time on the clock. They were now in Massilon territory, and the crowd was going ballistic.

Sam ran a post pattern on the next play, slanting toward the opposite corner marker, but it was actually a draw play and the tailback ran for a few, while nobody bit on covering Sam. The tailback was tackled after only two yards, but more importantly, he ate up a lot of precious time on the clock, and it was now third down.

Sam started his down-and-out on the quick snap, but planted and went right after just four steps this time, as they only needed a couple yards for a first down. Again, Justin was juked out of his jockstrap, and saw Sam pass the chain marker and add three more yards before he stepped out, stopping the clock.

He walked by Sam, both heading back to their huddles, and said, "Next time, punk, I'll plant your ass in the third row of the bleachers."

Sam's coach ran the same play into the huddle, and Sam looked at the quarterback, saying, "Tom, I am going down and in on a slant. Watch for me. Their safeties are coming up to back up the corners on both sides. When I ran the post, I was all alone. Nobody was covering over the middle."

Sam was far and away the best receiver, so Tom sighed and said, "Okay, man, this better work."

The ball was hiked and Sam tore down the right side of the right hash marks, and at the tenth step, he juked right and slanted inside toward the middle of the field, actually running directly at the far left cone in the end zone. When he made his cut, he saw the bent over body of Justin fly by, as the corner made his angle and attempted to cut in half the Muslim receiver who was now two steps away. The quarterback hit Sam in mid-stride, right in the center of the field, and he dashed into the end zone untouched, until he scored, and Justin speared him in the middle of the rear at the rear of the end zone. It bruised his spine.

A flag was thrown, Justin was ejected from the game, and Massilon was penalized on the kickoff, but it was too late for them anyway. There were only twenty seconds left on the clock after the kickoff, and McKinley's defense easily defended a couple Hail Mary attempts, winning the game 20 to 16.

Sam Ajamo was also a reporter/editor of the school paper, and spent a lot of time on the computer. He researched all he could the following week about Justin Hitchcock. Usama told his father what he had been doing, and the father concurred, feeling the son could develop some practical experience skills, especially in stealth.

It was the Tuesday following the game, and Usama sat inside Belden Village Mall waiting. He had gotten a picture of Justin from a *Canton Repository* article of an earlier game, so now he knew what he looked like without a helmet. Hitchcock's mother was someone Justin frequently visited at work. She was the manager of a woman's clothing store in the mall. Justin would drop by to squeeze money out of his proud mother, and was always successful, mainly because she felt sorry for him having to grow up with such a jerk for a father. Although she didn't realize it, her overcompensation because of her sympathy for the boy was helping as much as anything to make her son a jerk, too.

Usama looked up from his pocket game and his heart leapt. There was Justin Hitchcock walking down the mall toward him. He put his head down and pretended to play the electronic game. Justin passed by and walked into his mother's store. Usama simply stayed on his bench pretending to play his game. He could easily see Justin interacting with his mother in the store, which had no door, but simply an open front toward the interior of the mall. He could tell by the body language that the Massilon player was playing his mother, while two employees, both young women wearing their hair in French twists, watched in fascination. They seemed enamored of the well-built young man, who was also obviously putting on a show in front of them by being cute and charming with his mother. All of this was quite obvious and sickening to Usama. He saw the mother's hand go into the purse, pull out her wallet, and hand Justin several bills. He made a big deal about hugging and thanking her and giving her a kiss, then headed toward the mall with a wave and even threw his mom a kiss, which sickened Usama even more. He thought of his own mother, and quickly banished the thought, but his anger at Justin seemed to grow even more for some unexplained reason.

Usama followed Justin out of the mall and into the parking lot. He had not determined the type of car the young man drove. He followed Justin through the lot near the main entrance to the mall and saw him get into a red 1994 Sentra NSX. Why was Usama not surprised? The spoiled cornerback drove a flashy red sports car, just a few years old at that time. Usama made note of the license plate, and turned to go back into the mall. Once inside, he ran out the opposite exit and rushed to his own car. He knew Justin's address, so he headed south on Whipple Avenue NW, and would pass Myers Lake and then run into 172 after a few miles. From there, he would turn right, drive through Perry Heights, and would be in Massilon, which lay on the south-western outskirts of Canton, shortly after.

He caught up with Justin just after Myers Lake Plaza at Eleventh Street NW, and stayed back a comfortable distance. Usama followed the young man and dropped back farther when they pulled left off Lincoln Way after Perry Heights. He knew they were headed to Justin's, so he took the next street over. He wanted simply to see where Justin parked his car. The house had a double car garage door, but apparently the young man had to park out front of the house, at the curb. Usama smiled. That would simplify his plan.

Usama was thrilled that his father agreed to help him. It was 1:10 A.M. when his dad dropped him off at the end of the block and drove away. He had even duct-taped the little plastic button attached to the door frame of Usama's door, so that the light would not come on when Usama got in and out of the car.

Wearing his backpack, plastic gloves, and black jump-suit, he moved quickly and quietly down the street. A dog barked in the distance. A door slammed. Finally, he made it to the red sports car. Lying on his side next to the curb, he pulled the makings of his expedient explosive device from his backpack and set it under the car. He pulled an ice pick from his pocket and stabbed the gas tank. Gas started pouring out in a small stream. Usama set the jar down by the pool of gas, a large glass jar half-filled with beans. Next, he pulled a plastic bottle out of the pack and poured water in the dried beans until it covered them. Then, he pulled out a large lantern battery, which had two wires attached to it. The negative wire was hooked from the battery to a metal strip running across the top and a screw down inside the jar. The positive wire was attached to the top of a metal disk, which he had placed on the water covering the beans inside the jar.

He then tightened the screw down until it was close to the disk covering the beans. Halfway down the positive wire, Usama had stripped the wire bare and twisted both sides around each other, then wrapped them around a small bunch of blue tip matches. The matches were shoved inside a matchbook, near the match heads.

When the beans swelled up from the water, it would make the disk with the positive wire attached rise, until it finally touched the screw attached to the negative wire. This would complete the connection and make the wire hot, igniting the matches and matchbook. They would, in turn, ignite the spilling gasoline.

Usama was looking at his watch, when suddenly he heard a car. He squeezed under the sports car while headlights slowly approached. Could his father have missed the pickup spot? he wondered. The car slowed near his car, and Usama saw that it was a police cruiser. His heart stopped.

It went a short distance past the car and pulled up to the curb. He looked out and saw two officers open their doors and get out directly across the street from the house next door to Justin's. Usama grabbed the little snub-nosed Smith & Wesson Model 19 .38 of his father's, which he had tucked into the right cargo pocket of his black jumpsuit. The boy relaxed as they walked up to that house, and Usama heard the door open and then a man's voice and woman's drunken voice. They were arguing loudly inside their house.

Usama slid out from under the car, checked to insure he had left nothing, and sprinted down the block. His father pulled up to the corner and Usama jumped in. The elder man pulled away from the curb and was careful not to drive too fast.

His father spoke. "Usama, did those policemens see you?"

Usama replied, "No, Father. They went across the street, where some drunks were arguing."

"Allah be praised," the father said, "the Enlightened One, the wonderful prophet Mohammed, watched over you tonight, my son. Now we must go home and sleep. While we sleep and also tomorrow morning, your enemy will be weeping."

Usama barely slept, and had to prepare for school with about an hour's sleep. That was okay, though. His father had told him that such trials would train him to be a better warrior.

He got out of bed and turned on the TV. The four network television stations were out of the Cleveland area, so he turned the TV to WAKR out of Akron, smaller but also an ABC affiliate.

The local news came on and Usama and his father watched as a reporter showed firefighters putting out the blazing car right at daybreak, and reported that arson was suspected.

"Your training has started well, my son," his father said, as he stood and went to his prayer mat in the corner.

Usama felt powerful.

Sergeant Samuel Ajamo opened his eyes. He lay in a hospital bed in Germany, and a captain, followed by an E-7, came into his room.

"Sergeant Ajamo," the captain said, "how are you feeling?"

Usama responded, "Pretty sore, sir. A bit woozy, too."

"Pain medicine," the captain said. "The doctors are sending you back stateside until you're healed. They told me you'll probably get a little convalescent leave, too, so you can visit your folks before you come back here."

"Where am I going, sir?"

"Walter Reed," the captain replied. "For wounds received against enemy forces, Sergeant Ajamo, I am pleased to present you with the Purple Heart."

The captain took the Purple Heart from the SFC and pinned it on Sam's pajama top. He stepped back, and the SFC came to attention.

The captain whispered, "Present arms."

Both men saluted.

Then the captain whispered, "Order arms."

They dropped their salutes and both men shook hands with Sam. It was over as quickly as that.

"Fools," he muttered under his breath as the pair walked out the door.

Sam sat up slowly in bed and went through his things in the bedside drawer. He looked at the other men in the ward, and most were asleep. He found his sat phone and turned it on, lying back down. He pushed on the button for his phonebook, found the name he wanted, and pushed the button.

"Hello, Veronica," he said, smiling. "Hi, It's me. Sam Ajamo."

"Sam are you back from Iraq?" she cooed.

"No, not yet, but I am coming back for a little while. I am in Germany in the hospital, but they are sending me to Walter Reed. I got wounded just a little."

"Oh, Sam!" she said, making it sound like she was crying, "I am so worried. How bad are you hurt?"

"No, I mean it," he protested, "really, it is not bad. I got shot through the thigh, but it did not hit anything major. I am going to be fine."

"Oh, good. Thank God for that anyway," she said, thinking to herself, "Damn, he is my best contact in Iraq."

She went on, "Sammy, how could this happen? I am so glad you're alive. I'll help you when you get back here. Guess you're finally done with that nasty place."

"Oh, no. Do not make a fuss, please. It is really not that bad," he said. "They just want to let it heal from the inside out, so they thought it would be better for me to heal back there and get a break. Then I will return to Iraq."

"You don't mean it!" she said. "You are so incredibly brave. You don't want to go back, do you?"

"No, no, I want to, very much."

"Why? You can't mean it!"

"No, really. My work here is not finished. I have to rest now, but watch for me."

"Okay, what day will you arrive?" she asked.

"I don't know which day, but I'm sure it will be this next week."

"Good," she cooed. "Please be careful?"

"I will. You, too. Good-bye."

He put the phone away and closed his eyes, picturing Ronnie naked. Usama thought of the virgins he would someday possess in Paradise and wondered if any would look like Veronica. He drifted into a contented sleep.

RETURN TO DC

DC

Bobby Samuels jumped up, blinking his eyes and looking all around. His heart was racing, and he felt like someone had stepped on his grave. He saw all the files before him and darkness outside his window. He walked over to the coffeemaker, poured a cup of coffee, and added powdered creamer, shaking his head.

He had been poring over too many files for too many hours each day now, reading past newspaper accounts, after-action reports, morning reports, and all the pertinent information he could get his hands on. He wanted to leave for Iraq with some knowledge about what was happening.

He had come to a conclusion. He thought there might be an interpreter who had been moved from unit to unit where these unexplained attacks occurred. Maybe al Qaeda or the Ba'athists had infiltrated a couple of interpreters into U.S. units as spies, or in this case, as saboteurs. It had certainly happened in Vietnam a lot.

Looking at his watch, he decided he better go home, eat, and take a long shower.

He slept until the next morning but still felt like he needed a full week of sleep. He got ready and left for the Pentagon.

Ronnie pulled her car up near the exit at Walter Reed Army Medical Center, press credentials in the window. She greeted Sam, who was on crutches and wearing desert BDUs. She ran up and carefully hugged him. A specialist in hospital whites carried Sam's bag and tossed it into her trunk. He and Ronnie helped him into the passenger seat.

Ronnie hopped in and immediately said, "I am so proud of you."

Sam shrugged it off.

"Where do you want to go?" she asked.

He immediately said, "To eat some junk food!"

She laughed, saying, "Mickey D's it is."

Sitting in McDonald's, the two talked about news stories. When Ronnie's cell phone rang, it was Bobby Samuels.

"Hi, Bobby. I've been wondering why you haven't called. I missed you."

She winked at Usama. He smiled, but inside he felt a flame of jealousy.

"Oh," she said, paused, then went on. "Sure, that story I did on all those soldiers who got blown up near Mosul? Yeah, I can give you a copy. I have one in my trunk, in fact. Where? You won't believe this, Bobby. Have you eaten yet? No, I'm just kidding. I have a friend who just got out of Walter Reed with me. Yeah, Iraq. Okay, I'll meet you there in a half hour."

There was a small coffeehouse a couple blocks from the Pentagon, where Sam and Ronnie waited for Bobby

Samuels. Outwardly, Usama smiled when Bobby walked in, but inwardly he already disliked Bobby, especially when he gave Veronica a kiss when he first walked up.

"Bobby Samuels," she said, "I want you to meet a good friend of mine and fellow journalist Sergeant Sam Ajamo. Sam got shot in the leg in Iraq, but they just let him out on convalescent leave. Sam, Bobby."

They shook hands and Bobby said, "Thank you for your service to our nation, Sergeant."

Sam smiled awkwardly, and inwardly thought, "What a fool."

They all ordered coffee and made small talk.

Sam said, "What type of work do you do, Bobby?"

Samuels said, "I'm in marketing."

Veronica chuckled.

"Sam, he's an army cop, a C.I.D. investigator," she said. "Bobby, Sam is okay. He's a good reporter, too. He would know your real job before long anyway."

Sam said, "Oh, you're an MP. Wow! What rank, Bobby?"

Bobby replied, "Major."

"Ooh sorry, sir," Sam said, hating him even more, "I didn't know you were an officer."

Bobby said, "That's okay, Sergeant. I know. I wear civvies, because I really do not want to broadcast that I am a cop."

He gave Ronnie a sidelong glance and half smile, and her face flushed.

"I am really sorry, both of you," she said. "I forgot army protocol. I'm just not used to it."

Bobby thought to himself, "Yeah right, Ronnie, like you aren't trying to manipulate two men at once."

"Wow, Major," Sam said, "a C.I.D. investigator that is a major. That is something, sir. You must work the very top cases."

Ronnie said, "Yeah, and I know he's going to Iraq to investigate something big shortly, but he denies it. I think this article he wants has something to do with it."

"Damn her," Bobby thought. "What a big mouth."

Usama, however, had a different problem. He was listening at McDonald's when she said on the cell that the story was about the troops killed near Mosul. That was his work. This high-ranking army cop was going to investigate him. It took all of Usama's training and self-discipline to keep his emotions in check.

"Ronnie, dear, I do not know your source of information, but just because they were right before that does not mean they are correct now."

She sipped seductively on her coffee, then said, "Bobby, are you headed to Iraq or not?"

Bobby grinned and countered, "You said over a week ago that I was going. I'm still here. Now, I am an MP, so chances are good, that at some point, I will go to Iraq, but when I go is decided by the U.S. Army, sweetheart, not you."

"You did not answer my question, Major."

"Yes, I did."

"Are you investigating the soldiers that were blown up at Mosul?"

Bobby said, "Ronnie, I know you are a reporter and a good one, too, but I am a detective who happens to be a soldier. I investigate crimes, not battlefield incidents. That is for after-action reports, lessons learned, bomb damage assessment, but not for cops."

Sam was not buying Bobby's answers. His mind was working hard on this potential problem right now.

After coffee, Ronnie said, "Bobby, where are you headed?"

Bobby said, "Home. I have been at the office, working too hard. I need a long shower and a longer sleep."

"Fine" she said, "I am taking Sam south of Alexandria. We'll drop you off at your apartment, and you won't have to take the metro."

He protested, but she insisted, so they left together, with Bobby insisting that Sam sit in the passenger seat, so he would have more leg room.

Halfway to Bobby's apartment, Sam, wearing a beaming smile, turned to him, saying, "Major, as an enlisted swine in the army, I understand need-to-know basis, as well as clearances, but out of a reporter's curiosity, can I ask off the record, does the article interest you in regards to any investigation?"

Bobby grinned, and that alone answered Sam's question. The second thing that gave Bobby away was that he took too long to answer.

Bobby said, "Sergeant Ajamo . . ."

"Sam, please."

Bobby went on, "Sam, you already answered your own question when you said need-to-know."

Sam chuckled, "I respect your answer, Major . . . uh, what was the last name?"

"Samuels."

"Please, sir, do not lose patience with Ronnie or me. It is our job to ask questions, probe, and investigate, especially if we have hunches."

Bobby grinned. "You just gave my job description."

Usama Ibn Ajam-Vash gave his enemy a big smile and thought what it would be like to saw Bobby's head off while he screamed in abject terror.

He remembered watching the Nick Berg video and cheering "Allah Akbar!" over and over while the terrorist, who Usama knew was Abu Musab al-Zarqawi, used his long dagger, which looked to be a *khanjar* or *jambiya,* and sawed the young man's head off starting at the right rear side of the neck, so it would take longer and be more painful. Usama had prayed to Allah that he could do the same to an infidel before he was called to Paradise.

But because right then it was the expedient thing to do, Usama smiled again, saying, "I sure would not want your job, sir. It seems too dangerous."

Bobby laughed out loud, saying, "Sam, who's the one on crutches from a bullet wound?"

Ronnie started giggling, and Sam laughed even louder. Veronica pulled into a high-class gated apartment complex and rolled down her window.

Ronnie said, "5676?"

Bobby thought, "She doesn't miss anything," but he replied, "Correct."

She pushed the numbers, while Usama mentally made note of them. The large wrought-iron gates opened, and she drove through. Bobby's apartment was the second one in the back of the first group of buildings, and his rear deck faced toward a beautiful patch of woods. Privacy walls kept him from having any neighbors seeing him, or him seeing them while sitting on his porch. Usama's eyes quickly scoured every window and the door for weaknesses.

He said, "Nice apartments."

Bobby replied, "It's a place to sleep. I wish the security was better. We've had a few burglaries."

"Really?"

Bobby said, "Yeah, they never change the code on the gates, and don't patrol it at all. I have thought about getting a small dog, but it would spend half its life in the kennel, I'm gone so much."

Usama was analyzing and preplanning. This want-to-be cop would have to be eliminated.

Bobby got out and moved to the front window by Ronnie. He reached across, smiling, and offered his hand to Usama.

"Good luck with your healing, Sam," Bobby said. "You going back?"

Sam smiled, paused, and replied, "Yes, sir, I'm in it for the long haul. This is my war."

Bobby smiled.

Ronnie reached up and pulled him to her and kissed him.

"Go get some sleep."

"Thanks."

He walked to his apartment, and Sam noticed he unlocked a dead bolt and regular door lock.

They pulled out, and Sam lied. "It's a shame with nice places like this that they don't have better security."

Ronnie said, "I don't think Bobby has a worry. He used to be a Green Beret. Was in Delta Force, in fact."

Usama Ibn Ajam-Vash felt like someone had just stepped on his grave.

He forced a smile, saying, "He looks like someone you would never want to mess with."

Veronica batted her eyes at him, saying, "I don't know if you noticed, but he is someone I like to mess with."

Sam smiled. "I noticed."

Inside, he seethed with jealousy.

In Ronnie's mind, she secretly hoped she had made the younger man jealous. She had no desire or feelings about Sam. She just wanted to make him want her. She could tell that he did, although he tried to hide it.

Ronnie drove Usama to Fredericksburg, Virginia, where his father was going to pick him up, as he had been visiting two friends, also deep sleeper members of al Qaeda, living in Richmond, Virginia, where they would stay in obscurity until it was time for their mission to be carried out. She got off Interstate 5 on U.S. 17 and went into the town, where Sam asked her to drop him off near the Fredersickburg National Military Park. She wanted to stay with him, but he told him how shy his father was, and that he preferred seeing Sam alone. He even went into an elaborate story he ad-libbed about his father having agoraphobia.

Satisfied, she left him and his bags at a bench in a small city park, where he assured her his father would meet him. As soon as Veronica left he made several trips, struggling on his crutches, and carried his bags to the curb.

Usama also called his father.

"*Asalamalakim* [as-salam alaykum], Father."

"Hello. This is a cell phone. Are you there yet?"

"Yes, but do not come. I have had to make last minute arrangements. A new client popped up I did not expect," Usama said. "I do not like his goods, so I think I will cancel his contract immediately."

"Where is the client?"

"Where I just left."

"May Allah be with you, my son," the father said, understanding fully the nature of Usama's coded warning about Bobby and ignoring his own advice about being on a cell phone, he said, "*Ma as-salaamah.*"

Usama spotted a cab and flagged it over. He first went to the Virginia-Maryland train terminal and bought a ticket to Alexandria. Having the cab wait, he returned and had the driver take him to the closest Wal-Mart, again with the meter running. Usama bought some supplies in Wal-Mart and then had the cabbie take him to a feed store about two miles away. He was looking for one particular item, which he found and purchased. According to the cabbie, there was a Super 8 Motel near the train station, and he dropped Usama off there, gladly accepting the large fare. Usama rented a room and first took a nap.

He worked on his leg with the liquid from the feed store, and applied his newly acquired leg brace over the wound, wrapping his thigh muscle with an Ace bandage. Usama gritted his teeth and tried walking around the room without the crutches. It was not as bad as he'd thought it would be. The wound was healing quickly, and the antibiotics had apparently started knocking out the infection that had caused so much pain and swelling previously.

Out of his ruck he grabbed the medication he had stolen from the hospital. He put on plastic gloves and carefully mixed it with the medication from the feed store, in a Wal-Mart plastic jar with screw-on lid. He packed his backpack and put on the black running suit he had just purchased.

Usama then checked his room to make sure his bags were locked and he had forgotten nothing. He called a cab to take him to the train station. It was still daytime, but the sun was slowly inching its way down the western edge of the sky, like a child stuck on a garage roof.

It was well past dark when Usama disembarked near Bobby's home in Alexandria. He recognized the street and estimated it was about three blocks away. He was scared. Delta. Special Forces. Usama had not been up against an enemy like this before. He was walking without the crutches, and his leg hurt already. What if he had to run? he wondered.

Bobby was fast asleep when Usama made his attempt to break into the house. At the back door, he saw no evidence of a burglar alarm, so he decided that he was at least safe in that regard. He pulled a small wooden-handled plunger from the backpack, spit all over it, and pushed it up against the lower right pane of glass in the door. Next, he pulled out the glass cutter he had purchased and scored the glass all around the outside of the plunger. He tapped all over that area and heard the glass snapping. He patiently waited a full fifteen minutes to see if Bobby showed up, but Bobby had fallen asleep, fully clothed, across the bed, with the stereo playing. Finally, Usama popped the circle of glass out, attached to the plunger. He carefully set it down on a bush by the back stoop.

Hearing the music from within, Usama carefully reached through the hole and unlocked the door lock, then the dead bolt. He gently opened the door and stepped inside. He patiently waited for his eyes to adjust to the darkness, as he removed the small jar from the bag, unscrewed the top, and reached in, coating his left plastic glove with a substance like Vaseline. Next, he pulled a large sheath knife out, holding it in his right hand. Being careful not to touch anything with the coated plastic glove on his left hand, he adjusted the black ski mask so he could hear better.

Then he dropped to his hands and knees and started moving across the kitchen floor, slowly, ever so slowly, using the heels of his hands to brace himself. It took a long time, but Usama had spent years being taught by his father to be extremely patient in such a circumstance.

He was finally near the door to Bobby's bedroom, and he stood. Holding the knife in front of him, he carefully moved forward on the balls of his feet. His eyes were glued on the sleeping figure on the bed. He had climbed the stairs to get to this bedroom, and he mentally thought of his escape route if something went wrong.

A knowledgeable bow hunter, utilizing a practice of early Native American hunters, will never look at an animal he is stalking, but instead will look at a spot directly behind or next to the animal. Bow hunting requires a person to get much closer to his prey than a gun hunter does. Because of this, obviously, a great deal more stealth and wood lore needs to be applied. Animals, especially ones like elk and deer, whose lives are spent primarily being the prey and not the predator, develop a sixth sense. Warriors, very good warriors, also develop that sense to a certain degree. We all have it, and it is easily understood by simply remembering a time in your life when you were standing in a room and someone looked at you through a window or door. You got a shiver that ran down your spine just sensing someone was looking at your back. This sixth sense is a "sense of knowing."

Fortunately for Bobby, as a former Green Beret and Delta Force member, he had this sense developed pretty well. Also, fortunately for him, Usama's father did not know to teach his son such a lesson.

Feeling someone staring at him, Bobby's eyes popped open in the darkness. He saw the outline of a man only one step away from his bed, hand upraised with a large sheath knife in it. Bobby's head was toward the man. The figure stepped and stabbed downward, and Bobby Samuels kicked up over his head and hit the man's cheekbone, his foot sliding off the side of the face. He felt the knife plunge into his upper chest, and a moist gloved hand grabbed his face.

Immediately, Bobby tasted a really strong garlic taste in is mouth. Wide awake now, he jumped from the bed and faced the attacker, but he started to feel woozy, and where he was touched by the man, his flesh and tissue were hot, like Ben-Gay hot. The ex–Green Beret knew what happened immediately. DMSO! Dimethyl sulfoxide. It was a drug used more on animals like horses, to take care of sore muscles or tendons. It immediately penetrated the skin and produced a very strong taste of garlic in the mouth. It also heated, not only the skin, like Ben-Gay would, but also deep down into joint and muscle tissue. Feeling woozy, Bobby immediately knew someone had drugged or poisoned him, using the DMSO to make the poison penetrate into his body. He was losing balance. Bobby kicked at the figure but fell backward on the bed. He rolled by instinct, and the knife blade stabbed into the mattress where he had been. Bobby was a survivor, and his instincts took over, telling him he absolutely had to get the hell out of Dodge. He was so groggy he could hardly focus, and his stoned eyes darted in slow motion around the room. With enough semblance of sanity left, he made his courageous decision. He grabbed the pillow, shoved the figure with his foot, and holding the pillow over his face, dived headfirst through the second-story bedroom window.

Usama ran for the stairway. He knew the neighbors would be waking and reaching for their telephones, but he would try to make it to Bobby and slit his throat at least. Bobby was lying under a large tree with several broken branches on top of him.

Usama moved in closer, and Bobby's eyes opened up. He saw the assassin approaching, and he did what was totally natural to him. He remembered what his own Tae Kwon Do instructor had told all his children students.

The man, who was named Il Joo Choi, used to say, "So and a just and anyhow, if someone tries steal you, people not want get involved, so don't yell, 'Help!' But all people want to see big fires, so you yell 'Fire!' very loud. Then people will come and see you and help."

Bobby screamed as loud as he could bring it up, "Fire! Fire!"

He heard dogs barking and doors opening up, then the sound of a man's voice. "Hey, you over there. Hold it! I said hold it!"

Bobby looked and the assassin in black was gone. He passed out.

So far, Sam's leg was holding up okay, and he knew he had been seen. He made up his mind to insure at least no witnesses would be able to say he had a limp. His escape route was planned in advance, so he kept his head and moved fast. Usama was well away when he heard the first sirens approaching.

Bobby blinked his eyes at the light, and his head swam around a little, then he opened his eyes and looked up at the beautiful face of Captain Bo Devore. His mind went through a flood of confusions and emotion.

He smiled and softly said, "Bo, Bo, I love you."

Tears welled up in her eyes, and a smile spread across her beauteous face.

"What did I just say?" he said to himself.

Bobby came wide awake. He looked all around the hospital room, trying to figure out what was happening.

Bobby gave out a little embarrassed laugh, saying, "Did I just say, I love you?"

Bo could not speak; she just nodded affirmatively.

"I apologize," Bobby said. "I was hallucinating. How long since someone found me?"

Inside, she became very sad and let down, and did not understand this at all.

"Several days," she replied.

"Several days!" Bobby said, amazed. "What happened to me?"

Bo said, "You are very blessed, Bobby. Someone apparently broke into your apartment and somehow touched you with DMSO that was mixed with scopolamine. DMSO, as you know already, is kind of like Ben-Gay on steroids."

"Right," Bobby interrupted, "and when it penetrates your skin, you immediately have a real strong taste of garlic in your mouth. That is why I immediately knew what happened. What kind of poison did he give me with the DMSO?"

"It wasn't poison," she said. "Scopolamine is the stuff you find in patches you wear to stop motion sickness. In bigger doses, like you were given, it will make you woozy and then knock you out."

"I can't believe he didn't kill me," Bobby mused.

Bo went on, "He sure tried, Bobby. The FBI has agents working on this, besides our office. We think he must have been wearing rubber gloves coated with the compound and was going to touch you and knock you out, then kill you. He did stab you in the upper right quadrant of your chest. It went through your pec and stopped on the breastplate. Your lungs are okay. You were blessed." Her face got red and she added, "The surgeon said that your pectoral muscle was so well developed, it really helped halt the stab wound at the breastplate."

Bobby Samuels let out a sigh of relief, and thought about all the time he bitched to himself about lifting weights so hard.

Bo pictured what it would be like to lie in bed with her head on that hard chest.

"I kicked him in the face, and kicked him away from me, too," he said, startling her back to reality. "I can't remember after that."

She said, "You apparently covered your face with a pillow and went headfirst through the window. Very ballsy, Major. It seems you bounced off a red maple outside your window, fell through some branches, hit the bottom limb, and fell from there to the ground. Diving saved your life, though. Then, your neighbor said that he saw this guy approaching you and you screamed "Fire," several times, and the guy lit out like his tail was on fire. You sure used your head. It saved your life."

Bobby smiled. "I sure don't feel like it. What else is wrong with me?"

"Hairline fracture of the wrist and two broken fingers, hairline fracture of your left femur, moderate concussion, bruised ribs, pulled calf and thigh muscles, and other assorted bruises, which you will probably start feeling," she answered. "As I said, you were blessed. They could not believe you had so much presence of mind."

Bobby noticed a tear running down Bo's cheek.

"What's wrong?"

Bo gave a shushing gesture and replied, "I'm sorry. I'm

just so glad you're alive. You're my coworker and friend, you know. Hey, I'm the OIC on the investigation. When you feel better, we need to talk."

"Give me a cup of coffee with cream, please, and let's talk right now," Samuels replied. "By the way, where am I, Walter Reed?"

"Yes," she said, pouring two coffees from a pitcher, adding powdered cream to both. She handed one to Bobby.

"Any word on the guy who stabbed me?"

"He disappeared."

Bobby smiled softly, not surprised at all. Bo excused herself to go to the restroom, and Bobby stared out the window and felt his mind drift back. His eyes closed. She retuned to the room and saw him asleep. She kissed him on the forehead and walked out the door. Outside in the hall, two MPs with M-16 rifles snapped to attention.

"Carry on," she said. "You two keep a good eye out. Nobody but doctors and nurses to see him, got it?"

One was a spec-4 and the other a buck sergeant. "They will have to go through us first, ma'am," the spec 4 said.

She smiled and went on.

Bobby Samuels lay on his bed in the hospital and looked at the VCR/television provided for him. He was watching James Bond and laughed as he saw James get wounded and then basically recover from his wounds in less than five minutes. Bobby had just returned from physical therapy and was in severe pain and exhausted. He laughed looking at the video, and his laughter gave way to tears, then the tears gave way to crying. Embarrassed, he pulled his pillow over his face and cried hard into it. The army detective, ex–Green Beret, wondered what his combat buddies would think of him if they could see him bawling like a baby. Bobby had rehabbed from wounds before and hated it. He was frustrated and depressed. He was also angry at himself for his crying.

He sat up on the side of the bed and dried his tears, muttering out loud, "Stinking thinking! Knock it off, wuss!"

Completely worn out, he lay back down and chuckled at himself. He thought about how far he had come in life. Bobby thought back to one of the biggest changing points in his life, when he had also cried. We all have them, and his was quite obvious.

He had been acting out against the world. His mom and dad almost got divorced after years of marriage, and it about destroyed the young lad, who always tried so hard to get their approval. Prior to that, Bobby was the school spelling bee champion, had the highest grades in the school, and was very active in his family's church. He was also an avid Cub Scout, then Boy Scout. After the sudden separation, due to his father being SF basically, Bobby did a complete turnaround and was soon smoking, drinking, breaking into homes, stealing a few cars for joy rides, and getting Fs and Ds in school. By the age of fifteen, though, Bobby was still involved in athletics and excelled in them.

The army was his salvation. Bobby had failed the ninth grade and had to take the whole year over, so he graduated from high school at nineteen. He really felt like a loser. Bobby was drinking a lot, too.

Two things made matters worse: one, heavy drinking was encouraged by many in the army, especially in Special Forces; two, it was career-ending, just about, for an officer to get a DUI or any kind of trouble for drinking, so Bobby would really have to control it. He wanted to be an officer and a Green Beret. As the son of a Green Beret, he already was very gung ho entering the army, volunteering to attend Infantry Officers Candidate School, Airborne, Ranger, the U.S. Army Special Forces, the Green Berets. The army was more than happy to oblige. After basic training and ad-

vanced infantry training at Fort Benning, Georgia, he got
his orders for OCS, also at Benning, near the Infantry
School.

Once he did, there were many times he wished he never
had. TAC Officers in Infantry OCS made drill sergeants
seem like Sunday school teachers. For a number of
months, Bobby learned, he would be harassed mentally,
emotionally, and physically, almost twenty-four hours per
day. He could hardly get his hands on booze then, so the
army essentially helped him to control his drinking behav-
ior. Of course, this was all subconscious, as he was not
close yet to admitting to himself that he had that kind of
problem.

The candidates had to keep their rooms prepared for inspection twenty-four-seven. Candidates in the sixties and
before, under blankets and holding flashlights, would
spend most of the nights spit-shining the brown tile floors
with Birdseye diapers and Butcher's red wax. The floors
were so highly polished that the candidates would get out
of their cots, make them, step on one of the open terraced
dresser drawers, grab the door transom, and swing out onto
the narrow rubber runner rolled out each morning and
rolled back up before morning inspection. The bottom of
the legs of all the furniture in their rooms had Kotex pads
taped under them so they would not scuff the floor. The
only difference in Bobby's time was that they used a
buffer, with pieces of army blanket to apply the final polish, while several other guys stood guard at each end of the
hallway.

They wore tailored, triple-starched BDU uniforms, and
each day burned every little loose thread off them with cig-
arettes. They used a black Bic pen to go over each letter on
their name tag and each letter on their U.S. Army patch.
They used a black Magic Marker to go around the outside
edge of the Infantry School patch, which had a sword in

the middle of it with the words below that: "Follow Me." The candidates wore polished black helmet liners, with a round circle on the front and the letters "OCS." A diaper was carried inside the helmet liner webbing, which had Pledge furniture polish on it to shine the helmet when rest breaks were taken. Additionally, candidates carried a little cotton ball soaked in Brasso in the webbing, to use on their belt buckles and collar brass, which read "OCS."

During each day, the candidates would be required to low crawl through Raider Creek, near the Infantry School, or their company barracks lawn. This would mean another change of uniforms and spit-shined boots. After highly shining the boots, they would then be covered with a liberal coat of floor polish, which made them really shine. Besides all the harassment, Bobby's company wanted to win the Tactics Tiger Award, so any candidate who drifted off to sleep during the classes on tactics, strategy, weapons, and many other combat-related subjects at the Infantry School would get a hard elbow smash to the rib cage from the guy sitting next to him. There was a mutual agreement among all the candidates that nobody was allowed to get mad for that. Nobody ever got sleep, so this was incredibly difficult, staying awake during classes, even knowing you would probably get bruised ribs.

The changing moment, though, came when it was a Sunday afternoon, and Bobby was summoned to his TAC officer's office. Bobby knocked on the door and Lieutenant Jones growled, "Who is knocking on my door?"

Bobby hollered, "Sir, Candidate Samuels, sir!"

Jones snapped, "Come in here, Samuels!"

Bobby walked in the door, marched to the front of the desk, and sharply saluted. "Sir, Candidate Samuels reports!"

The TAC Officer returned the salute and said, "At ease, Samuels."

Bobby snapped his left leg out a foot, feet at a forty-five-degree angle, and folded his hands smartly behind the small of his back, saying, "Sir, Candidate Samuels, yes, sir!"

Jones relaxed and said, "No Bobby, dispense with the normal formalities and just say, 'Yes, sir,' and stand at ease in a relaxed way."

"Yes, sir!" Bobby replied, now worried that maybe he was about to be told of a death in the family or something similar.

"In fact," Jones added, "sit down in the chair there and relax, Samuels."

Now Bobby was really worried. Lieutenant Jones had never treated any of the candidates like they were human beings. Something was terribly wrong. He sat in the chair.

The TAC Officer said, "Samuels, I think you have the makings of a good officer, but you have a ways to go to get there. Next week is the thirteenth week review board, and I'm going to have to take you before the board and kick you out. Samuels, I want you to take a voluntary recycle."

Bobby felt like he had been hit in the stomach with a sledgehammer. Now it was decision time, and this would be a defining time in his life. He made up his mind instantly.

His shoulders suddenly went back, and he stood up, at attention.

Bobby said very firmly, "No, sir."

Jones jumped up from behind his desk and said, "What did you say?"

"No, sir!" Bobby said even more emphatically. "I have a mission for myself to accomplish and that is to graduate with this company, sir."

Jones shook his head. "Candidate Samuels, I think you could make a good officer someday, but if you do not recycle, voluntarily, I will have you kicked out of OCS. Are you crazy?"

"I might be," Bobby said, "but I will never be a quitter, the rest of my life. I will not quit, sir. You will have to throw me out. My dad is a retired Special Forces command sergeant major, sir. I gave him my word, and if I break my word, I would rather face you than him, sir."

"Get out of here, Bobby!" Jones said, disgusted.

Bobby said, "Sir, Candidate Samuels, yes, sir!"

Bobby went down the hallway of the barracks and went into the latrine. He immediately went into a stall, locked the door behind him, and started crying, punching the wall in anger with both fists. He did this for a full ten minutes. Then, out of habit, after several months of scrubbing and spit-shining everything, he pulled toilet paper out and started cleaning the blood spots off the wall, where his knuckles hit. Bobby heard the latrine door open.

He glanced under the door and saw a pair of spit-shined Corcoran jump boots striding across the latrine floor and knew it was a candidate.

The voice was familiar, Red Little. "Hey, Snake-eater, you in here?"

It was Bobby's nickname because of his father and his strong desire to be a Green Beret himself.

"Yeah," Bobby replied.

"Lieutenant Jones said for you to report to his office ASAP!"

Bobby said, "Thanks, man."

He came out of the stall and looked at himself in the mirror. He was wearing his Sunday afternoon relaxation clothes, spit-shined jump boots, triple-starched BDU pants, army belt and belt buckle (highly polished with Brasso inside and out), and a spotless T-shirt, with his last name neatly stenciled in black six inches below the collar and centered. He made sure everything looked fine and ran out the door, down the hallway, and knocked on Jones's door frame.

The Tac Officer roared, "Who is knocking on my door?"

Bobby yelled, "Sir, Candidate Samuels, sir!"

The second lieutenant bellowed, "Get in here!"

Bobby walked in the office door, stepped up in front of the desk, saluted sharply, and said, "Sir, Candidate Samuels reports!"

Jones returned the salute and said, "Stand at ease."

Bobby went to parade rest, while Jones said, "Samuels, I want to see improvement on your academics, but you have the highest leadership rating in the whole company. That last live-fire FTX [field training exercise] we were on, you had three really positive ORs [observation reports] written about you, and one was written by me. I'm not kicking you out. Just seeing if you would stick to your guns."

"Sir, Candidate Samuels," Bobby replied, "may I ask a question, sir?"

Jones said, "Yeah, go ahead."

"Sir, Candidate Samuels, what if I would have taken the recycle, sir?"

Jones grinned. "I would have let you, if you didn't have the *cojones* to see this through. What are you grinning about? Do you think I'm funny looking?"

"Sir, Candidate Samuels, no, sir!"

"I don't believe you," Jones replied. "You get outside and low crawl through the lawn sprinklers until they shut off!"

Bobby was really grinning now, and he left the office, ran out the door, and started low crawling through the wet, muddy yard. He knew he would not even be able to lift his arms and legs in short order, but Bobby was on cloud nine. This was a major turning point in his life.

Bobby got out bed and started doing ab work on the floor. He would, like everyone, have stinking-thinking days, but he made it a practice never to let them last very long. He was in pain and really sweating now, but he had to get to Iraq. A nurse walked in the door, took one look at

Bobby and the grimace on his face, and rushed out into the hallway yelling for a doctor.

She ran over to Bobby and grabbed his arm, as he opened his eyes in shock. He had heard her yelling in the hall, but did not know that it was about him. Bobby was so used to nurses coming in and out of his room at all hours, he had not really paid any attention when she came in, his eyes closed in pain and concentration as he did his leg raise exercise.

Bobby said, "What are you doing, ma'am?"

He looked even more shocked as two doctors and another nurse ran into the room. One doctor immediately knelt down beside Bobby.

The nurse said, "Are you all right, Major Samuels?"

Bobby said, "No, I am sore from doing abdominal exercises just now, plus rehab earlier today."

The nurse's face turned about five shades of crimson, and she spoke to the two doctors. "Doctors, I am sorry. I thought he was on the floor in excruciating pain, when I came in here."

Bobby laughed, saying, "I was!"

One doctor chuckled, then the other, and soon, all five were laughing uproariously about the incident. Bobby returned to his bed, and the medical personnel left. He would sleep well that night.

Bo came in around dinnertime and sat down with a recorder drinking coffee, while Bobby sat up in bed eating a very bland dinner.

A little testy, Bo said, "You had several calls on your voice mail from Veronica Caruso."

Her voice seemed a little strained to Bobby, but then it returned to normal as she went on. "Do you know who the attacker was?"

Bobby said, "No clue. Black tight clothes, maybe spandex, about six feet tall, two-hundred pounds maybe, but he could be a little taller and heavier. Athletic movements. What are you guys thinking?"

Bo said, "Well, we aren't taking any chances. There are two MPs outside your door. You've seen them. There have been break-ins in your apartment complex, averaging almost one per month, so that is the most obvious."

Bobby said, "Scopolamine and DMSO?"

"We know, we know," Bo replied, "but it could be someone with a science background, or who has worked in operating rooms."

"Operating rooms?"

She said, "I spoke with an anesthesiologist here, and he has used scopolamine to relax high-stress patients before surgeries."

"I know," Bobby replied, "but it sure seems like it is a professional. You better run a good investigation on anybody close to Colonel Adolpho Rodriguez, the rapist at Fort Benning. Also, check to see if anybody I busted, especially on violent crimes, has recently gotten out of the stockade."

"Already checked," she responded, "and we contacted the PMO [provost marshal's officer, like the military police chief] at Benning. I spoke to him personally, and he has his best guys on it."

Bobby said, "To me, the person who has the most to gain by my death is Rodriguez, so he should be at the top on the potential suspects list."

Bo said, "He is."

She headed toward the door, turned, and walked back, saying, "By the way, Major. You told me your father drummed a saying into your head."

Bobby said, "What's that?"

Bo sat down again. "He always told you, 'Give a sergeant a job, then don't tell them how to do it.' In this case, a captain, not a sergeant. You concentrate on recovering, and I'll concentrate on solving the crime."

He grinned, gave a mock salute, and responded, "Yes, ma'am."

She left after an hour, and Bobby was asleep soon after.

Usama Ibn Ajam-Vash was desperate. He had to kill Bobby, or the man would be found out. He had called Veronica a few days later, and during the conversation, he said how much he enjoyed meeting her friend. Ronnie said she had not heard from Bobby, but she voluntarily started telling Sam about him. Because of Ronnie's nature manipulating men, she also could not help herself, so she laid it on thick telling how good a cop Bobby was and how tough he was.

She had no clue that he was on his sat phone less than an hour away from her and within five miles of where she'd dropped him off. He had even checked his Black-Berry first and got the weather conditions in Canton, Ohio, and made a comment on the weather there.

Usama knew from the conversation that Bobby would eventually figure out that he was the Saboteur.

It was around three o'clock in the morning when the male nurse, carrying a small tray covered with a green sterilized towel, and wearing operating room garb, including a mask and surgical gloves, came into the room, nodding at the MPs as he passed between them.

This was not unusual, but the nurse walked so quietly into the room, and so carefully, that the sixth sense in Bobby went on guard.

While in northern Iraq with the Kurdish tribesmen, on patrol before the Gulf War started, Bobby noticed that, even in enemy-controlled country like that, the Kurds would not be as cautious as he would like while patrolling.

Then, all of a sudden, with no given signal, they would immediately get very quiet and purposeful with each step they took. It was as if each man sensed the presence of the enemy. Every single time this happened, Bobby would soon find himself in some type of contact with Saddam's soldiers, or they would spot some with binoculars. He soon learned that true warriors like the Kurds have that keenly developed sixth sense of knowing.

That sense had taken root in Bobby, years before, and he was now at full alert, but from experience, he lay still, feigning sleep, and slightly opened his eyes. He saw the form of the male nurse gliding across the room. It was too fluid, too graceful for a nurse bringing in something sterile. The movement was that of a skilled warrior, stalking.

Bobby was ready this time, and waited, watching through squinted eyes. He made his breathing seem relaxed and long, as if in deep sleep. There was a ballpoint pen on his nightstand. He would grab it and drive it into the throat of the assassin. Then he thought, "What if it is simply a nurse?" He immediately cursed himself for being in denial. It was the man from the other night, who was here to kill Bobby.

Bobby knew that in self-defense situations such as this, the natural tendency is to attack too early, so he made himself be patient. The shadow drew closer. It was now only two steps from the bed. Something came out of Usama's shirt and flashed in the moonlight, a knife blade. Bobby's hand went forward with his pillow in it, and the knife slicing through the air cut into the pillow. Bobby's fingers closed around the pen, but a hand grabbed him by the wrist.

Bobby screamed, "Fire! Fire!" and this caught Usama totally off-guard for the second time.

He released his grip on Bobby as he heard screams and yells in the hallway and footsteps running toward the room.

A fire alarm went off. Bobby could not move like normal, but adrenaline and tough-mindedness took over, and he was out of bed. He immediately rushed for the doorway and flipped the light switch on. Usama had propped the back of a chair against the door handle on an angle, but Bobby did not notice this as he moved away from the light switch.

Knife in hand, Usama stood facing Bobby. Bobby's eyes darted about the room, searching for a weapon, and he spotted the mop and bucket in the corner. Usama saw it at the same time and knew he would be no match with a knife against even a wounded Green Beret with that mop in his hand, which would turn into a deadly spear within a millisecond. The MPs kicked the door in finally, and a doctor and nurse ran into the room and all pulled up short, in total shock at the sight of the two facing each other.

Bobby grabbed the mop as Usama lifted a metal chair, placed it in front of his face, and ran for the window. Bobby stomped the mop, breaking the handle near the mop head. He threw it like a spear right before Usama crashed through the window, and it stuck in Usama's left shoulder muscle, as a bullet from the MP E-5 (buck sergeant) ripped past his ear. The window crashed. The nurse screamed, and Usama pushed the chair away from his body. He would land on the roof of an ambulance several stories below.

The Muslim killer braced himself and landed on the balls of his feet, screaming in pain, but he was operating on full adrenaline now. His knees flexed, and he sprang off onto the blacktop and did a shoulder roll, which broke the tip of the spear off in his shoulder muscle. The pain was excruciating, like the pain in his ankle, knee, and thigh, but he blanked out all pain for now.

Usama ran back to the ambulance, jumped in, started it, turned on the flashing lights, and tore out of the driveway.

He turned on the siren for two blocks, then pulled off on the side of the road, removing his ski mask. He flagged down a car coming up behind him, and the woman driving home from her work as a barmaid figured the ambulance had broken down and needed help. She stopped and had started to get out as Usama ran to her door.

"What's wrong, Doctor? Did you have—" The blade of his knife choked off her words, as it crashed into her windpipe.

She fell to the road holding her throat, as he jumped in the car and tore off into the darkness.

In the meantime, Bobby watched from the hospital window and knew that Usama, once off the hospital grounds, would probably not be caught. Nevertheless, he ran to the phone and called Bo, who in turn alerted the Office of Homeland Security, and she also called a friend who was one of the Secret Service agents guarding the president. Within minutes, all available forces were on the alert hoping to avert the escape of a would-be killer who had infiltrated Walter Reed Medical Center and tried to kill an MP army major.

Usama removed the hospital garb, revealing the black jumpsuit underneath. He drove the hijacked car around several blocks and then headed to the small shopping center parking lot where he had parked his rental car, a nondescript Ford Taurus. He returned to his motel in Fredricksburg an hour later and headed to his room, his suitcase in hand. He had kept it with him in case he had to make a quick getaway. Usama also carried the woman's purse from the hijacked car. He felt now it was more important to nurse his wounds and get into a new disguise, so he would retreat in his room for now.

In the bathroom, he ran hot bathwater and also filled the sink with hot water. Usama looked at his back in the mirror and started washing the blood off. It seeped from the wound. Putting on a bathrobe, with a towel over the wound, he went to the ice machine and got a bucket of ice.

The killer poured aftershave over his hands and the wound, and with the Leatherman needle-nose pliers he carried in his suitcase, he grabbed an end of the piece of wooden spear and pulled it out, while shaking all over from the excruciating pain. Blood gushed out, and he was glad, as it would clean some of the remaining splinters and dirt out, too. Next, he cleaned the wound thoroughly and then washed it with mouthwash. He placed a washcloth over it and then a bag of ice, while he soaked the rest of his sore body in the hot tub. Before long, the bleeding stopped.

Usama found several mini-pads in the woman's purse, so he put one on his wound and taped it in place with the duct tape he carried in his suitcase. Having taken three ibuprofen, he lay down with the bag of ice over the washcloth on his ankle and slept for hours, after placing the "Do Not Disturb" sign on his door.

For three days, Usama ordered delivery food and only left the room the second night to secretly hide the woman's purse in the motel Dumpster. He saw on the news that she had died from his stab wound to her throat. It meant nothing to Usama. It was a woman and an infidel at that.

In the meantime, the FBI and other agencies combed the Washington, DC, area looking for the killer. A classified all-nation alert was put out on the assassin, but he stayed busy in his motel room relaxing and watching HBO and FOX News.

Mortezah never told anybody she was from Iran. She, too, like Usama's father, had always referred to herself as a Persian. To her, it sounded more classy and proper and did not cause as much trouble. She worked hard cleaning rooms in the motel that Usama was staying in and took great pride in her work.

Mortezah was in the motel office with the head of housekeeping when the two FBI agents came in and showed the picture to the motel manager. The picture made her catch her breath, as she recognized "the Muslim from 314."

The ASAC, assistant special agent in charge, the FBI agent actually in charge, had been a CPA for years, got POST-certified as a cop and thanks to his uncle, a noted liberal from Massachusetts, got into the Academy. He had been an agent for ten years.

He said, "Why are you helping us and being so cooperative?"

In near perfect English, she said firmly, "I am an American, sir. I happen to be from Iran, and I happen to be a Muslim, but we are not all terrorists, you know, Agent. I am cooperating because that is what a good citizen does."

He went into the lobby, his face as red as a strawberry. Backup agents started arriving in unmarked cars, but this did not go unnoticed by Usama. He saw cars with no chrome, dark colors, four doors, no vinyl roofs, and men in business suits but wearing rubber-soled shoes you could run in easily.

A Hispanic maid had just emerged from Usama's room and was frightened, as the Secret Service and FBI agents descended on the room from both ends of the hallway. Outside, on the roof and in the parking lot down below, there were more agents, armed to the teeth. There was also a Blackhawk in the air overhead, with plenty of electronic goodies on board.

The ASAC gently grabbed the frightened maid and said, "Don't be afraid. Is he in there?"

Through glossy red lips, she whispered, "*Sí*. He ees sleeping, señor."

"Thank you," he whispered. "Hurry up and get in the elevator. We'll wait until you are out of the way."

He watched and waited while the elevator came back up and offered its little advising bell to say it had arrived. A rookie female FBI agent tried to speak, but the ASAC held his index finger up to his lips in a shushing gesture.

The largest agent there walked forward with a piston-type device, which was quietly placed against the door. It was a powered battering ram, and he hit the trigger and the door flew in, as the officers stormed in, yelling, "Federal agents! Do not move!"

The ASAC looked around and could not figure out what had happened.

He sat down on the bed and said, "Son of a bitch! How could he have escaped?"

The rookie agent came up and said, "Sir, I think I know."

Furious, he turned on her and screamed, "What? What do you know, Clemens?"

Clemens replied, "I tried to tell you in the hall, sir. That maid you let on the elevator was wearing way, way too much makeup for a maid who has been on duty all day, and she had no perspiration signs anywhere."

"Oh, son of a bitch!" he yelled, kicking the bed; then he dashed out the door. "Come on!"

Usama was already two blocks away in traffic when the Blackhawk got the call to watch for a car or person leaving the hotel lot. The entire hotel was cordoned off and would be thoroughly searched for hours.

Usama was gassing up at the Breezewood Rest Station on the Pennsylvania Turnpike before the mall surveillance tapes had indicated what type and color car he was driving, and it was parked too far away for any better identification. He had several of the turnpike's tunnels behind him, and each one of those ridges between Usama and DC seemed like one more protective barrier between him and the powers that be.

At the same time, on the orders of General Perry, Bobby was being wheeled into a makeshift private medical care facility in the basement of the Pentagon. There, he would continue to recuperate and take rehab, with whatever equipment was needed being brought in for him. On the orders of the USSOCOM commander at MacDill AFB, Florida, a team of four men from Delta at Fort Bragg were put on a C141 jet and shuttled to Washington, DC. They were brought into the briefing room and were told by a J-2 lieutenant colonel what had happened with Bobby Samuels.

General Perry entered the room, and the civilian-clad, long-haired, and some even bearded, men jumped to attention.

The general said, "Carry on, gentlemen. Look, I have to get back to Iraq, and my train is at the depot."

They chuckled.

"You men probably know Major Samuels, or know of him. He was one of yours, and I need him healthy and in Iraq, ASAP. You four are to keep him alive while he heals."

One of the men, who was actually a master sergeant who had served with Bobby, said calmly, with a Southern accent, "Suh, you git on outta here and don't worry. We got the major's back, General."

Perry stood and walked to the door. "Anybody gives any of you any shit, forget channels, get ahold of me. My aide is in the hall, and he'll give you my sat number. And I won't worry."

The four walked into the makeshift hospital room, and Bobby just grinned. He finally felt safe and could actually rest.

At the hotel in Fredericksburg, Mortezah described Usama as having a big belly and being about 230 pounds, but maybe six foot four, and clean shaven. The manager described him as being average build and maybe five foot nine with a beard. They did not do much better with artist's renderings of the suspect. Even the ASAC estimated the Hispanic maid as five foot seven and maybe 150 pounds. That became the description the FBI adopted, because he was a "trained and experienced agent." The rookie had Usama's height, weight, and description correct, but unfortunately, the ASAC got her shipped to the FBI field office in Grand Junction, Colorado. She had been a Brooklyn, New York, homicide detective but joined the Bureau just like her father and two cousins had: Another case of someone in power simply burying talent.

THE SANDBOX

Iraq

The buck sergeant carried his bag into the tent and looked around. Off in the distance, he heard the sound of automatic weapons and heavy machine-gun fire, followed by a muffled explosion. Suddenly, a battery of 155 howitzers not far from the row of tents sent marking rounds, followed by a fire for effect on some distant target.

A spec-4 walked into the tent and sat on his bunk. He looked at the sergeant and walked over and shook hands.

"Welcome to the 817th Transportation, Sergeant. Name's Harrigan, Rod Harrigan," he said.

"Pleased to meet you," Bobby Samuels said. "I'm Bobby Samson."

"How long you been in the Sandbox, Sarge?"

Bobby replied, "Three days. Processed in to division, then brigade, and finally made it here."

"Did you get the first sergeant's Red Ball Express speech?" Rod asked.

Bobby chuckled and replied, "Sure did. He sure takes his MOS serious doesn't he?"

Rod laughed. "More than anybody I know. His dad was the command sergeant major of headquarters and headquarters company at Fort Eustis, Virginia, or some shit like that."

Bobby laughed, saying, "I hope Patton isn't out here, waiting on us to deliver supplies to him."

Rod said, "Top sure as hell thinks he does. Why'd you get into transportation?"

Bobby lied. "Don't want to shoot anybody or get shot at. How about you?"

Rod said, "I was a long-haul trucker back in the States."

"Really? Who'd you drive for?"

"Independent," Rod answered.

"What did you drive?"

Rod grinned broadly, "Peterbilt!"

Bobby said, "Is that your favorite?"

"For long hauling, yeah," Rod responded. "How about you?"

Bobby said, "I didn't do any long-haul trucking, but I am kind of partial to the KW."

Rod said, "Yeah, the Kenworth's a great truck. I guess it would be my second favorite."

Little did he know Bobby had driven his cousin's Mack a few times before leaving for Iraq, because he would be posing as a buck sergeant with a transportation MOS.

Bobby said, "Usually don't get shot at in a KW or Peterbilt."

Rod opened a care package and produced a Nature Valley granola bar. He handed another to Bobby.

"Thanks."

Rod said, "Getting shot at isn't what is so bad. It's the IEDs [improvised explosive devices] and damned suicide bombers. And I don't know why, but they just about always seem to want to use white pickups."

"Has this unit lost any guys to attacks?" Bobby asked innocently.

"Are you shitting me? Just a few months ago, when I was a newby," Rod responded, "we had seven guys and two chicks killed. I got a Purple Heart out of it."

Bobby said, "You got wounded?"

Rod chuckled and said, "Yeah, I got my ass fragged. A lot of guys say that, but I literally got my ass fragged. I got several pieces of shrapnel in the ass, and still have one piece in the left cheek of my ass. It is kind of stuck into the edge of my tailbone, so they left it for now. You wanna see it?"

Bobby shook his head, grinning. "I've seen wounds before."

Rod said, "That was a weird attack, too."

This was exactly what Bobby had wanted. "Oh?"

Rod eagerly went on. "Yeah, you know, when we drive, we have these devices in our trucks that . . . Well, these ragheads use garage door openers and cell phones mainly to detonate IEDs, and these trucks have high-frequency jammers that jam the signal from those things until after we pass."

"Really?"

Rod said, "Yeah, plus when you drive, if you're smart, you always watch for debris along the road, dead animals, or spots in the surface that could have been dug up, explosives buried, and patched up. I always watch for stuff like that, especially abandoned vehicles along the road. Anything suspicious, I give it a wide berth, Sarge."

"Makes sense," Bobby added.

Rod went on. "So when this truck blew, it was sitting still, and we were waiting on the lead vehicle. Everybody was pissed. The lead vehicle had a bad thermostat and almost blew its radiator."

Bobby said, "Did they replace it?"

"Sure," Rod replied. "Oh, was Top pissed. Man, does he believe in PM."

Bobby said, "Preventive maintenance."

Rod nodded, going on. "So anyway, we're all stuck boiling in the sun, and I was bent over checking the back of my truck, when that sucker blew. They found plenty of pieces of shrapnel from one-five-five rounds, but it looked like they came from inside the truck, I mean in the cab, and in the cargo area. I mean, that is just my opinion. I'm no cop, but how could it blow from the inside out?"

Bobby said, "Curious."

"Curious, hell, Sarge!" Rod said. "If that's true, any one of our vehicles could get sabotaged. We have good security, and it's all American infantry, not locals."

Bobby said, "Anything else make you suspicious?"

"Yeah," Rod responded. "Top wanted that sucker hooked out right away, so investigators could look at it, without being exposed to enemy fire. We were on Death Alley when it blew, so he didn't want to expose our guys to fire."

"Gotta hand that to Top," Bobby offered.

"Yeah, you're right." Rod went on. "So anyhow, they brought in a Chinook, and I thought they'd need a flyin' crane, but that Chinook hooked it out slicker'n seal shit."

"Wow," Bobby added. "What did they do with it?"

"Brought it here," Rod said. "It's in the motor pool, with the disabled vehicles."

Bobby's heart leapt. Finally, a break in the case, he thought.

"You got me so interested, I'd love to take a look at it," Bobby added.

Rod said, "Hell yeah, man, I mean, Sarge. C'mon, I'll show you."

Bobby snatched up his M4A1 rifle off his bunk and followed Rod out the door. They walked between a row of large wall tents with sandbags running up the sides, and past two large buildings, which apparently served as headquarters for the transportation unit. The buildings looked to Bobby as if they might have been some official Ba'athist or government facility, but not large enough for a presidential palace.

As they passed by, a second lieutenant came out of one of the buildings and down the steps.

Rod whispered, "Our new S-4 [supply officer]."

Bobby nodded as he passed by. "Morning, sir."

The lieutenant stepped up in front of Bobby and Rod, angrily snapping, "What is your name, soldier?"

Bobby said, "It is Sergeant. What's your name, Lieutenant?"

The second lieutenant got even more red-faced, his skinny little shoulders scrunched up to almost the height of Bobby's lower ribs.

"Sergeant What?"

"Sir, it is Sergeant Samson. I still did not get your name, Lieutenant?"

The little officer bristled some more, and said, "My name is Lieutenant Numinauz. I'm the S-4 here. Now, first of all, stand at attention when I address you! Secondly, why didn't you salute me when you saw me, Samson?"

Bobby looked at Rod, saying, "Rod, you go on. The lieutenant and I are going to have a private chat."

Looking at Rod, still red-faced, the second balloon fumed, "As you were, soldier! You stay put, while this sergeant learns about protocol!"

Bobby noticed the unit's first sergeant sticking his head barely out the door at the top of the steps, a slight grin on his face. He just watched. Three other soldiers walking to, or from, shower rooms or latrines in the compound, heard the commotion and walked up behind the lieutenant and watched from a safe distance. Bobby Samuels was simply irritated at the stupidity of the young wet-behind-the ears butter bar.

Numinauz went on. "Samson, when you men see an officer approaching, you better not avert your eyes, and you better salute or—"

Bobby interrupted, "At ease!"

The lieutenant was totally shocked and taken aback and got quiet, almost snapping to attention.

Bobby said, "Lieutenant, my name is not Sampson, it is Sergeant, and you may call me by that, my first name, not my last. Number two, you do not salute officers in a combat zone or a sniper will zero in on you and put one between your running lights. Number three, Lieutenant Numbnuts, or whatever your name is, your NCOs can make you look good, or they can look the other way when one of your men that you look down on tosses an HE grenade under your bunk while you're sleeping and frags your sorry, know-it-all ass. Guys like you are the reason officers get fragged anyway. Now, in the future, with all due respect of course, sir, you treat your NCOs with respect and dignity and listen to their advice, based on their years of experience, and they will keep you alive and make you look like a hero. Or you can keep acting like an idiot, and you'll go home in a body bag. I normally speak to all people with respect, dignity, and friendliness, and I expect to be treated in the same manner. Do I make myself damned clear, Lieutenant?"

Bobby almost laughed, noticing that the lieutenant was standing at attention. He heard a chuckle from the first sergeant.

The lieutenant just could not move or say anything. He just stood there, not knowing what to do.

Bobby turned and said, "Come on, Rod."

They walked on to the motor pool, leaving the lieutenant still standing, dumbfounded, on the walkway at the base of the steps.

"That was just awesome, Sarge!" Rod said enthusiastically. "I have never seen an officer dressed down like that!"

Bobby just kept walking, saying, "Maybe it'll save his life. He's just young and scared to death."

"Scared?" Rod said.

Bobby smiled. "Sure, that's why he was barking."

"Barking?"

Bobby laughed, saying, "Yeah, it helps keep my sanity since I'm a career man. When someone starts yelling at me, no matter what rank. Or even in civilian life it works. I never take what they say to heart. I just look at them and picture them being a dog that they look similar to, and their words to me become barks, growls, whimpers, whatever."

Rod thought for a second as they kept walking, then said, "That is awesome! I'm gonna start doing that, Sarge. A dog. That friggin' lieutenant reminded me of a Chihuahua."

Bobby replied, "Life is too short, Rod. Helps you keep things in perspective. I think it would stop a lot of fistfights."

Rod chuckled. "Hell yeah! Thanks, Sarge!"

They went to the motor pool, at the far end of the compound. There, they found several disabled vehicles, including what was left of the truck that got blown up.

Bobby wished that he was alone, but he wasn't, so he had to say something. "You know, I wish you wouldn't have said anything. I have a really inquisitive mind. If someone gives me a mystery, I want to solve it."

"Me, too. Let's pore over this thing!" Rod responded enthusiastically.

They looked all over the truck, and it was very obvious to Bobby that it had blown up from the inside out. He searched every inch for the next two hours, and found several things. For one, he did not find an entry hole anywhere in the truck skin, where it had been hit with a rocket, missile, tank round, LAW, or RPG. Every hole, whether gaping or small, in the entire truck had the metal skin peeling out from the hole, instead of inward. This clearly, definitively proved that either the truck hit a mine or it exploded from the inside out.

So the C.I.D. investigator had to determine if the truck did, in fact, hit a mine. That was simple to check. Bobby thoroughly examined the undercarriage and, again, found shrapnel wounds going outward and down through the bottom of the cab. The frame was bent, but bent downward, not upward.

He also found pieces of the firewall with holes that were made starting from the inside of the cab. So, next he checked what was left of the truck's interior, and it was almost totally shredded, but there was clearly a blast pattern, which started under the driver's seat, which was essentially gone.

Of course, he did not share all the things he was spotting with Rod.

Bobby really pored over the cab interior, looking for something, anything small. He noticed brown stains all over and realized it was dried blood and flesh. He found pieces of shrapnel from a 155-howitzer round. Then Bobby found something curious. It had what looked like part of the U.S. flag and a round edge on one side, jagged on the other. It had, on the edge, the letters "elly—Stal" and was cut off on both sides. At the bottom of the stars-and-stripes field was what looked like a symbol of the top of the Saint Louis arch maybe. The thing looked like it could be the corner of a commemorative coin, or a badge, or maybe a large pin. Bobby slipped it into his pocket, wondering if it could belong to the saboteur.

He and Rod finished looking and Major Samuels innocently asked, "Find anything?"

Rod kind of threw his shoulders back and said, "Yes. Did you see the brown all over the inside? That was dried blood, man. Also, it didn't look like anything hit it. I think it hit a mine, a big-ass one."

Bobby said innocently, "Could be."

They were heading back toward their tent and spotted a commotion at one of the tents near headquarters. Several soldiers were laughing and playing around with something. They walked up, and a young PFC was holding up what looked like a giant lobster. Bobby had seen them before.

Rod said, "Look, a camel spider, man. They don't hurt humans, but they're so big, they eat rats and mice I heard."

Bobby walked up to the PFC, saying, "Can I have that when you're done with it?"

The young man handed it to him, saying, "Sure."

They walked away, with Bobby holding the camel spider, which was the size of a dinner plate almost.

Bobby said, "Actually, you weren't quite correct. These things can hurt you. They inject you with a poison that works like a local anesthesia, and they eat your flesh without you knowing."

Rod said, "You just got to Iraq, Sarge. How do you know that?"

"I read," Bobby lied, not wanting to let Rod know he was in Iraq when Rod was probably in the first grade.

Bobby said, "They call them camel spiders because they jump up from the ground and attach themselves to camel's stomachs, inject them, and start eating the camel's guts."

Rod said, "They can jump that high?"

Bobby said, "They can run twenty-five miles per hour, too. Have it all over Michael Jordan."

Rod said, "Who's that?"

Bobby just gave him a curious look and walked into his tent.

Rod said, "Wasn't he a basketball star?"

Bobby nodded.

"I'm a football fan myself," Rod responded. "Hardcore Steelers fan."

Something about Rod's innocent comment gave Bobby a mini adrenaline rush, but he didn't know why.

He said, "Where can I get Internet access around here?"

"Freedom Calls bank of phones and computers is only about a klick away," Rod replied. "Of course, the S-4 has access, and the CP, too."

Bobby said, "Thanks."

He got up and placed the camel spider inside a plastic sandbag and carried it out the door of the tent. He walked to the unit headquarters building and specifically into the S-4's office on the north end of the building. Bobby didn't see anybody at the makeshift counter. There was a note on the counter: "Supply NCO out. Be back at 1630 hours. Holler for the S-4 in case of an emergency." A staff sergeant's signature was scrawled below that.

Bobby got the camel spider out of the bag, tossing the sandbag in the corner. He'd really had no definitive plan when he entered the building, but now he did. He placed the spider on top of the counter, slammed his palm down on the counter about five times, and heard Lieutenant Numbnuts shouting and cursing from his office in the back, as Bobby, chuckling, ducked out the door, and stood right around the corner of the sandbagged building.

He heard the lieutenant inside say, "Who wants to talk to me? Oh shit! Oh holy shit!"

Bobby suppressed his laughter as he heard footsteps and peered out, seeing the back of the young officer, as he darted for the main door of the command post.

Bobby darted also into the SF office, hopped over the

counter, and ran back to the S-4's office. He sat down at the computer and typed in his access code and password.

He sent a message to Bo in his office: "Research any and all commemorative coins or large pins or badges minted celebrating the St. Louis arch, especially with letters outside right top "elly—Stal" ASAP. Give me results with emergency e-mail message to this headquarters CP to Sergeant Bobby Samson. Attach it as a Word document. Need this yesterday. Do not reply. Thanks. BS."

Bobby heard someone coming in the door of the S-4 building, and he quickly signed off, opened the lieutenant's window, peered around out back, and quickly went out, dropping to the ground. He walked back around the building and could hear people inside talking about the spider.

He went into his tent and lay down.

Rod said, "What did you do with the camel spider?"

Bobby closed his eyes, saying, "Gave it to Lieutenant Numbnuts."

He heard Rod chuckling as he relaxed. Bobby drifted off to sleep thinking about his old Delta Force teammate Brand "Boom" Kittinger, the best SF engineer/demolition NCO he had ever met. Bobby was going to need Boom's services, and hopefully very soon.

Bobby heard a muffled explosion in the distance and opened his eyes. Why had his heart leapt when Rod made the comment about football and basketball? Where in the hell was the inside man who was killing Americans? It was hot, Bobby thought; he would sleep on it for now. He started to drift off and wondered again about Boom Kittinger.

7

BOOM
Colombia

"*Mi amigo,* you are American, no?" the rough-shaven desk clerk said for no reason other than to make conversation.

The tall, slender man walked past the desk, giving the clerk a cursory glance. The sidelong glance from his piercing hazel eyes seemed to penetrate right into the clerk's mind, and the clerk sweated more than usual in the humid Colombian air.

Two flights up and half a hallway down, Sergeant Major Brand "Boom" Kittinger unlocked his door and entered the musty little room, which had been his home for the past two days, since his arrival in Bucaramanga. He would take his place, once more, behind the curtains, peeking out with the ten-by fifty-power Tasco binoculars. Enrico Pablo Vaccario had passed by five times already in the past two days, and the street corner below was the one place where he could not avoid passing when coming to, or from, the giant walled compound.

His eyes hurt from so much staring, so he stretched out on the too-short bed. As he had done so many times in his life, Brand thought to himself, "What the hell am I doing here?" His whole life, he had been told by loving, sincere family members or friends to "get a normal job," "be more responsible," or "start acting sensibly." They all meant well, but he could not. He was what he was, the oldest member of the super-elite Delta Force, headquartered in the old stockade at Fort Bragg, North Carolina, for so long, it was a joke with members and former members about being prisoners or "livin' in the stockade."

Brand thought back just a few days, to when he was sitting in a smoke-filled room in a small building in downtown Fayetteville, North Carolina, not far from the Airborne and Special Operations Museum. He and others were gathered around a beat-up long table, all sipping cups of coffee from Styrofoam containers. The looks on their faces and their different styles of clothing were of such variety, it was like a small convention of opposites was being held. One, a surgeon, wore an expensive gray and blue pinstriped suit, with a blue shirt and maroon "power" tie. The lady next to him was dressed like a homeless bag lady, and the one next to her was a housewife in a flowered shift, and she had a sandaled right foot, which never stopped moving up and down in anxiety-filled restlessness. Brand—he never used his nickname at such meetings—was next, dressed like a cowboy in solid classy Western clothes, his usual dress. He grew up out west and the West never left him. Beyond him was a police officer, apparently having just gotten off duty after a full night, judging by his red-rimmed eyes and many yawns. There was a lieutenant colonel and a master sergeant he recognized from Smoke Bomb Hill. The ring of people went around the table, as diverse as one could imagine.

The doctor finished what he was saying and said, "Thanks. That's all I have."

Everyone in the room simultaneously said, "Thanks, Jerry."

Smiling, Brand said, "My name's Brand, and I'm still an alcoholic."

Everyone said, "Hi, Brand."

Brand said, "You know this is a good subject today. Step four. Man, do you know how hard that is to make a fearless and moral inventory of yourself? I am great at being able to list other people's faults, but my own—phew! I have always been different. I don't seem to think the way that people say is the norm. I don't know why. I didn't say to God, when I was a little boy, that I wanted to be an alcoholic when I grow up. I just am, and after all these years, I know that I can have a happy life without taking that first drink ever again. In fact, I do have a happy life."

He paused and said, "No, that's not totally true. I am lonely. I think I've been alone most of my life, but I am happy overall. I guess it is mainly my job. I take great pride in it, and that helps me stay sober, too."

The housewife said, "What is your job, honey?"

Brand said, "I distribute Lego's, Lincoln Logs, and fireworks, and I really move lots of merchandise."

The lieutenant colonel, who recognized him and knew he was a Green Beret engineer/demolition sergeant who could expertly build a bridge or expertly blow one up, laughed uproariously at Boom's job description.

Most in the room gave funny looks, but the field grade officer winked at Boom, who winked back.

In his hotel room, Boom blinked several times, returned to the chair, stretching his arms and back. He continued his surveillance, sans optics, and blinked his eyes again against the afternoon sun. The three-car convoy would be easy to spot without artificial assistance, and the other spots were already scanned with the binocs. Boom had a plan. Now he just wanted to make sure the plan would work.

He had been given a mission and was working Opcon (meaning under the Operational Control) for some government spooks, who were also connected with DEA. He presumed it was the CIA, but did not care. He was serving his country and took great pride in that and in being the best.

The electric gate started to open and the lead car, a black HUMMER, full of bodyguards with MAC-11s and folding stock automatic AK-47s, came out of the shadows of the trees into the bright sunlight. Without picking up the binoculars, Sergeant Major Brand Kittinger knew the men in the vehicle would be looking left and right for hidden assassins. Next, came the long, black armor-plated Lincoln Town Car limousine, a tank in a prom dress. This would contain Enrico Pablo Vaccario. Finally, the third car, a backup and twin to Enrico's limo, also loaded with bodyguards and assorted weaponry, emerged, bringing up the rear.

Brand stared at the long limo, pictured the gold-toothed smile of Vaccario within, and caught himself playing with the heavy dirty-brass-colored coin in his pocket, something he did when he was nervous. He pulled it out and looked at it, wondering if he had ever actually really read the words inscribed upon its head and tail. In silent complaint against aging, he roughly jerked his 175-power Wal-Mart reading glasses from his pocket and actually studied the coin for the first time.

On the heads side, it read around the outside edge of the coin: "Special Forces Association Rocky Mountain Chapter." Then inside that outer ring was the Roman numeral X, from the original SFA decader insignia, atop the Special Forces crest with crossed arrows on a crest and the words "De Opresso Liber" (Liberators of the Oppressed). Below that, the letter *c*, which Brand had not really figured out the meaning of and had never asked. Below this were large Roman numerals IV/XXIV overlaid on top of a background of a mountain range, designating his chapter numbers. Then below that was a little box with the number 8 inscribed.

On the tails side, the coin read around the outer edge: "Charles Hosking—Alexander Fontes" and the words "De Oppresso Liber." Inside the border was a green beret with a diagonal dagger behind it. Then large crossed arrows behind a raised bar with Brand's name engraved on it. Then, finally, another crest below that with a horse overtop a lightning bolt.

Green Berets, and former Green Berets, like Boom, many times carry these challenge coins everywhere, lest they run into any comrades who might whip out their own coin and yell, "Coin check!" The tradition being that whoever was without his coin had to buy drinks for everyone.

Boom looked at the coin and thought back three decades to his first adventures in the army, and introduction into Special Forces. He had done it all, seen it all, and been everywhere, but he wanted more. It was maybe an addiction to adrenaline highs and a sense of knowing you are the best in the world at your job. A little over thirty years and still going. He loved his job. He had a ranch out in Colorado and that was where he would retire.

Brand had been lucky. He had very little gray showing in his hair or mustach. He wondered if any gray was now showing in Vaccario's or if he, in the way of the Hispanic males down there, dyed his hair jet black, until the day he was no longer conducting drug deals.

He thought about the gray-and-black-bearded Bin Laden. He was noticeable; six foot five, maybe even six foot six, but only 160 pounds, and walked with a cane. Numerous aliases: the Emir, Usama bin Muhammad bin

Laden, Shaykh Osama bin Ladin, the Prince, Abu Abdal-
lah, Mujahid Shaykh, Hajj. He even sometimes referred to
himself as "the Director." The leader of al Qaeda, "the
Base" was good at hiding, but he loved all the notoriety.
After all, how many FBI Ten Most Wanted fugitives had a
multimillion-dollar bounty on their heads by the FBI? He
loved getting young zealots to die for him while he hid in
hideouts surrounded by many bodyguards, Boom thought.

Then came that black day in America. Boom got sad as
he recalled waking up on that sunny September morning.
He'd reached over and felt the softness of the beautiful
blond-haired woman lying next to him, and then he'd heard
words coming from the large-screen digital television in
his bedroom. He sat up and looked at her, tears flowing
down her cheeks. Boom looked at the television, which she
had turned on ABC's *Good Morning America*. Kittinger
was looking at smoke and flames billowing out of the top
of the World Trade Center's Tower One, and then a jet
came into the picture and passed behind the building, slamming into Tower Two, out of camera sight, but flames and
debris shot out the side of it and the result was painfully
obvious. His mind became suddenly alert.

The blonde looked over at him, saying, "I'm scared."

He wrapped a protective arm around her and stared at
the television screen.

The days following were very busy for Boom. He immediately went to the stockade and waited for the calls
from Washington to Bragg and MacDill AFB in Florida.
As predicted by himself and many who had spent time in
Special Forces and Special Operations, the United States
had been attacked, mercilessly and without warning. In
spite of the 1993 bombing of the World Trade Center, the
USS *Cole,* the Marine barracks, embassy bombings, and
other events, the terrorists had caught us with our guard
down. They had preyed on the weakness that so many "old

countries" looked at as the Achilles' heel of America, over-materialistic values. Waving lots of cash in front of businesspeople apparently did not wave red flags enough to provide an early warning. For money, we had literally partially trained the terrorists to attack us. On top of that, the terrorists targeted a symbol for American commercialism. None of these things mattered to Boom. He was a warrior and his country had been attacked. If he was even being considered for retirement before, that did not happen now as the think-tankers at MacDill, Bragg, and DC had already had his name high in the mix, while teary-eyed firefighters were still looking for survivors in the smoldering ruins. His assignment would be what it had been before: Blow up bad guys and the places they hide.

Boom wrote down the time as the three cars stopped at the intersection, the length of time they paused, and jotted down a Roman numeral next to the other three of them, as that was the number of times the Lincoln limo stopped within two feet of the same exact spot each time. The other times, it was less than five feet. The margin of error would be very adequate for Sergeant Major Kittinger's mission.

He wanted to go out and search for some good food. Boom had a busy sleepless night ahead of him.

An hour later, he was seated in a small restaurant three blocks away. The place was small, clean, and had a good fare of American food, as well. He had been in there only five minutes when an American in khaki shorts and a golf shirt approached his table. The man was very tanned and well built. He introduced himself as Tom Smith, and Boom chuckled as he stood, and they shook. Tom stood almost a head taller than Boom's six foot one inch, and was built like an NFL tight end. When they shook hands, he placed a folded piece of paper in Boom's palm, which Boom immediately placed in his front pocket.

Tom said quietly, "I'm DEA, sir. I do not know why you're here. Need-to-know basis only, but that's the addresses of two safe houses. Each has a car waiting to take you to the Lima Zulu [landing zone] outside of town where a sterilized Blackhawk will pick you up. Two Apaches will be in the air to accompany you. You are top priority and everyone is on alert to assist you in any way you need. Good luck, whatever your mission is."

They shook again, smiling, and Tom waved, walking away, saying over his shoulder, "See you back in New York at the museum, Professor. Good luck!"

Boom smiled broadly and waved.

It was funny how things could be in the army; hidden away most of the time, the Old Man [commanding officer] thinking about new training exercises to kill time between insurgencies, hijackings, and the like. Now they needed him, and it seemed like he was the unknown celebrity of the week. He liked it after so much time. It was unfortunate that it took the tragedy of 9/11 to awaken our sentries, he thought. He'd had several different short tours in Iraq and Afghanistan, but he was glad to get missions like this one, too.

It was hard to eat, because he was excited about the night's upcoming adventure. Would he survive it? he wondered. He would return to his room, soak in a hot tub, and take a nap.

It was well after midnight when Boom exited his room, but this time by way of the balcony. It was now the twenty-first century, but Boom relied on the decades-old improvised Swiss seat. He opened the fake bottom of one of his suitcases and produced a long coil of nylon climbing rope, a shorter length about six feet long, a simple climber's snap link, and bowing to the new century, a pair of Teflon-coated climber's gloves, instead of leather. He wrapped the six-foot length of rope around his waist, tying a square knot, then wrapped both ends around and under his buttocks, and tied them a square knot at the other end, forming the climber's Swiss seat, an expedient seat to use for rappeling. He then looped the rope over the railing of his balcony, having earlier thoroughly checking the railing, bolts, and concrete floor. He doubled the rope and sent the double lines down to the alley below.

Next, Boom put his black backpack on, containing the contents of the false bottom in the other suitcase. He slipped over the edge of the balcony and wrapped the doubled rope twice around the snap link on his right hip, making sure it was not on the hinged door on the side of the link. He tightened the aluminum nut to hold the hinged part in place. Leaning out over the alley ten stories below, he made sure his body was parallel to the ground, bent his knees, and pushed his body out into space, moving his right hand from the small of his back out, and using the left hand to hold and guide the rope above. Boom fell swiftly and silently toward the asphalt below, moving his right "braking" hand back behind the small of his back to slow his descent and stop his feet inches from the ground. He then pulled down on one side of the doubled rope and released the rope from above. He coiled it and cached it behind a trash can and moved silently down the alley. Next, he removed the manhole cover closest to the street.

He knew he was totally exposed now. Brand had a fake ID, but he was a Green Beret sergeant major, an army lifer, even if he did sport a goatee. If he was caught doing a civilian in South America, nobody in Washington, MacDill, Langley, or anywhere officially in the U.S. would know who he was. He would be on his own.

At the end of the alley, he waited, cautiously surveying the street left and right. Kittinger started out into the street but jumped back as he heard noises at the corner. Two couples, obviously very much "in their cups," appeared down the street and started chatting, stopping near the corner. All four were carrying glasses of amber liquid.

Boom got the impression they were not planning on leaving soon, so he had to think. There was no traffic and no other people. He looked around and found a good-sized stone in the alley. Spotting a classy restaurant across the street, he tossed the rock from the shadows. It crashed through one of the windows and an alarm started ringing. The *policia* would soon arrive, but he only needed less than a minute. The alarm had the desired effect. Like most people, not wanting to get involved, the two couples disappeared around the corner.

Boom ran out into the street and removed the manhole cover, which was a distance he had eyeballed from the intersection. He quickly crawled in, as he heard a siren in the distance, and closed the lid above him. Boom went down the ladder and opened the top of his black backpack. From within, he extracted a fold-up battery-operated lantern and turned it on. It gave off a lot of candlelight power. He placed this on his forehead, held in place by a sweatband. He reached into the bowels of the pack and retrieved a large shape charge of U.S. Army vintage, with its identification numbers and writing removed by acid. He also pulled out a number of plastic-wrapped blocks of Composition C4 plastic explosive. Military shape charges are cone-shaped and blast in one direction, and are generally used to blast holes through walls, bunker roofs, tank sides, etc. Boom ascended the ladder and quickly attached the shape charge to the bottom of the manhole cover. Next, he placed blocks of C4 up against the cover, as well. Finally, he inserted an electronic blasting cap into the shape charge and another into one of the blocks of C4. A wire ran from each to a small remote-control receiver with a self-sticking plate on the back. He placed it against the steel side of the shape charge and inserted the wires. Then he pulled the lit-

tle cotter pin on the side of the receiver and breathed a little sigh, as he realized he had not been blown to
smithereens, something he went through every time he
pulled a safety clip or pin on any pyrotechnic or explosive
ordnance.

Boom went down into the sewer and headed back toward the nearby open manhole he had uncovered when he
first left his room. Minutes later, he was climbing out and
low crawling on Kevlar padded elbows and knees to the
edge of the alley. One officer was across the street inspect-
ing the window. The alarm had been shut off. Boom retrieved the rope and crawled back into the sewer, closing
the cover above him, in case the officer snooped around.
Resting his back against the crumbly sewer wall, he then
methodically started tying overhand knots in the long rope
about every three of four feet. When he had tied enough to
reach his balcony, he stopped and recoiled the rope.

When he emerged an hour later, the officer was gone
and the street was silent. Boom moved over under his balcony and removed his backpack. He withdrew a small
black Barrett pistol-grip crossbow. He cocked it and inserted a bolt with a weighted blunt end. The end of the bolt
was attached to the line, and he aimed through the four-
power scope that was attached and fired. The bolt shot up
slowly and arched across the balcony and fell down on the
other side, the rope falling across the balcony's ten-foot
width, and the bolt landing in the alley. Next, Brand took
the end and pulled the rope across the balcony until the
knotted portions were in place. He then tied the other end
of the rope around a large steel drum, securing it with a
bowline knot. He ran over to the other end hanging down
from the balcony and started climbing, the knots providing
easy hand- and footholds for him. Within minutes, he
climbed over the balcony railing and pulled up the rope.
Brand gasped for air, but he was not done. He reached out

far with his scalpel-sharp Cutco sheath knife, grabbing the rope beyond it. He cut the rope, then tossed the end out toward the street. It fell into the shadows on the far side of the drum.

Brand grabbed a bottle of springwater and headed for the shower. The water felt great. He moaned as he twisted under the warm water, and tried to work all the kinks out of his aging back. His legs shook from exertion, as did his arms. He was closer to fifty than forty and the bruises were starting to last longer.

Boom had been a recovering alcoholic for over two decades now, and he thought about how nice a cold drink or beer would be right then. He settled for the bottled water.

He slept.

The next morning, Boom Kittinger awakened early and, moaning, reached for a bottle of extra-strength Tylenols and swallowed some with warm water from the bottle on his nightstand. He stretched and jumped out of bed, immediately looking in the mirror at his love handles and moaning again, although most men his age would kill for such small love handles. When he was in his twenties, he ate everything in sight, and his waistline was thirty inches or less, but now he could look at food, and it would go to the waistline. He constantly worked to keep his waist down to thirty-four inches. Boom raised his legs together straight up, pointing his toes at the ceiling, and placed both hands at his sides, palms down, about three inches above, and parallel to, the floor. He slowly did fifty sit-ups, then simply crossed his left arm over his body and did fifty more, feeling it pull the stomach muscles on that side; then he repeated the move with his right hand. Boom's abs ached now, and he rested for one minute. Then he pointed both toes down, and with his legs together, raised his feet until his heels were six inches above the floor. His hands were folded behind his neck. He counted to two-hundred slowly while he held his feet still. Now his stomach had had its grueling morning workout, but the mirror showed the daily ritual. In his late forties or not, Boom had some ripped abs.

Next, he dropped down and did fifty slow push-ups, being careful to hold his body position completely straight and go down to almost touching his chest to the floor. Following that, he repeated the exercise with his feet up on the bed. Then he got on his knees and placed his hands, palms up, under the bed frame and lifted repeatedly as if doing curls. His biceps burned. The shower felt great afterward.

Boom took his seat by the window and made sure the red light lit on the remote control device when he turned it on. He shut it off, poured a cup of hot tea from the automatic coffeemaker, and poured more hot water from it into an MRE ration. He ate and watched, knowing that Enrico would soon be leaving the compound to go to breakfast.

The cocaine lord could not get out of his own house fast enough. He was hungry, no, famished, after a long night of sex, drugs, and booze.

Five minutes later, the SF NCO spotted the large electronic wrought-iron gates opening. He immediately armed the remote detonator. The red light came on, and he waited. The American assassin checked the viewfinder on a little broadcast-quality Sony digital video camera, and pushed the record button. Next, he zoomed it in a little more, assuming he would get the limo in the exact spot again. A minute later, the HUMMER was stopping at the intersection and Boom felt his hand sweating. The limo was in place perfectly.

Boom spoke softly, saying, "This is for all the little kids you've poisoned, you sorry bastard."

He squeezed the trigger on the detonator and a millisecond later, Ka-Boom! The manhole cover, with Enrico on top, crashed through the roof of the limousine. The driver was propelled through the windshield, along with the steering wheel, and the upper half of one of the bodyguards crashed through the right side window. The limo itself went skyward, folded in half just behind the middle, and turned over upside down. Most of Enrico's body, atop the manhole cover, shot skyward and dropped in a large arc, almost achieving seventy feet in height at the apex. It was a mess. The windshield of the second limo in the drug lord's normal caravan had been shattered by the twisted trunk lid of the main limo, and the lid decapitated both bodyguards in the front seat of the third car.

Boom zoomed in on the scene and got everything as thoroughly as possible. He then hid the camera and binoculars in the false bottom of the suitcase. Next, he ran around his room and made sure any suspicious items were hidden in a similar fashion.

Numerous bodyguards and cartel cadre members flooded out of Enrico's compound, all sprinting for the accident site.

Now Boom ran into his bathroom, splashed water all over his face, and held his breath for two minutes. He darted for the door and ran downstairs, eyes wide open. Acting totally panicked, he rushed up to the clerk, who had just returned from the front door.

The wide-eyed Green Beret screamed, "What was that? Are we under attack?"

As calmly as possible, the clerk answered in very broken English, "No sweat, sir. No sweat. Ees okay. Evereetheeng ees okay. Please, doan worry, señor. Eet was a car bomb. Mebbe a, whatyou say? Mebbe drug dealers mad at each one another. Blow up car. Doan worry."

Boom said, "Worry! Hell, I don't want to get killed down here for no reason. Get my bill ready. I am checking out."

Disappointment in his voice, the clerk murmured, "Sí, señor. Eet ees ready."

Boom ran to the stairs and yelled over his shoulder, "I'll be right back!"

In the room, he grabbed his luggage and wheeled it downstairs. He hurriedly checked out, acting scared to death the whole time. Boom made it to the closest safe house and never even entered. He was whisked away in an old sedan by someone he thought was a tattered-looking local. When they were on their way, however, the man shocked Boom by speaking with a very thick south Texas accent.

"Ya goin home?"

Boom replied, "Yep."

"I envy you," the man said. "I wish ah was goin' home right now. I'd wrap mah lips around the business end of a longneck Lone Star beer, and then mebbe follow it with another."

Kittinger said, "Why don't you go home?"

"I will," he said, "in about two weeks, when my assignment's done."

"CIA. Independent contractor," Boom thought, "probably ex-SF, maybe a SEAL. He can pick and choose assignments. Agency loves it. No threat to anyone's career. What the heck," he thought, "I'll just ask."

"So," Kittinger said, "were you in Group?"

"Weren't we all," the man said. "I mean management consultants like you and me."

He winked and gave Boom a broad grin.

Boom did not let him know he was still in Specops and not a civilian. The man did not have a "need to know," which actually was more important than a clearance.

The driver went on, "First in Okie. Eighth in the Canal Zone. Was in the Tenth in Bad Toelz and Fort Devens; also did some time in Det-A. Fifth at Campbell. Third Herd. Even worked Training Group for a while."

"Instructor?" Boom asked.

"No, CO," the man answered, looking out the window to the left.

Kittinger felt his face redden. If the man was the commanding officer of Training Group, he was a retired full bird colonel at least, and Boom asked him if he was maybe a sergeant first class or master sergeant. Here the man was ushering him around, and then Boom realized a couple things. They were SF. The man would not care if he was compared with an SF NCO. It would be an honor. Secondly, he was ushering Boom in a car collecting his government pension, plus making sixty to one hundred thousand a year more to pick and choose assignments he wanted to work for the Company, which was the term many SFers used for the CIA.

In less than a half hour, Sergeant Major Boom Kittinger was safely on a Blackhawk helicopter and lifting skyward.

Flying over the Colombian countryside, he was handed earphones with an attached microphone and a voice on the other end: "Great work, Sergeant Major Kittinger. Great work. By the way, this line is digitally scrambled and is secure. Our preliminary reports indicate you successfully affected mortal transience on Vaccario. You nailed one of the biggest traffickers of cocaine in the world. He has been poisoning our children."

Boom said, "Thank you, sir. Affected mortal transience? Do guys sit around a think-tank conference table and come up with these terms?"

There was laughter in the background, and the voice said, "Very funny. The Blackhawk will be taking you to a long strip with an AC-130. You'll have a short flight and then hop on a C5A jet. You'll be debriefed on the C5A and will land at Peterson Air Force Base in Colorado Springs. You'll get one more debriefing in the Isolation Facility at Tenth Special Forces Group headquarters at Fort Carson. I assume you have been there?"

Boom said, "Many times, sir."

The voice said, "Isn't it past Group headquarters?"

Boom said, "Roger, sir, next right, then it's on the left just before the rappelling tower."

"Near the rigger towers?" the voice asked, referring to a tall-ceilinged tower building where parachutes were hung, checked, and repacked by parachute riggers.

"Affirmative."

The voice went on. "You're going to Tenth first, because the SECDEF wants a quick read, and of course, since the Seventh is responsible for South America, you'll get debriefed at Bragg, too, then MacDill."

"Most of the people transporting you today just know the mission is Tango Sierra, but have no idea what it is," the man on the phones said. "Be sure you do not discuss your operation with anyone other than the debriefing personnel. This is a very clandestine operation, and we cannot read about ourselves in the papers."

"Wilco."

The voice added, "Just for your own personal information, Sergeant Major, the president said, 'Thank you and God bless you.'"

Boom felt a shiver of pride run down his spine.

8

MOVING TIME
Iraq

Bobby felt a chill run down his spine as he hopped out of his bunk. It was not quite daylight. He heard light snoring from the end of the tent.

In the chow line, he was speaking with Rod about professional football, when a clerk/typist from headquarters walked up to him. It was an Asian-American female PFC with a weight problem, but a very pleasant smile.

"Excuse me, Sergeant Samson," she said. "You are wanted in the Old Man's office ASAP."

Bobby acted surprised, "I am?"

She seemed sympathetic, saying, "You're not in trouble, but I think you have an emergency e-mail. I hope everyone at home is okay."

"Thanks," Bobby replied. "Catch you later," he called as he left Rod in the chow line, following the young woman out the door.

After an "attaboy" from the first sergeant for the butt-chewing of the S-4, Bobby was led into the office of the assistant S-3, who was on sick call for heatstroke. The S-3 clerk connected Bobby with his e-mail and left the office, closing the door. The air-conditioning was a nice reprieve.

The Word message from Bo was short and sweet: "Dear Bobby, I'm so sorry to tell you, but your uncle from Saint Louis just dropped over dead. There is not a single clue why. I wish I could give you better news. So very sorry. If there is anything at all I can do, please let me know. Love, Bo."

Bobby hit reply. "Dear Bo, Got your message. Thanks. Try the same thing in regards to the NFL team the St. Louis Rams. You want to help? Send me air-conditioned BDUs. Love, Bobby."

Bobby left the headquarters and had to go out as the NCOIC (noncommissioned officer in charge) on a convoy the following day. He rode shotgun in Rod's vehicle, and they delivered some MREs to elements of the 101st Airborne.

The next day, he heard back from Bo: "Dear Bobby, It is just so sad that there is not a single clue about the death of your uncle. So sorry. When I have been in the tanning bed and the sauna every day, I think about you. Love, Bo."

Bobby grinned.

He left the S-3's office and walked into the first sergeant's day room, smiled at the first sergeant, and closed the door.

The man looked at him strangely, but smiled and said, "Sergeant Samson. What's up?"

Bobby said, "Top, it is time for me to move on. I need a chopper to take me to Baghdad."

The first sergeant shook his head slowly, then sarcastically said, "Well shit, Samson, you want me to grab some money out of the cup and flower fund so you can get a whore and some booze while you're there?"

Bobby started laughing. "Top, I am not Sergeant Samson. I am Major Bobby Samuels, a C.I.D. from the PMO in the Pentagon."

The first sergeant was shocked and jumped to his feet, snapping to attention.

Bobby laughed. "Top, at ease, please. Relax. Man, I can't believe they have you so conditioned here like that. This is your office. You have enough stress."

The first sergeant relaxed, visibly, and poured two cups of coffee.

"Thanks, sir," he said. "Cream? Sugar?"

"Cream. Thanks."

The first sergeant continued. "That just took me off-guard. It came from left field."

Bobby said, "That truck where you lost so many a couple months ago."

The first sergeant said, "Yes, sir. Major, that was a friggin' inside job."

Bobby said, "You positive?"

The first sergeant said, "Sir, I have been a transportation NCO so long, I signed the requisition for Jesus to ride that burro into Jerusalem."

Bobby chuckled. "Road guard for Sherman's March through Georgia, huh?"

The head NCO didn't miss a beat. "Hell, sir, I had mechanics providing PM on all his wagons before the march, haying his mules during, and feeding the mule shit to his staff after."

Bobby really laughed.

The noncom got serious. "Sir, I am really glad you are investigating this. I told them at the time it was sabotage, but the damned know-it-all . . ."

He hesitated and Bobby grinned again, "Officers in this unit, you were about to say."

Top chuckled and nodded. Then he said, "Stand by, sir. Sandy!"

The young PFC who had summoned Bobby for the emergency e-mail stuck her head in the door, and he said, "Get me an ETA on any choppers coming in, and if there aren't any, get on the horn to your friends at Brigade or Division and tell them we need a chopper to take someone to Baghdad, and it is top priority."

"Wilco, Top. Is the boss going to Baghdad?" she replied.

"Naw, Sergeant Samson is going," the first sergeant responded. "Get a bird in here ASAP."

The door closed, and Bobby said, "Thanks, Top. Like much of the army, guys like you make things happen and keep going regardless of whose in charge."

"Thank you, Major."

The first sergeant's shoulders went back a little.

They spoke for another hour, and Bobby learned that a Blackhawk had an ETA of one half hour, so he shook hands with the first sergeant and returned to secure his gear. Rod was inside, writing to his girlfriend.

Bobby started packing his gear, and Rod asked, "Did you have a death at home, Sarge?"

Bobby smiled softly and shook his head.

He said, "Why don't you walk with me?"

They went outside, Bobby carrying his ruck and weapon, and they headed toward the headquarters.

"Where we going, Sarge?"

Bobby ignored the question, saying, "I have to be leaving, pal. I hope you stay in the army. You're a good truck driver, and I think you'll be a good transportation sergeant major someday."

Rod said, "You do? Wow. Thanks, Sarge. I'll tell you what: Watching you the past couple days, I know what kind of sergeant I want to be."

As they walked up the steps into the headquarters, Rod said, "Where are we going?"

They went in, and Sandy the clerk nodded at Bobby, saying, "Top, Sergeant Samson is here!"

"Send him in!" came the muffled voice.

They walked into the first sergeant's office, and he stood up almost at attention, but Bobby quickly dismissed it, saying, "Top, as you were, relax, please?"

Rod looked like he had just been shot.

"What?" was all he could get out of his mouth.

Bobby said, "Top, do you know this soldier?"

"Harrigan?" Top said. "I sure do. Damned good driver. How ya doing, young man?"

"Fine" Rod responded. "Thanks, Top. Thanks a lot. What's going on?"

Bobby said, "Top, I bunked with Rod here and became well acquainted with him, and before I leave, I just wanted to make sure you know him, and I wanted to tell you I think he is an excellent candidate for E-5."

Rod said, "Thank you, Sarge, uh I mean, sir. What is happening?"

Top said, "Well, Major, I appreciate you bringing this to my attention, and I'll see that it happens as soon as possible, sir."

"Major!" Rod said, "Top! Please tell me what's going on? You can't be a major. You're too good of a sergeant!"

Hearing the distant sounds of the Blackhawk, Bobby smiled and stuck out his hand. "It was great knowing you, Rod. Top will explain it to you later."

Rod said, "What should I call you?"

Bobby clapped him on the shoulder, saying, "Sarge is fine. I felt honored to be called that."

Bobby shook hands with the first sergeant and grabbed his stuff, heading out the door. The two just stared after him, both shaking their heads.

* * *

Veronica had a press pass around her neck, but the men who were passing her in the halls of the Pentagon did not look at the pass. She had a small slit in the side of her skirt that showed just enough of her very well-shaped leg, and her blouse could not hide her ample bosom, no matter how the blouse fit, but this one looked tailored to accent her body. But her overall looks, her long flowing hair, the high cheekbones, pouty mouth—everything just always made men stare after her.

She walked through the door that read "Criminal Investigation Detachment" and was one door away from Bobby's office, when she turned in, and said, "Specialist Berken, how are you?"

The C.I.D. clerk turned from her filing cabinet and said, "Hello, Miss Caruso. I'm fine. How are you today?"

Specialist Jennifer Berken had her dirty blond hair up in a bun. She, too, was striking looking, despite the military uniform, especially the very, very light powder blue eyes.

Ronnie said, "Call me Ronnie, please? And I am fine."

Specialist Berken said, "Very well. What can I do for you Ronnie?"

Veronica said, "Actually, since Major Samuels is not here, why don't you let me take you to lunch? I had some other business at the Pentagon, and am starving and I want company. Come on. We'll have fun."

Jennifer smiled and said, "Thank you. I would love to. I just have to check out."

She grabbed her purse and walked into another office, by Bo's, and returned. Talking and giggling like two schoolgirls, the two women made their way outside, turning many heads as they walked several blocks to Ronnie's waiting stretch limousine. A tall black chauffeur with a broad smile held the door open for them, and they climbed inside. He got into the front and pulled the limo away from the curb.

Ronnie started to roll up the partition window, but stopped it and said, "The Sheraton, George."

She finished rolling the window up and leaned toward Jennifer, staring into her eyes.

She said, "I have missed you, Beautiful. It's been almost two weeks."

Jennifer pouted, saying, "You know my number."

Ronnie said, "Oh, come here."

She pulled Jennifer to her and their lips met for a long time, their bodies mingling together in familiar fashion.

It was close to an hour later when Jennifer emerged from the bathroom, her hair back in a bun and makeup freshly put on very lightly. Ronnie lay on her back on the king-sized bed, still totally nude.

Jennifer sat on the bed.

Ronnie said, "I'm going to stay here and take a nap. George will take you back, sweetheart."

Jennifer leaned down and kissed her passionately again and stood, saying, "I love you, Veronica. Bye-bye."

She walked to the door and blew a kiss.

The door closed and Ronnie reached for the phone and dialed.

She said, "Sam, how are you doing? . . . I'm fine. Hey, I got something for you."

There was a pause, and she chuckled. "No, Sammy, you can owe me a big one, but not that kind of big one. Why? Because I am a professional, sir. . . . Remember, you were curious about what happened to my friend Bobby Samuels? I finally found out where he is and what he is doing. He went to Iraq, just like I predicted. . . . You are! You're going back after getting wounded? How soon will you leave, Sam? . . . That quickly? . . . Oh, really. I'll miss you, Sam. Promise you'll write, and also let me know if you get any scoops you want to share. . . . Anyway, let me tell you what Bobby's doing," she said. "You might want to do a human interest story on him after he is done."

They spoke for another hour, and then, totally spent from the passionate hour of lovemaking with Jennifer, Ronnie really did take a nap.

Thanks to the 1st Expeditionary Red Horse Group and the 447th Air Expeditionary Group, Usama Ibn Ajam-Vash, al Qaeda terrorist aka wannabe jihadist Sergeant Sam Ajamo, was able to forgo a military aircraft and was landing on the thirteen-thousand-foot runway at Baghdad International Airport on a commercial aircraft at almost the exact same time that Bobby's Blackhawk was only sixteen kilometers away, touching down inside the Green Zone, just outside an opulent former Presidential Palace.

Bobby looked at the four-story-tall marble palace, built in the shape of a ziggurat, or stepped pyramid, and large enough to hold five football fields inside one floor. It was surrounded by miniature palm trees and rose gardens. Even as the skids of the Blackhawk touched down and the doors opened, Bobby could smell the beautiful fragrance of roses, and he thought of Arianna.

Sam could literally smell the stifling heat of the desert, as his plane opened its doors. He thought of the prophet Mohammed and his ancestors, and how much he wanted to kill as many infidels as possible. Usama had spoken to the PIO, or public information officer, of the Third Infantry Division and was looking for assignment there as an imbedded reporter. It would be a start to search for and kill Major Bobby Samuels, before he could unravel the mystery. Usama knew Bobby was working undercover, so he could not just check unit records to find him.

Bobby was soon inside a secure room in the palace and was on a safe phone calling the Pentagon. General Perry had taken off for the USA to meet with the secretary of defense. Bobby was finally put through to him.

He heard the voice in Washington. "General Perry here. This is a secure line."

Bobby said, "Good morning, sir. This is Major Samuels, and I am on a secure line calling from your Hotel Quebec [headquarters] in Baghdad."

The signal was scrambled as it hit the satellite miles and miles in space above Bobby's head and descrambled back into the general's phone in the Pentagon, all in milliseconds.

"Bobby, how's your search going, young man?" the commander asked.

Bobby replied, "I have found some evidence, sir. We definitely do have sabotage going on, at least so far in one of the units I infiltrated. I have an investigator back there at DA, Captain Bo Devore, checking morning reports and unit personnel records for me, to see if one name pops up in more than one of these units. If we can come up with that, we have our man."

The general said, "Are you telling me, son, that some treasonous son of a bitch in our army is sabotaging our own units?"

"Sir, a good investigator does not jump the gun on identifying a perpetrator," Bobby replied. "I am not sure yet of anything."

A little impatient and anxious, the general snapped, "Why not?"

Bobby said, "No excuse, sir."

The general got embarrassed and replied, "Good answer, Bobby, but not necessary. It just frosts my balls to think that some swinging Richard in one of my units is killing my men. Bad enough fighting the enemy."

Bobby said, "Sir, whoever this is, he is the enemy."

"You are right about that son, and I mean it, when you identify him, I do not want any Abu Ghraib controversy or any other hand-holding, nose-wiping liberal media types turning the son of a bitch into a celebrity."

"Sir, believe me," Bobby said, "that will not happen. This is guerilla war, and he is a guerilla fighter who is not playing by the rules of the Geneva Accords. He set the rules for engagement, which are totally nonconventional. I am a cop, but before that, I am an American, and I am SF. He will be dealt with in an SF manner. You have my word on that, sir."

"Good, son," the general responded. "I have your back, and so does the CINC on this."

Bobby said, "No problem, sir. In that regard, I need an SF sergeant major named Brand Kittinger, but he goes by the nickname Boom. He was or is Delta for years, and has a Tango Sierra clearance. If he could be briefed on this—my mission, I mean, sir—and told I will need his help."

"I have even heard of Boom Kittinger!" the general interrupted. "It is as good as done, Major. We'll find out what swamp he is hiding in around the world, haul his ass in here, brief him, and ship him your way after he volunteers. I'll brief him myself."

"Thank you, sir," Bobby said.

"Keep after the Bear, son," the general replied. "My G-2, Charlie Sierra Mike [command sergeant major], and a couple others there know about you. If you need help and cannot reach me, they'll handle it. Jump on the horn anytime. Perry out."

Bobby heard a dial tone and hung up, satisfied.

He had to find some SF guys.

Bobby checked around the Green Zone and found some contractors who had served with him in Group. They were living in a large house and walled courtyard that had been the home of a high Ba'athist official. Bobby wanted a drink, and they would have hidden booze.

* * *

Everyone sat down at the table with a deck of cards. One guy was a former Navy SEAL, one was a former Marine, and five guys were former SF. An Iraqi housekeeper was just finishing up dusting when they sat down at the card table, and she quietly left, with one of the guys bolting the courtyard gate behind and then the large barred interior doors. One of the SF guys, who had briefly been with the HALO Committee with Bobby, walked over to the conspicuous pair of crutches leaning against the corner. He grabbed one and unscrewed the bottom.

Glasses were pulled out, and the guy with the crutch started pouring Jack Daniel's from the bottom. Bobby grinned broadly. Soda was brought out and poured into some of the glasses, where requested.

The bartender, retired SF Sergeant First Class Rey "Chi-Chi" Rodriguez, said to Bobby, "It's amazing. Every time one of us comes back from a leave, we seem to have a leg injury."

Bobby could not believe how nervous he felt. He had made up his mind he could only drink one drink, and it was bothering him to think about just having one.

The men played poker and talked first college and then professional football. There was a lengthy discussion about which division was better and tougher, the NFC or the AFC, with the older men at the table favoring the NFC and the younger favoring the AFC.

Then they started talking about the Hall of Fame and the Hall of Fame games. Chi-Chi grew up in Casper, Wyoming, so he was automatically a Denver Broncos fan. He talked about traveling to the Hall of Fame game for the Class of 2004 and how awe-inspiring it was to watch John Elway get inducted into the Pro Football Hall of Fame. This was followed by a half hour talking about how much better Elway would have fared in the stats if Mike Shanahan would have been his coach his whole career. Then one of the men who grew up in Jacksonville but was always a Miami Dolphins fan argued that Dan Marino was the greatest quarterback of all time.

Finally, the SEAL chimed in, "Terry Bradshaw was the best quarterback of all time. Four Super Bowls, that's what it's all about, man, but I grew up in Buffalo, and I have to tell you, I will always be a Jim Kelly fan."

Chi-Chi said, "Kelly was a nice guy, but he was no Elway."

The SEAL said, "I know, but you know, I went to his 2002 Hall of Fame ceremony in Canton and heard him and Stallworth, and—"

Bobby jumped up.

He said, "Wait!"

Bobby was excited. He ran to his duffel in the corner and dug a plastic bag out from a small metal box. He looked at the piece of coin he found and walked over to the SEAL and handed it to him.

The SEAL said, "Where did you get this?"

Bobby said, "Not important. I just wondered, could this say Kelly—Stallworth?"

The SEAL said, "Sure. That is a piece of the commemorative coin from the Pro Football Hall of Fame. See the top of the football, that arch there?"

Bobby said, "I thought it was the Saint Louis arch."

"No, man," the SEAL replied, "it's the football arch over the Hall of Fame building. Right there. That is part of the names Kelly and Stallworth on the outer ring of the coin."

"Thank you," Bobby said. "I gotta go. Thanks a lot!"

Chi-Chi hollered, "Where you going, Bobby?"

Bobby said, "Something important! Thanks, guys!"

The man who served on Bobby's team said, "I'll drive you! Somebody lock up after us!"

Neither spoke during the drive back to the former Hussein palace. This man was someone who spoke very little anytime. He also knew Bobby would tell him if he needed to know. The men just knew him as P.S., and they all thought it stood for his first and last name. It didn't. His name was simply John Smith, Brigadier General John Smith, and the P.S. stood for "Problem Solver."

They arrived at the big compound and entered the gate in the heavily armored Swiss vehicle P.S. drove. When he stopped, Bobby simply turned and shook hands.

The look said, "Thanks," and mutual respect showed in each man's eyes.

Bobby soon had Bo Devore on the secure phone and told her of his find. He shared with her that he had a hunch that the coin had belonged to the saboteur.

During his investigation, Bobby had tried to picture the spot where the coin piece was found, and the worn and nicked part of its edge made him feel like it might have been used as an expedient screwdriver, which it had been. When Sam rigged the bomb, he had to unscrew and loosen two bolts under the driver's seat to fit part of the package underneath, and he did not want to draw attention to himself by leaving to get a larger screwdriver. He had really chewed up the edge of the coin using it on the tough metal, so he'd simply left it there under the seat.

On a hunch, Bobby decided to call Ronnie, so he used his sat phone.

"Hello, Veronica here."

"Ronnie, it's Bobby Samuels."

He knew she had to know he was in Iraq, since she knew before he ever did that he would be going. He decided to call her and throw her off.

"Honey," she cooed, "I have been so worried. Where in the world are you?"

"Baghdad," he replied, "but I'm going to be leaving for Mosul in the morning," he lied.

He was actually going in the morning to the 3rd Armored Cavalry Regiment, originally out of Fort Carson, Colorado, but now stationed at Camp Stryker, just a little south of Baghdad.

"Why didn't you call me before you left?" she said in a pouty voice.

Bobby replied, "Well, your sources are great. I did not know until the last minute that I was being deployed, so I couldn't call anybody."

"So what are you doing over there, Bobby?"

"I'm working out of the provost marshal's office here, teaching classes to Iraqi police detectives, as well as local C.I.D. investigators, on investigative methodology, case building theorem, and using forensics to reinforce hunches. It is really boring, but at least I am eating great."

"You are!" she responded. "I thought soldiers are always poorly fed."

Bobby said, "Are you kidding! You know how they complained about Haliburton? We get a gourmet menu in their canteens—fresh fruits, veggies, various dishes. I'm getting fat."

"Yeah sure," she said sarcastically. "Not with that washboard you've got, baby. I miss laying my head on it. I miss having you inside me."

"That nasty teaser," Bobby thought to himself. "I can't believe she had to say something like that to try to manipulate me and make me horny."

He said, "Ronnie, you keep thinking about me, and I'll do the same about you here. I really miss you."

She cooed.

Bobby said, "So what's the latest news out of Iraq?"

She laughed, saying, "You're there! I'm here, honey! You should know more about what's going on than me."

Bobby replied, "Fat chance. You have more sources than anybody. You know what's going on all over the place."

While he was speaking, she was typing an e-mail onto the laptop of Edward Ormonds, a network reporter at the al Rashid Hotel.

Dearest Edward,

You have seen Major Bobby Samuels at dinners with me, the ex–Green Beret who I did the big story on a few years ago. He is at the army's headquarters in Baghdad. Stake it out and watch for him and follow carefully. Please advise. Could be big story.

Love and kisses,
Ronnie

"You give me a lot more credit than I deserve," she replied. "I mostly guess at things."

While they continued talking, Bobby, sitting at a secure computer, wrote to Specialist Jennifer Berken.

Jennifer,

Pass to Captain Devore's eyes only. Her computer is down. Going by convoy tomorrow at O-dark hundred hours to Camp Stryker, south of Baghdad. Will be under with the 3rd Armored Cavalry Regiment while I investigate. Leave messages on Sat mail. Will check often.

BS.

Bobby finally bid Ronnie adieu and hung up.

* * *

Usama Ibn Ajam-Vash was still at the airport waiting for his transport to northernmost Iraq. He'd been told he was being embedded with the 173rd Airborne. His phone rang and it was Ronnie. She told him what she had just learned from Jennifer about Bobby's new investigative assignment. Sam carefully promised her to notify her the moment that Bobby uncovered the person or persons sabotaging army units in Iraq.

He had to move quickly. Sam made several calls. He finally got the call he wanted: Sit still and wait at the airport. In one half hour, Sam was approached by a broadly smiling Iraqi police officer.

The man stopped at the seat by Usama and in a low voice said, "Hello, Sergeant. The sun shines today on the desert. Does it not?"

Usama replied in an equally low voice, "Not as warm as the look of the Divine Allah."

The cop whispered, "*Atastatti an tatahadath bil-arabiyya?*"

Usama looked about nervously and whispered, "Yes, I can speak Arabic."

The officer said, "*Hayaa natakallam bil-arabiyya. Linatruk hunaa.*" ("Let's talk in Arabic. Let's leave here")

Usama stood, saying, "*Hayaa binaa.*" ("Let's go.")

Five minutes later, the cop, who had walked away, met Usama in the restroom. When the stall area cleared out, both men dashed into a stall, closing the door. Usama sat on the commode with his feet down and the cop sat cross-legged on Usama's ruck, leaning his back against the stall door. They made sure nobody could see them through the crack on either side of the door.

Whispering and using sign language at times, Usama

handed a photograph of Bobby to the Iraqi al Qaeda spy posing as a cop. He told him where Bobby was and what his plans were.

Bobby smiled broadly when he saw Army Armstrong, the intel sergeant on his ODA with the 5th Group at Fort Campbell, Kentucky. He was walking out of the G-2 office when the two spotted each other. Even with the salt-and-pepper beard and native dress, Bobby had no trouble recognizing Army. They walked up and hugged each other and pumped each other's hand enthusiastically.

Bobby said, "Army, what the hell are you doing here? I heard you retired."

Army replied, "Captain, you are a sight for sore eyes. I did retire. I'm a civilian."

Bobby said, "Then call me Bobby please, besides I'm a major now. I came back in after nine-eleven."

Army said, "Okay, Bobby. How have you been?"

Bobby replied, "Busy. I'm a C.I.D. investigator now and am working on a case."

They had to suspend speaking for a few minutes while two Apache attack helicopters flew low overhead and disappeared beyond the HQ walls.

"What are you doing these days?"

"Private contractor," Army replied, "not for Blackwater, Dyncorps, or any of them. I'm with the Company."

Bobby said, "Figures."

Army said, "It's great. I'm not an employee, a private contractor. I can pick and choose assignments pretty much, and I'm making a hell of a lot of money. But the work is boring as hell."

Bobby said, "Yeah, right. Hey, I'm hungry. Let's go to the mall and talk."

Army said, "I'll go you one better. Let's go to the Jaa'i

Amerikky Restaurant. I think it means the Hungry American Restaurant. We can get a really good cheeseburger and fries there, and cold beer."

"Let's go," Bobby said.

Army said, "I'm serious, too. Nothing like what you would expect for my type of background. If you are a used car salesman with no military background, but can speak fluent Arabic, Farsi, whatever, they'll shit their pants trying to snatch you up. If you are SF, Specops, any type of background like that, the little old ladies in the Company's Management of Human Resources section seem intimidated."

"Thought it changed since nine-eleven," Bobby said.

"Some," Amy said. "But you know Uncle Sam. The bureaucratic wheels always turn slowly, no matter who is in the pilothouse."

They went to Army's heavily armored SUV, and Army introduced Bobby to a giant of an Iraqi man, apparently a bodyguard, armed with an folding stock AK-47 and crossed bandoliers, who Army said was simply named "Charley."

Bobby had his hand engulfed by Charley's. He nodded and said, "*Marhaban. Kayfa I—haal?*"

Charley looked pleased, as were many Iraqis who heard Americans speak any Middle Eastern language.

He replied, "*Bikhayr. Kayfa l-Haal?*"

"*Al-umuur aadiyya,*" Bobby responded.

Charley looked down at Army as he held his door open, saying, "You friend speak Arabic really good."

Army smiled and hopped in. Charley was trained but did not spot the two vehicles following him. They wound their way through downtown streets in Baghdad and suddenly pulled up quickly in front of the restaurant. Charley looked all around, not noticing the one carload of Iraqis passing by, or even seeing the other, which pulled up to the curb fifty meters back.

They indeed were served really good cheeseburgers and

fries, and Bobby had a cold beer in a plastic milkshake glass, while Army drank a chocolate shake. Two Iraqi men and two women came in together and sat at the table behind Bobby. Normally, the ex–Green Beret cop would sit facing the door, but he knew Army covered his back.

After fifteen minutes, Bobby knew something was up, when the owner and the young man serving went to the back quickly. Bobby heard a staccato of loud explosions right by his head on both sides that made his ears ring, and he reached for his guns, but his hands stopped in place as the Uzi was placed against the back of his head, and he heard the safety being clicked off. His head was pressed forward into the table, but not before he looked at the twitching bloody bodies of Army and Charley. A black cloth was wrapped around his eyes and face, and his hands were cuffed tightly behind his back.

A hand grabbed him roughly by each arm, and he was forced outside. Bobby heard the opening of a car trunk, and he was roughly tossed inside. He heard the car doors being closed, a muffled voice commanding, "*Asri!*" ("Hurry!"), and then the car took off at what felt and sounded like a high rate of speed.

All Bobby could picture was the tape he'd studied of screaming American hostage Nick Berg having his head sawed off with a long knife by masked terrorist leader Abu Musab Al-Zarqawi, starting at the right rear of Berg's neck, while two other terrorists pinned his arms behind his back and screamed, "*Allah Akbar!*" ("Allah is Great!") over and over again.

A shiver ran down Bobby's spine, and he tried to listen for any sounds he could hear to backtrack later to wherever he was being taken. While he listened, he tried to work his cuffs off his wrists. The ride started turning into a long one as time passed.

Bobby decided right then and there that, no matter what,

if they started cutting his head off, he would never scream, no matter what. He would sing the National Anthem.

Then he thought back to the amazing story he'd heard about his own father. Before he left for Iraq, he really wanted to hear more from Spook about his dad's exploits in Vietnam, and he was amazed what his dad had not told him. Bobby knew now that he would have to try to measure up to the old man. His dad had been captured in North Vietnam and become a POW during his second tour in MAC-V-SOG.

Honey's cell had large stone walls and floor, with a small drain, which also served as his toilet facilities.

He got his food and water, sparingly in a small pan, brought to his cell by the guards. Honey had also managed to get a four-foot length of bamboo, split lengthwise, in half. He would hold this up through his door window during the frequent rains and catch the little bit of rainwater dripping from a hole in the ceiling in the hallway. It would run down the bamboo, and he would drink the few drops he could get. There was a narrow entranceway as you opened the door, maybe six feet long and five feet wide. The ceiling was ten feet high. The guards would look through the small barred window in his door hourly, at the very least, and so far, had not taken away the piece of bamboo.

His best friend had been tortured and killed, and Honey was finally ready to make his move. There was a torrential rain pouring outside, monsoon force winds. Honey drank as much water as he could get through the bamboo.

He waited at the door and watched for the guards. He heard footsteps and saw two coming, engaged in a loud conversation about making *nuoc mam,* a pungent fish sauce quite popular in both North and South Vietnam. One was still verbalizing about his mother's *nuoc mam,* while the other casually looked in the window and saw an empty cell.

His eyes opened wide, and he screeched, "*Choi oi!*"

This was the most commonly spoken vulgar expression in Vietnamese, although the words actually meant "Sun-Rock."

His partner glanced in and fumbled for the key to the giant padlock on the big teakwood door. In seconds, the two opened the massive door with a creak and ran in, forgetting until too late to look up. Honey had climbed up the wall with both feet on one wall of the entranceway and his hands on the other. He braced himself directly above the door in the entranceway.

Too late, the two realized that he had to be above them, but his elongated body landed on both just as they looked up. This gave Honey a chance to smash the bridge of one's nose with a head-butt as he landed. The guard let out a scream of pain and grabbed his nose with both hands, as Honey jumped to his feet and punched the other wide-eyed guard on the base of his chin with a vicious uppercut. He followed it, almost simultaneously, with a left hook punch to the jaw that numbed his own arm to the shoulder. The little man's jaw made a loud cracking sound, as his eyes rolled back in his head and he fell face-forward, his face then making a dull thud as it smashed into the stone floor.

The first, blood streaming from his nose, dived at Honey's torso with a short scream. This yell was choked off by a guillotine choke applied when Honey directed the diving man's head between his right rib cage and under his right arm, which immediately wrapped around the man's neck. Honey reached up under the man with his right hand and grabbed his own shirt as high up as he could and grabbed tight. He then stood on his tiptoes, as the choke hold lifted the guard off the floor. Honey's bicep was cutting off the blood flow to the brain, from the side of the neck through the carotid artery. The crook of his elbow was cutting off the man's air as it squeezed against his Adam's apple. Honey's forearm, reaching up high to hold his own shirt, was across the other carotid artery, and the man stopped moving in less than eight seconds. After a few more seconds, he began moving again, going into convulsions. Honey kept his tight choke hold; and mere seconds later, a foul odor filled the room as the man's bladder and bowels involuntarily let go. In less than a half a minute, the guard was dead, and Honey let the body drop to the floor.

He wanted the desired effect, which would be to terrorize any guards bent on pursuing him. When they saw this man's body and figured how he died, Honey wanted them to think long and hard about pursuing him for very long. To that end, he grabbed the hair on the first guard and smashed his face into the floor several times to kill him also, and make him look pretty frightening to whoever found him. Honey grabbed the keys and his bamboo stick and headed toward the door. Looking into the hallway, he saw and heard nobody. This was what he had hoped for with the monsoon raging outside.

Honey sat down and quickly rubbed the end of the bamboo pole on the stone floor until it had a sharpened point. He then ran for the main door of the building, checking each cell window for other prisoners. As he thought, there were none. He had mainly been held in this separate building, so he could not even tap Morse code on stone to communicate, like most of the Americans did.

Honey made it to the main door and looked out. There was a small thatch-roofed guardhouse outside his building and overlooking a large courtyard. Inside, barely protected from the raging storm, was one lone guard, but he was armed with a Chicom AK-47 automatic rifle, loaded with a banana-shaped thirty-round magazine of copper-jacketed

7.62-millimeter bullets. If Honey could get his hands on that, he thought.

Kang Li Fat was the prison warden. He was not Vietnamsee but was in fact a Red Chinese officer working for years in Vietnam as an NVA advisor. He was always frightened yet intrigued by Bobby's father. He worried constantly that this man would eventually escape. In fact, by this time, the prison boss was totally fascinated by the tall Green Beret sergeant. He reminded him of himself. With the monsoon blowing with such ferocity, Kang Li got up from his bed, where he had been participating in the countrywide custom of *poc*-time, a mid-afternoon nap at the hottest time of the day. He strapped on his U.S. Army forty-five automatic and slipped on a pair of sandals.

All Honey could think about was getting his hands on that AK-47. He carefully unlocked the big door, just as Kang Li unlocked the door at the far end of the big building on the other side of the courtyard. Kang Li scrambled inside the big hallway and shook the water off his clothing.

Honey slowly went out the door as the guard peered across the courtyard in the direction of the big building. The guard's name was Nguyen Van Hoe, and he had grown up in the Haiphong area. His father used to beat young Hoe with a bamboo rod every time the boy did anything that did not please the old man. Consequently, Hoe grew up a victim and was always trying to win the approval of anyone in authority.

He had fallen asleep once while sitting at a table in the main building, and at two-thirty in the morning, Kang Li Fat decided to check on the prisoners, a thing he was wont to do when the mood struck him. He came upon Nguyen Van Hoe asleep at the little table in the main hallway. He viciously shoved the electric cattle prod he carried with him into the man's left ear and taught him a severe lesson about falling asleep on guard duty. As Hoe fell from the chair screaming and onto the stone floor, Kang Li, a sadistic grin on his face, continued pushing down on the cattle prod.

This incident had occurred fourteen months earlier, and after being caned and reprimanded in front of his fellow guards, he was assigned to the little guard shack outside Honey's building.

Kang Li Fat's outburst was now his own undoing, in that Nguyen Van Hoe had a permanent hearing loss in his left ear. Also, he was much more afraid of Kang Li than of any escaping prisoners, so his eyes remained glued on the door of the main building, watching for his maniacal overseer. This gave Honey the opportunity to rapidly sneak across the twenty feet from the door to the edge of the guard shack. There were two tower guards, but these men clearly had ducked out of sight from the raging storm, and both were huddled down inside their towers.

Honey made it up to the side of the shack and worked his way along the stone wall. As he leaned up to peer inside the open window on the man's left, Nguyen Van Hoe felt his presence. He turned his head, but it was too late. The expedient bamboo spear was the last thing he saw. His eyes opened wide in horror, but the point of the spear went straight into the left eye and penetrated his brain. The man had a brief moment of joy at the instant realization that one of Kang Li Fat's prisoners was escaping, but he could not be tortured for it. The next millisecond, Hoe thought no more. Honey grabbed the AK-47 and darted across the courtyard and came face-to-face with Kang Li Fat, as he came out the door of the main building.

Honey was bound and determined to locate and free the other Americans and the twenty pro-American Montagnard tribesmen and two pro-American VN/Chinese Nung prisoners in the other buildings, but now here was his arch enemy. For a second, the two stared at each other, more in fascination than surprise, shards of rain pouring down their faces and making both blink involuntarily. Then, while Kang Li clawed for his Colt .45 automatic, Honey raised the AK and, grinning, squeezed the trigger. Click! The weapon was jammed. Now it was Kang Li's turn to grin, and Honey's turn to react in shock. Kang Li pointed his pistol directly at Honey's face and pulled the trigger. Click!

He dropped the pistol and covered his left fist with the palm of his right hand, raised his left leg up slightly, moved his hands in a somewhat circular movement to the side and back to his front, and bowed to Honey. Not copying the kung fu gesture, but using his simpler karate tradition, Honey put his hands on the side of his legs and bowed, eyes glued on his enemy all the while. Stepping into a cat stance, Kang Li raised his hands and looked like a praying mantis in the way he held them.

With a loud yell, he lunged forward and threw a vicious sidekick at Honey's face, and the Green Beret ducked and jabbed upward with his bamboo spear, already clean of the blood of Hoe because of the heavy rain.

It penetrated the back thigh muscle of the Chinese killer, and he screamed in excruciating pain, and it exited through the top of the leg. Blood squirted out in throbbing bursts, stemming from the puncture of the femoral artery. Honey laughed out loud, as Kang Li stared at him from the muddy ground. The American made the fallen Kang Li scream again, as he put the bottom of his left foot against Kang Li's thigh and yanked the spear out with a pop.

The color was gone from the commandant's face, and Honey Samuels raised the spear and was about to thrust it into Kang Li's chest, when something stopped him. He looked down and saw the arterial bleeding in the leg, and Honey held his weakening foe down in the rain with his foot as the life drained out of him and the struggling slowed.

Honey looked down at his dying enemy and whispered

between clenched teeth, "Kang Li Fat, I told you someday I would kill you for all that you have done, and today it has been done. You can die with the fact that I escaped, and you could never break me."

He spit on the Chinese officer and stood there until the man man died. As quickly as that, it was over for his arch foe.

He bent down and grabbed Kang Li's pistol and took off for the wall. He heard a whistle and turned to see Kang Li blowing a little steel whistle he feebly held up to his lips. Honey ran back and shot Kang Li Fat in the forehead, twice.

Honey scaled a thick tree by the wall and went up and over, as two shots from the towers clipped the stone near him. He heard alarms going off seconds later, but he was already at a dead run on weary legs, pushing himself through the driving gale. He dodged down Hanoi alleys and between shacks and buildings, trying to make sure he was angling downhill. His theory was that he would eventually make it to the river, if he could keep going downhill.

Honey's legs felt as if they were filled with mercury, and he felt as if his lungs were going to burst, but nothing was going to stop him from making the relative safety of the river. Then he ran around a corner and crashed head-long into a police officer, the man's helmet flying into the raging little stream running along the edge of the street and being carried out of sight right away into the steel gray of absolute humidity.

Honey looked down at the cop, who was trying to draw his .38 special revolver. Samuels jumped forward, raising his right foot high. The blade of his heel came crashing down on the man's solar plexus and the wind left him in a gush, eyes opening with instant panic. Cocking his knee and now a step closer, Honey struck out sideways with the blade of his heel, and the sidekick caught the North Vietnamese cop in the throat, crushing it. He started strangling, as Honey grabbed his pistol, holster, and ammo belt.

The Green Beret sergeant disappeared into the darkness; and within minutes, found himself on the banks of a large river. As he ran along the bank, he found a log and tossed himself into the river clutching the wood.

Once in the water, Honey hung on for dear life, kicking his legs only lazily. The current helped move him at a high rate of speed, and soon the town and its buildings were behind him, and he could barely make out the forms of trees in the emerald green jungle on both sides of the river, because the downpour was still so heavy.

The escaped POW felt tremendously guilty because he had wanted to save the other POWs. Then he started feeling stupid because he did not kill Kang Li all the way at first, and it really bothered him. Then he simply felt relief, and Honey just started bawling. He cried and cried, and shed tears of total relief and joy. Honey had cried in captivity, but always in private and very quietly. Here, he was in the wilderness with a screaming, howling monsoon blotting out any sounds he might make and destroying any possibility of someone on shore seeing him. He cried the cry of a broken heart, and the floodgates really opened wide. He cried so hard, it gave him a headache, and his throat, and even his stomach, hurt.

He would need food and shelter. Honey Samuels had to make it south through hundreds upon hundreds of miles of enemy territory. It would be many days, and much more danger, before Honey saw an American face again, but he was on his way. He was a Green Beret and had great pride in that. He could live off the land and eat anything. He could defeat any enemy, in any number. That was his attitude, and Honey knew he would make it. He did, but he never spoke about it when Bobby was growing up.

* * *

Now Bobby, Honey's son, was in the same situation. He was an American soldier who was a POW. He must escape, just like his dad did. He must survive.

Bobby automatically listened for any identifying sounds, while he worked on getting loose. Why did they kill Army but capture him? he wondered. He had no clue that Usama Ibn Ajam-Vash had said he wanted a video or DVD of Major Bobby Samuels having his head cut off while he screamed.

Bobby remembered he had a Special Forces boot knife tucked away in his boot, and he reached down for it, not realizing it had been taken away. Calming himself down and thinking, he twisted his body around and started feeling behind him with his cuffed hands, his fingers finally finding a piece of metal sticking through the fender well. It was a long, skinny screw. Bobby still had the piece of commemorative coin in his pocket. He kept tilting his hips and shaking until he got it to drop out of his pocket.

Bobby twisted, got it in his hands, and got himself in place. He finally started unscrewing the screw, and soon was unscrewing it with his fingers. It came free.

Now Bobby carefully squirmed around and dropped the screw on the trunk floor. Then, careful not to lose it, he twisted around and started placing his mouth on the floor. He found the screw. Bobby used his lips to pull the screw up, and he tried to hide it in his mouth, but it was too long. They would find it. He was very frustrated. Bobby was a Christian and he prayed now, and asked for an answer.

Bobby Samuels sobbed, then stifled it, as the answer came to him. He must survive. Bobby spit the screw out onto the same spot on the floor of the trunk and twisted around again, until he felt it with his fingers. He grabbed it

and slowly raised his cuffed hands and pushed them down
the back of his pants. Bobby gritted his teeth and slowly,
carefully inserted the long screw into his rectum. He asked
God to protect him. It felt like he had to have a bowel
movement, and Bobby fought the urge to evacuate the
sharp metal object.

No sooner did he get the screw in place than he heard
excited voices from the cab and the car slowed. Bobby
heard the distant sounds of a mosque while the car slowed.
He heard a gate being opened, and the car was apparently
pulled through the gate, which was closed behind them. It
stopped and the engine was turned off. The trunk opened,
and he was roughly jerked out, as he felt the screw tear into
his rectal tissue. Ignoring the pain, Bobby tightened his
sphincter muscle and held it like that, while he was
marched inside the house and taken upstairs.

They had not left Baghdad, as he heard city sounds and
experienced many stops on the way there. He felt he was in
a neighborhood area.

Bobby was taken into a room, where his blindfold was
removed. To his surprise, none of his captors wore a mask
or scarf. This told him one thing. He was going to be
killed, definitely. He knew he could not afford to be in denial.

Two men stripped him naked, and he thanked God that
his parents did not have him circumcised, as this was
pointed out by one of the captors making a derisive remark
about Jews. They went through his clothes and removed
everything, and one took the clothes out of the room.
Bobby was still blinking his eyes when the apparent leader
entered the room, and Bobby was amazed when he saw the
resemblance of the older man to Abu Musab al-Zarqawi.
When Bobby thought of the Berg beheading, he could not
have imagined how much Usama Ibn Ajam-Vash had
watched the tape as well.

Bobby listened carefully, trying to decipher the fast spoken conversation.

The apparent number two leader spoke in good English. "Major Samuels, you will be released and not killed if you do not try to escape, and we collect the ransom for you. Do you understand?"

Bobby nodded affirmatively, but inside he thought, "You lying piece of crap." One of the other young men checked all over Major Samuels, even under his testes, and inside his mouth, but not up his rectum.

They dressed him in orange coveralls, which sent another chill down Bobby's spine. He could see only a courtyard outside and blue sky, but he was thankful the blindfold had been removed and he could see anything. The window was barred. His feet were left bare, and his handcuffs were attached to a six-foot-long chain sticking out from the wall. When they put the cuffs back on him, Bobby pushed his arms forward, so the cuffs actually went a little higher up the forearms and consequently were not quite as tight and painful when he let them slide down onto his wrists.

Finally the guard left, and Bobby immediately pushed with his rectal muscles, and felt the screw come out. It only took a few seconds of shaking a leg and it was on the floor. He bent down and grabbed it, and started wiggling it, like a rake, inside the left handcuff lock. But to pick a lock, you had to have a rake and a pick, the standard burglar's tools.

A guard came in carrying a camera tripod, and Bobby stopped moving and dropped his head down. The guard set up the tripod and left the room.

Bobby knew what was coming and furiously started working the makeshift rake, but he needed something to put pressure inside the lock and twist it to the left, while he tried to trip the little tumblers inside. He backed up against the wall, listening to the voices from downstairs.

Bobby recognized the voice of the leader who resembled Zarqawi, saying, "*Sa-a'uud qariiban! Sa-antahii qariban.*"

Then a door closed loudly. Bobby felt very desperate. He understood the words.

The leader had said, "I will be back soon! It will be done soon."

They would soon bring a video camera into the room, maybe some lights, and hang a flag, maybe a banner on the wall. They would drug him so he would not fight back, and they would decapitate him with a knife. Bobby calmed himself, knowing he had to in order to survive.

Bobby pushed the opening of the keyhole against the corner of one of the bolts holding the chain. He fit the screw in next to it, and while he kept pressure to turn it, he slowly stuck the screw, acting as his rake, in the lock, pushing down each little tumbler one by one, while twisting on the keyhole in a clockwise direction. Finally, he felt he was pushing down the fifth and last one, and the cuff sprang free.

Bobby let out sob of relief and looked skyward, mouthing the words, "Thank you, God."

Then he looked back up and whispered, "Help me get through this, Dad."

By now, FOX News had already reported Bobby's kidnapping, and General Perry had been informed, along with the commanding generals of USSOCOM, Special Forces, the secretary of defense, and many in between. Members of Delta knew who Bobby was, and they were patrolling, rattling cages, and many Pave Low helicopters were filling the Iraqi skies, more than ever.

Bo Devore was glued to her TV in her apartment, crying her eyes out.

Bobby was now working desperately on the right cuff, when he heard the stairs. Two Iraqis came in, one carrying a camera and the other a light on an aluminum stand.

One looked at Bobby, smiling broadly, and pretending

like he was making friendly conversation, saying, *"Sa'aq-tuluk."*

The other laughed.

Bobby pretended like he did not know the man had just made a joke for his buddy by saying, "I'm going to kill you."

Bobby nodded, smiling, and said, "Hello, how are you?"

The two men nodded and, laughing, left the room. Bobby turned back to the cuff and forced himself to relax.

One minute later the right cuff was off. He had no time for thank-yous now. Bobby moved to the tripod and broke off one leg. He ran over to his clothes and quickly put his BDUs and desert boots on. Bobby even found his Special Forces boot knife lying in his boots. He clipped it on to the back of his belt.

He started to rub the end of the tripod leg on the floor to sharpen it to a point, but he heard steps again. Bobby got behind the door. The same two men came in carrying a long table, and Bobby lunged from behind the door, running the tripod leg all the way through the first's back and through the man's heart and out his chest.

The other man started to scream, but Bobby's handle-first knife throw from just six feet away turned the scream into a gurgle of blood. He quickly stepped up to the man and slashed the knife left to right, ripping the throat open. The man fell to the floor, clutching at his throat in sheer panic. He died quickly.

The former Green Beret searched the two men and found only one long knife, but at least the door was now open. He moved quickly to the stairs, and slowly started down, his knife in one hand and the tripod leg in the other. The two women from the restaurant walked down the hall passing by the stairway, and both looked up at Bobby simultaneously. His right foot snapped out catching the closest one on the side of the jaw and sending her into the other, slamming both into the wall.

They both started to stand and Bobby's knife lashed out, slicing both of their throats in milliseconds. The secondary leader, SKS in hand, ran into the room ready for action. Bobby threw his boot knife, and the man ducked back as it flashed by his face. The knife bounced off the wall and back toward Bobby, and the barrel of the SKS came out and started searching fire on automatic all over the hall-way. Bobby dived down onto the floor and rapidly low crawled toward his boot knife. He grabbed it and stood back against the wall, as the barrel almost touched his chest and fired. Bobby gritted his teeth, grabbed the hot barrel with his left hand, and slashed the terrorist's left wrist with the other. Blood started pumping out all over, and the man grabbed his wrist and started screaming with what sounded like a woman's voice.

Bobby yanked the SKS from his hands and butt-stroked him with it as hard as he could, pulping the killer's face. Bobby hit him five more times, until he was certain the man was dead.

He searched the man's pockets and pulled out the ciga-rette lighter of an American soldier; then he kicked the body. Bobby also found a cell phone. He ran upstairs and grabbed the orange coveralls.

Bobby used the lighter to start setting fire to everything in the house that would burn. He then dialed the operator and a voice came on saying "Marhaban."

Bobby gave his telephone credit card number and called his office in Washington. It was nighttime there. No an-swer. Bobby hung up and called the Pentagon main num-ber. He finally got the officer of the day.

He said, "Listen. You have to call command here in Iraq ASAP. Tell them I have been a hostage and just es-caped but there are more boogeymen in the area. My name is Major Bobby Samuels. I have set the inside of the house on fire, and will wave orange coveralls when I see a chopper overhead. I know that I am near a mosque, and I am in Baghdad or one of its adjoining cities. Do you understand?"

The OD said, "Yes, sir," even though he was a lieutenant colonel. "You are all over the news, Major. Great job! Stay on the horn. I am calling Iraq right now. Stand by."

Bobby said, "Wilco."

The terrorist leader who looked so much like Zarqawi was one block away when he saw the smoke pouring from the house. He immediately went down another street and headed for the closest al Qaeda safe house, a mile away. He had never seen so many American helicopters in the sky at one time. He would leave for Mosul in the morning.

A Pave Low helicopter and a Blackhawk helicopter both spotted the dark column of smoke from the burning house interior at the same time, and banked toward it. Bobby was in the courtyard, frantically waving the orange coveralls, when the crew members spotted him and started cheering, as did the five Delta Force members in the Pave Low.

While the choppers hovered, the five Delta Force members ordered the pilot in closer. They dropped down into a hover over the roof and all five jumped down, one spraining his ankle badly. They immediately did a house search and came outside, shaking hands enthusiastically with Bobby. One opened the gate, and within minutes, military vehicles started showing up.

A half hour later, Bobby was in Corps headquarters G-2 getting debriefed. Two hours later, he was at Baghdad International Airport climbing aboard an Air Force C5A Galaxy monster jet heading back to Washington, nonstop. Refueling would be done in the air.

9

HOME SWEET HOME

DC

When Bobby flew into DC, he was taken immediately by ambulance to Walter Reed Army Hospital and thoroughly examined and checked out by two doctors and a psychiatrist. Afterward, he was taken to the Pentagon. Even though his telephone and cell phone were unlisted numbers, they rang nonstop. Bobby stopped answering either phone, and his voice mail boxes filled up in less than an hour.

Bo saw him in the hallway and almost could not contain herself. She signaled him with a nod and stepped into the women's restroom. Bobby grinned at the two MP guards with him, and they smiled back. He slipped into the restroom, while they remained at alert in the hallway.

Bo threw her arms around him, holding him close, and he winced, but he held her, too, loving the feel of her body against his, but scared by it, too. She stepped back and began crying, and soon after was crying hysterically.

Bobby touched her arm and said, "I know. It's okay."

He walked out and left her there sobbing. Bobby and the two MPs walked quickly down the hallway. You do not keep four-buttons waiting in the army.

Ronnie stepped out of the doorway of Jennifer's office and threw herself into Bobby's arms and kissed him. Bobby looked at the MPs, who were grinning broadly and shaking their heads. His eyes darted around, and fixed on one spot: The face of Jennifer Berken.

Bobby now knew the leak for sure.

Ronnie stepped back and smiled up at Bobby, but gave a quick nervous glance toward Jennifer. Bobby now really understood.

He did not let on.

Veronica said, "Oh, Bobby. I was so worried about you! Come into the office and tell me all about your escape, everything."

Bobby smiled at her and said, "Sorry, Ronnie, no comment. I have to go. Bye."

He and the MPs took off down the hallway, and he whispered to one, "Check back and see if she goes into the C.I.D. reception office." One MP was white and the other was Iroquois.

The Native American looked and said, "Affirmative, sir."

Bobby said, "Thank you, Specialist."

They went to the conference room, and General Perry and his aide entered a minute later.

Bobby snapped to attention, and felt it in his right hip and left arm. The general walked up to him and shook his hand vigorously.

"Outstanding, my boy! Out-frigging-standing! Hooah!" General Perry enthused. "You made us all proud! You made all soldiers look good, Bobby!"

Samuels said, "Thanks, sir, very much, but I only did what we are supposed to do."

The general said, "Hah! I am submitting you for the Medal of Honor, lad."

Bobby's knees got weak.

"The MOH, sir," Bobby said. "I feel very humbled, General, but I didn't save anybody's life but my own."

General Perry replied, "On the contrary. I think your actions will inspire our troops everywhere, especially if they are captured. You did not get out of that situation without keeping your wits and really using your head. Besides some ball-to-the-wall hand-to-hand combat. The lessons learned from your experience will probably save many lives of future POWs. Besides, you're alive, so the liberals in Congress will probably downgrade it to the DSC [Distinguished Service Cross] anyway."

Bobby said, "Sir, how long will my debriefing here take? I need to get back to Iraq and get that son of a bitch quickly. He set me up, but he also killed a really good man."

"Oh yeah," the general said, "the private contractor. Shame."

General Perry accepted a cup of coffee from a DRO [Dining Room Orderly] in the corner and said, "Hot tea, Major, correct?"

"Coffee, cream, sir, decaf. Thank you."

"Sit down, Bobby," the general said, ignoring his aide's protestations and carrying both cups to the table.

"Major," the general said, "it will take a bit. As I told you, our lessons learned may save a lot of lives."

"Sir," Bobby said passionately, "I have to nail this slimeball bastard. I need a couple days stateside to take care of a problem I discovered here, but then I just have to get back over to the Sandbox. I was set up, and someone tried to kill me here. We had a leak here in DA, but I have uncovered it. I want to plug it and then get him. But I need to take care of the leak before anything."

"We have a leak here in the Pentagon!" General Perry

said indignantly. "You mean someone here is responsible for getting you captured and maybe many killed. Is that what you are telling me?"

"General," Bobby said, "I have it handled. Believe me."

"Keep me posted."

"General Perry, you will be the first to know. I promise, sir," Bobby said enthusiastically. "In fact, sir, I promise I will do all the debriefing they want. I'll teach a class at Carlisle even, but I have to take care of this and then get back to Iraq and locate the killer first. With your permission?"

"Absolutely!" General Perry said. "Again, if there is anything you need to accomplish your mission, just ask. Incidentally, we found you Sergeant Major Kittinger, and he is on his way here."

"Thank you, sir," Bobby said. "Now, by your leave, sir, I have to get back to work."

Bobby stood and the four-button followed suit, shaking his hand and clapping him on the shoulder.

Bobby left the conference room, picking his cell phone out of his pocket and speed-dialing Spook. He spoke to the sergeant major briefly and promised to send a courier immediately to pick up what he wanted. Less than a half hour later, two MPs showed up at Spook's house, ran to the door, and accepted a large cardboard box from Spook. Bobby was spending the night in the Pentagon and was going to sleep in the bed provided for him when he was wounded. He had learned that the makeshift hospital room was still there, and he did not want to take a chance on his place, even though there was security posted all around it. He knew what the news media would be like, or thought he did anyway. He correctly figured they would be like circling vultures.

Bobby next called Bo Devore and asked her to pick up a steak dinner for both of them and get back to the office, and bring clothes for work the next day. She arrived an hour later, around 6:00 P.M., with a chateaubriand for two on a giant Portobello mushroom, salads, and a bottle of Chianti. Bobby saw the wine, and sarcastically thought, "Oh great, just what I need." Then the thought itself irritated him.

Bobby took the food from Bo, leading her into the abandoned C.I.D. office's little conference/interrogation room. He placed the food down on the table and ran down the hallway, returning with a Sprite for himself. There was no way he was going to drink right now. He could not trust himself to stop.

They ate, and Bobby told her of his plans. Bo was excited, especially since she would help bring down a competitor. They sat for an hour after eating, just talking about the Saboteur.

"There is a connection between Berken and Veronica," Bobby said, "and I could sense it when I saw the look she tried to hide when Ronnie kissed me in the hallway."

Bo's face turned bright red when Bobby mentioned this, and he got a slight sheepish grin on his face, thinking, "What the hell did I say wrong?"

Bobby's cell phone rang, and he walked over to the door to the C.I.D. offices. The two MPs handed him the box from Spook's.

Walking back to Bo, a smiling Bobby said, "Come on, girlfriend. Give me a hand."

She smiled and followed him. They went into the C.I.D. reception office carrying the box of supplies from Spook. At Jennifer's desk, Bobby took out a teddy bear, with a built-in alarm clock in the center. Bo looked at him wondering what was up, as he ran to his office and returned a couple minutes later with a color card printed out with a yellow rose on it and the words: "Specialist Berken, Thank you for all your hard work helping this office run so smoothly. Sincerely, CPT Devore & MAJ Samuels."

He placed the card next to the Teddy Bear clock, which he positioned under her desk lamp.

Bo said, "What the hell?"

Samuels winked and pulled a small air purifier from the box and placed it on top of one of the file cabinets. He found a plug and plugged it into the wall between the cabinets.

Carrying the box and smiling at the grinning captain, he said, "Follow me."

Shaking her head, she followed him into the conference room. He pulled a small digital video recorder and monitor out of the box, and plugged it in, turning it on. He turned up a small antenna in the back and played with the knobs. Bo grinned as she looked at the split-screen shot of Jennifer's office from the tiny cameras in the center of the clock in the teddy bear's chest and from the hidden camera in the air purifier.

Bobby walked into the room while Bo watched, and he said in normal tones, "Testing one, two, three, four, five."

He returned to the conference room and looked at the monitor, adjusting the volume. He then did a stop tape, rewind, and playback.

"Cool, but where are you going to keep the monitor and recorder?" Bo asked.

Bobby said, "I am going to ask General Perry to see that the person upstairs is moved out of their office right away, for air-conditioning repairs, and we'll lock it in there."

"Do you really think Jennifer and Veronica are lovers?"

"I saw the look she gave her, Bo," he replied. "She tried to hide it, but she was jealous."

"Now, do you have the pictures you showed me of that suspected Taliban drug smuggler from Afghanistan?" he asked.

"Yeah, why?"

"Did Jennifer ever see the photos?"

Bo, really curious now, said, "No, why?"

Bobby said, "We're going to hang the photos all over the office bulletin board in Jennifer's office, then cover each with a sheet of typing paper just hanging over it, so you can't see it unless you lift it up. Then, when she is there, you will ask me tomorrow morning if I am going to expose the identity of the Saboteur I had been investigating in Iraq. I'll hint at it and so on, then we'll leave for the day."

"And the curiosity will eat away at Veronica, because Jennifer will call her as soon as we leave," Bo added.

Bobby said, "Exactly, my dear. You should have been a C.I.D. investigator."

"I am."

"Okay."

They finished preparing the office with two miniature mikes, then Bobby called General Perry's aide and apologized for the after-hours call. He told him about his desire to get the office directly above Jennifer's by the next morning, and the lieutenant colonel said the general had told him that Bobby was to get anything he wanted immediately, no questions asked. The colonel told him that by start of business the next day, the office would be available, and he could just go there. Further, there would be a "Construction Off Limits" tape placed in the hallway barring entrance to the office.

Around 9:00 P.M., Bobby led Bo downstairs to the makeshift hospital room.

They walked in, and she said, "What are we doing?"

Bobby smiled. "We are on stakeout, kind of, in a way, Bo. We better get some sleep while we can."

Bo grinned and said, "Sleep?"

Bobby said, "Okay, bed rest. You sleep on the bed. I'll push two of those chairs together."

Bo said, "You don't need to do that, Bobby. I trust you. You can sleep on one half the bed. I mean it. I trust you."

Bobby grinned, replying, "I don't."

He pushed two stuffed chairs together.

All night long, Bobby thought about Bo sleeping a few feet away.

She awakened several times in the darkness and just stared at Bobby's sleeping form. She wanted to be lying under one of those well-muscled arms, so badly.

Neither of them slept well that night. They both got up early, showered, and got ready.

Bobby and Bo entered the office about five minutes apart the next morning, with Bobby going in first, drinking a cup of coffee.

Jennifer said, "Major Samuels, thank you so much, sir, for the teddy bear clock. It is so cute."

"Well," Bobby said, "Captain Devore and I were talking and chuckled about how many times you forget your wristwatch and would ask us the time, and also how hard you work, so we thought it was a natural."

Bo came in shortly after and had a similar conversation with Jennifer.

Bo and Bobby both drank coffee and looked at the surveillance photographs of the drug dealer that looked like they were taken in Iraq but were actually taken in Afghanistan. Jennifer sat at her computer and tried to act disinterested, but her ears were tuned into every word like satellite dishes.

They talked about the guy as if Bobby suspected him as the Saboteur, so Jennifer, consequently, really had her heart pounding in her chest. She could not wait to tell her lover about it.

Jennifer was desperate for Veronica, not realizing she was being played, too. Ronnie had plotted picking her up several years earlier, just to get information on Bobby

Samuels. She always held a little back, and would not give that one last little kiss when saying, good-bye. She would have to be asked by Jennifer to say, "I love you." The result of all this was that Jennifer chasing after her withdrawn lover, always trying to prove how much she loved Ronnie. Her heart ached for her.

Jennifer Berken grew up in Detroit, Michigan, the little sister of two much older brothers, and they followed in the footsteps of their stepfather. Her dad left the family when Jennifer was five years old, because he could not "handle another minute of that overbearing, controlling bitch," his description of her mother. Mummy, heartbroken, hooked up with the first man that came along, and Jennifer ended up with a life sentence, without having committed a crime, except for being an innocent little girl.

Her stepfather, Keith, was an autoworker and made good pay. He also attended Bible college and took great pride in that fact. Every Sunday morning, wearing one of his cheap K-Mart suits, he took the family to church, with little Jennifer dressed up like a little Shirley Temple. He made sure he had a large Bible, with a large leather zippered Bible cover, with a large cross on it. He always wore his scuffed plain brown shoes and white socks. What was humorous was his taste in ties. Maybe that was his statement, his chance to stand out from the crowd. He paraded around church looking down at most and preaching to those who would listen. The help-starved minister gladly accepted him as a Sunday school teacher for the youth.

Jennifer would never forget his Sunday school lessons, especially the one when he talked about hell. He asked how many children had ever been burned, maybe scalding their fingers on a hot stove, or whatever. Then he would describe hell as being hotter than any of those burns they ever experienced. He asked how many had been in a cave before, and asked if they had ever toured a cave where the guide turned the lights out. He described hell as being even blacker than that. His description of hell went on for an entire class, and she had nightmares for weeks.

The worst part was that after church every Sunday, they always went to a restaurant, usually a different one each week. Keith would pick out a table in the center of the restaurant where all could see them praying, and they would all hold hands, while he prayed loudly. When the bill came, he would always find something to get angry and berate the waitress about. That way, Jennifer quickly deduced, he would not have to leave a tip. It got to the point where she absolutely dreaded going to a restaurant, even with friends.

She could never, after that, hold hands with anybody to pray.

By the time she was in sixth grade, changes started happening to her body and to the way he treated her. Her two brothers, who were emotionally abused by him, had already been having her fellate them for two years by then, using intimidation and coercion to get her to perform the act. She mainly did it to get their approval and keep from getting picked on, and it was the start of Specialist Berken's career as a people pleaser.

Before she finished the summer vacation prior to seventh grade, Keith had her in the sack. Her mother knew deep down inside, but did not want to be alone, desperately did not, so she remained in denial. In a perverted sense, it was a relief for her, so she would not have to perform his idea of wifely "chores," which Keith had convinced her were Biblical.

There was hardly a night now that Jennifer did not picture her stepfather over her sweating and panting heavily as he pumped inside her furiously. He used to tell her it was their "secret" because he did not want to hurt her mom by telling her how they felt about each other. This was always humorous to her because she hated him.

Jennifer dated in high school, but only for appearances. Sex was used to get what she wanted and to control men, but she actually had her first sexual affair where there was any real emotion involved with a woman, her best friend, Candy. From then on, she preferred the softness, intimacy, and tender caresses of women.

Veronica, on the other hand, was simply a manipulator, out for herself, always. She had learned how to use her beauty and sensuality to manipulate and control men, and women as well. She got sexual satisfaction, too, but mainly by conquering and maintaining control over a conquest. Ronnie was, quite simply, a tigress.

Bobby said, "Jennifer, please get Veronica Caruso on the horn for me. She should be at her network office, I would think."

"Yes, sir," Jennifer said, dialing without thinking that she was not looking up the number. "Hello. Ms. Caruso please."

There was a pause and her face turned red. "Yes, I am fine. How are you? Can I speak to Ms. Caruso please? Yes, Ms. Caruso please?"

Bobby pictured a friend she had made on the other end of the line giving her a hard time, and Jennifer was squirming like a worm on a hook.

Bobby remembered that some philosopher had said something about liars having to tell a hundred truths for each lie, just to cover it up. Then he grinned to himself, as he thought about the great deception he was pulling himself.

"Ms. Caruso. Good morning, ma'am," Jennifer said.

Bobby winked at Bo, both thinking Ronnie would hate the "ma'am" bit.

Jennifer went on. "Ms. Caruso, this is Specialist Berken at the central C.I.D. at DA. Major Samuels wanted to speak with you, ma'am. Thank you, here he is."

She handed Bobby the phone.

"Ronnie," he said, "how are you?"

"Fine . . . No." He chuckled. "No comment, Ronnie. That's not why I called. I was wondering if you had any news guys in northern Iraq? . . . No, just curious. . . . No I don't know who it is yet, if I'm even working on such a case. Damn, see how good you are! . . . No comment," he said. "I have to go, really. . . . No, never mind. Thanks anyway." There was a short pause. "No, thanks. I'll probably skip lunch altogether; I have so many places to go today. . . . No, that's okay. Bye, Ronnie," he said and hung up.

He looked at Bo. "I'm gonna go meet with a FOX News guy and see if they have any tape of this Muhammad Aswar guy in northern Iraq. I have appointments all day after that. See you tomorrow, Captain."

Bo replied, "I have an appointment, too, sir, with my gynecologist at Walter Reed actually. Then I am going to run over to the Heritage Foundation and look at some photos a friend there has for me. See you tomorrow, Major. In fact, let me grab my purse. I'll walk out with you."

Jennifer said, "Good day, ma'am, sir. Should I refer calls to your cell phones?"

Simultaneously, Bo and Bobby said, "Yes," as they walked out into the hall.

Bobby walked back in and said, "By the way, those covered photographs and what we were discussing are classified TS. Shhhh!"

She smiled and said, "Yes, sir. No problem."

Fifteen minutes later, when they unlocked the door and went into the office on the floor overhead with the box of equipment and got it set up, Jennifer was already about to hang up. They heard her say, "I know you can't speak, but I love you."

Not knowing Jennifer's phone had been bugged by Bobby, too, Ronnie responded, "I love you, too, baby. See you shortly."

Two cups of coffee later, Veronica Caruso arrived at the C.I.D. office. Jennifer stood and shook hands with her and acted professional. Bobby was concerned at first, but that was up until Jennifer walked to the door, looked out in the hallway, closed the door, and locked it.

She walked up to Veronica, and they gave each other a long, passionate kiss, with Jennifer fondling Ronnie's right breast right in front of the teddy bear camera.

Bobby said, "We need to catch them looking at the photos and talking about them."

The two detectives, with a detached attitude, watched and listened to the two lovers for the next hour, as Veronica performed oral sex on Jennifer, and they looked at each photo, while Jennifer told Veronica all that she knew. Finally, Jennifer said she had to get to her office with the digital photos she'd taken of the photos.

Bobby and Bo stood up and high-fived each other. Bobby called the office just as Jennifer was unlocking the door. He asked if Veronica was there, and saw the shocked look on her face, as she answered.

Bobby said, "Do you know the command conference room, where you brought me those files?"

"Yes, sir," she said, nervous and showing it on the monitor.

Bobby said, "I need you to ask Veronica if she can accompany you to that conference room. This pertains to the case I am working on and is very important."

"Yes, sir," Jennifer said, as she signaled Ronnie back into the office from the hallway.

She told Veronica, who squealed and hugged her, saying, "Honey, he is giving me an exclusive on the story!"

She gave Jennifer a kiss, and they both looked at the open door and giggled. They went out as Bo and Bobby gave each other knowing looks. He pushed a button and made a backup DVD of the tape in the monitor. Then he made a second and a third. He put them in protective jackets, and the digital master tape as well, which showed both camera angles in split screen. For brevity's sake, they would later be edited by someone on an Avid Express editing console, but for now, Bobby and Bo walked down to their offices to put one of the backups in the safe, as well as the raw master digital tape. Bobby handed one other DVD to Bo and said, "Lock this in your own safe at home or a safe deposit box if you have one."

Bo said, "I do."

She stuck it in her purse.

Bobby called General Perry's aide. "Morning, sir. It is Major Samuels. . . . Fine, Colonel. Would you please tell the general, sir, we are all on our way to the conference room, and tell the Old Man we got what we want. . . . Roger. . . . No, I'll handle it all. Thank you, out."

They walked briskly toward the conference room, and two additional MPs appeared out of nowhere, it seemed, and joined the two guards at the door.

A portable cart with an IBM computer on it was by the wall near the end of the conference table, and was plugged into the wall. Veronica and Jennifer were already seated at the table and accepting cups of coffee from the two white-coated orderlies.

Bobby and Bo were greeted very warmly by Veronica and finally noticed Jennifer standing at attention.

Bobby said, "I'm sorry. As you were, Jennifer."

They all sat down as the orderlies continued to pour their coffee. And the door opened as General Perry walked in, followed by his orderly and two MPs.

All jumped to attention and General Perry said, "Carry on! Hot tea for me, young man, and I know the good major here wants a coffee with cream and two sugars."

The aide grinned, nodding at Bobby. Bobby nodded at the MPs, and they went out the door.

The tea and coffee was delivered to one and all, while Bobby said, "Veronica Caruso, the commanding general of all coalition troops, General Perry. General, this is—"

The general interrupted. "The lovely Miss Veronica Caruso, I have seen many of your stories, although I must confess I almost always watch FOX News."

"General, this is Specialist Jennifer Berken from our office," Bobby said.

Jennifer looked like she was going to faint, and the general, Bobby noticed, stood at attention while meeting both women, and Bobby thought to himself, "Cool."

"And this, sir, is my partner in crime, or rather crime-busting, Captain."

Again, the general, shaking her hand, interrupted, saying, "Captain Bo Devore, C.I.D. investigator, received a Purple Heart for wounds received and Bronze Star with V device for valor while commanding MP elements in the first week of the War on Iraq."

Bobby grinned at her with pride, and her eyes glistened with such recognition. Ronnie begrudgingly thought she would have to do a story on her and maybe get into her pants.

The general said, "That was a handy piece of under-cover work you did posing as a prostitute a few months back, Captain." He looked at her chest and grinned, "Nice bust."

"Sir?" she said shocked.

The general chuckled and said, "That was a nice arrest, Captain."

"Oh," she said blushing deeply, but she knew he was joking and being flirty. "Thank you very much, sir."

He suddenly got serious and sat down, saying, "All nonessential personnel will leave the room."

The orderlies left, and Perry nodded for his aide to leave

also. This left the general, the two women lovers, and Bobby and Bo.

General Perry said, "Major Samuels, shall we proceed?"

Bobby walked to the machine, and the general said, "Have my aide come back in."

Bo opened the door, and the lieutenant colonel came in and walked to the computer as if he'd known this would happen. Bobby grinned, handing him the DVD.

The general looked at him sternly. "Frank, I have all of your loyalty totally, don't I?"

The field grade did not hesitate. "Absolutely, sir. Total loyalty, sir."

He gave the four-star a knowing look the man understood. This man would follow him to hell and back. Perry winked and smiled at his aide.

Bobby looked at Jennifer and said, "Before we begin, Specialist Berken, I have to tell you something very important and you need to listen very carefully."

She looked shocked until he started; then she looked horrified.

Bobby went on. "Specialist Jennifer Berken, under Article 31-Bravo of the Uniform Code of Military Justice, you have the right to remain silent, do not have to answer any questions, and or make any statement. You have the right to consult with a JAG officer, a military lawyer, at no cost to you, or to speak with a civilian lawyer at no cost to the government of the United States, or both. And you have the right to have either or both during questioning. If you decide to make any statements or answer any questions, they may be used as evidence against you in any court-martial, nonjudicial proceeding, administrative proceeding, or civilian court. Do you clearly understand your rights under Article 31-Bravo of the UCMJ as I have explained them to you?"

She started gagging and ran to the wastebasket in the corner, where she started throwing up while tears poured out of her eyes. The general jumped up and poured her a glass of water, which she gulped.

Veronica, furious, jumped up and said, "What the hell is—"

But she was shoved down hard by Bo, who shocked everyone by interrupting, saying, "Sit down, Media Bitch, and shut up. You're next."

General Perry grinned.

Bobby said, "Specialist Berken, do you clearly understand your rights as I explained them?"

Jennifer said, "Yes, sir."

Bobby nodded at Bo, who turned to Veronica. "Ms. Caruso, you have the right to remain silent during questioning. You have a right to have an attorney present during questioning. If you are charged with a felony and cannot afford an attorney, the court will provide you with an attorney. If you relinquish your right to remain silent during questioning, anything you say can and will be used against you in a court of law. Do you clearly understand your rights as I have explained?"

Ronnie, indignant, said, "I'm a civilian, Captain!"

Bo said, "That's why I just gave you your Miranda rights, Ms. Caruso. Do you understand them as I have explained them?"

Caruso angrily snapped, "Yeah, and I want my attorney."

She stood and Bo shoved her back down roughly. "No, you don't, Bitch. Just watch the DVD and then tell me you want an attorney."

As if that was the cue, the lieutenant colonel said, "Major, before I start, do you want me to add color bars and tone to the beginning?"

Bobby said, "No, thank you, sir. Go ahead and roll it."

They stared at the tape, and everyone else turned to look

at the two shocked women, who were now speechless. Soon, the general was being treated to not only a porn show, but also a soldier giving away what she thought was top secret information to a reporter. Both women cried, as they watched themselves poring over the photographs and discussing them, as well as performing oral sex and other intimacies.

Finally, Bobby said, "Have you seen enough, General?"

Bo looked at Ronnie, now sobbing heavily, and said, "Hey, Veronica, would you like to cooperate or did you want your attorney here?"

Ronnie sobbed, "I'm ruined."

Bobby said, "No, Ronnie, but you are now paid back for the way you betrayed me."

Ronnie said, "You used me."

Bobby said, "In spades, baby. You could write a book on that. Now, do you want your attorney or to cooperate?"

Veronica, bawling, said, "I'll cooperate! I'll cooperate!"

The general jumped in. "You need her, Bobby, or just Miss Caruso here?"

Bo answered, "Just Veronica, sir."

General Perry said, "I don't need your cooperation, Hot Lips. Tomorrow, you will be leaving the army with an Undesirable Discharge Under Less Than Honorable Conditions. I do not give a shit what the regs say. Colonel, tomorrow she is gone. Whatever has to be backdated, waivered, or forged, we will get it done. You will get no GI or VA benefits either. If you want to try lawsuits, a book, anything after you get out, we will save this DVD. Understand?"

Jennifer nodded meekly, but Veronica boldly said, "She won't do anything or I'll have a hit put on her. You understand, you little slut?"

Bo said, "You are so sweet, Ronnie."

Bobby could not help but laugh. The general grinned, too. Jennifer put her head down and cried even harder. It was actually the lowest point of her life, but very good, too, as it became the day she stopped being a people pleaser.

Veronica was cold and masking now.

"What do you want from me?" she said.

General Perry shocked Bobby again by jumping in and saying, "For starters, a news special on the courage of our fighting men and women in the war on terrorism, as well as the courage and wisdom of our president and commander in chief."

Veronica said, "On my network? You have to be shitting me, General. Besides that is blackmail."

Bo said, "Yes, it is. What are you going to do about it? I'll tell you what you'll do, Lolita. All you have to do is spread your legs with someone, and you will make it happen. You seem to be good at that. Understand?"

Bobby, the aide, and the general laughed out loud this time. They did not expect this from the beautiful MP captain.

Ronnie said, "I will make it happen, General."

Bobby said, "You are also going to help us nail the saboteur, and if you're a good girl, I might even let you do the news story on it. Oh, by the way, Ronnie, using sex to get your hands on government secrets and passing them on to the enemy, which you have done, is punishable by death."

Veronica fainted, literally. She hit her head hard on the tile floor, bruising her cheekbone. The lieutenant colonel and Bobby jumped up and ran to her.

Bo grabbed Jennifer's glass of ice water and tossed it in Ronnie's face. She sat up gasping and sputtering. Bobby lifted her up, and she sat in her chair.

Veronica was now sobbing uncontrollably, and the tears this time seemed genuine.

She said, "General Perry, I would never betray our

country or our troops. Never! I will do whatever you want. I am so sorry! Please believe me!"

Bobby said, "I do, General. She is the connection to the saboteur, but I would not believe she intentionally would give him information to put troops in harm's way, or to get me captured."

Veronica was shocked. "Do you think I would have gotten you captured?"

Bobby said, "Ronnie, I have checked, and you have been the one link that enabled the saboteur, through the info you have gotten from Jennifer here."

Bobby stopped, and then said, "Wait a minute! Where did you tell me your friend, what's his name?"

"Who?" Veronica almost screamed.

Bobby said, "Sam, yeah Sam Ajamo. Where did you say he is from?"

"Canton, Ohio, but not him, Bobby," she said. "He is a sergeant in the army. He just got over a leg wound and is back in Iraq already."

Bobby looked at the general, saying, "Sir, I pulled a piece of a commemorative coin, about a third of a coin, out of the wreckage of one of the vehicles that he killed a bunch of soldiers in. It had been used as a makeshift screwdriver and was from the Professional Football Hall of Fame."

General Perry cut in, "In Canton, Ohio."

Bobby said, "Exactly. A reporter. He goes from unit to unit, probably picking the assignments he wants, and works from the inside killing our men and women."

Veronica said, "Bobby, it does not make sense. Sam is a red-haired, blue-eyed American. He is not the al Qaeda. He is not overly greedy, or too ambitious."

Bobby said, "I am not saying he is, but we have to find out, and you will not contact him, except when I tell you to."

"Yes, sir," Veronica said meekly, and then paused and added, "but what if there is a developing story in Iraq? He has been my best source over there. He is so nice, and he earned the Purple Heart. I just cannot see him as a spy."

Bo jumped in saying, "You sure as hell ain't Barbara Walters, honey, and this ain't a democracy here where your opinion matters. You will do exactly as you are told, no more, no less, or you will end up in front of a firing squad. Do you understand that?"

Ronnie's legs buckled, and she sat down again quickly, and started bawling and shaking all over again.

"Yes, ma'am," she said very meekly.

Her right cheekbone was now swollen very badly and her right eye was discolored. She reached up and touched it gingerly and started crying harder again.

Bobby grinned at Bo and shook his head. She turned her head, and General Perry did the same thing. The general's aide was doing the same.

Two of the MPs were summoned, and the lieutenant colonel spoke with them. They stepped over on each side of Jennifer Berken, and she rose.

She said, "Major Samuels, General Perry, sir, may I ask one fa—"

General Perry cut in. "No! Just for a chance to have sex with someone, you sold out your fellow soldiers. I don't care how rough your life has been, or how you want to color it. You're getting off easy, so deal with it. Get her out of here!"

She sobbed as the MPs grabbed each arm and escorted her from the room.

Bobby said, "Send in the other two."

The two remaining MPs entered the room and stood on each side of Veronica.

Bo said, "Gentlemen, escort the TV star from the buildings and grounds of the Pentagon."

As they were going out the door, Bobby said, "We will contact you shortly."

As soon as Veronica was gone, the general walked over to Bobby and Bo, grabbing them each on the shoulder with a beefy hand. He was grinning from ear to ear.

"Outstanding!" he said enthusiastically, "You two make a great team!"

Bo gave Bobby a sidelong glance, and he shuffled his feet uncomfortably.

General Perry went on. "And you, Captain Devore. What a hard-core badass! I love it! I have three very expensive cigars in my office. Come on, let's go share a smoke."

Bobby said, "Sir, thank you, but I have to get back to Iraq immediately."

Perry said, "Horsehit! I'm leaving at o-dark hundred tomorrow morning. You can hitchhike with me. Come on."

"Thank you, sir," Bobby said, grinning at Bo.

"Oh, by the way," General Perry said, "your old pal you requested, Sergeant Major Kittinger, is riding with us. Flying into Ronald Reagan tonight on the red-eye. Aren't too many Vietnam veterans still in the army, and he and I can swap lies and tell each other war stories. You can listen."

"Great, thank you, sir," Bobby said, and turned to Bo. "When we finish our cigars, I would like for you to contact your buddies at Homeland Security, and quietly talk about Ronnie, have them monitor her phones, mail, and e-mail in case she gets flaky and this guy Ajamo turns out to be our perp. I also need you to do a complete BI on him and his family."

"Wilco, Major," Bo said.

As they walked along, the general looked at each of them wondering if there was more to their conversations than he understood.

A few minutes later, they were in the center of the Pentagon in the courtyard, each smoking a large cigar.

Bobby said, "These are good, General Perry. Where did you get them, sir?"

"Small tobacco store in Falls Church."

Bobby looked at Bo and said, "Did I tell you, Captain Devore, what happened to me at that big drugstore in Falls Church last summer?"

Bo said, "No, sir."

The general said, "First, will you two stop with the military protocol with each other. You work together closely. Give me a break. Now, go ahead."

Bobby said, "You just would not believe what happened to me there last summer."

Curious, she said, "What?"

Bobby replied, "Well, I was going into this store to buy new nail clippers, just before dark, and was almost to the door. I had to stop because a splinter from my deck had somehow gotten into my cowboy boot and was sticking in the side of my foot."

Bo made a face.

He went on, "I had to literally remove my boot and dig it out. While I was messing with it, an elderly woman, maybe eighty, came outside, and a little girl came up at the same time with a dog on a leash."

The detective beauty was getting interested in this story.

"The little girl was probably the cutest little thing I have ever seen."

"Really?" she said.

"Yes," Bobby went on. "She had a frilly white dress with red lace all around it, little white gloves with red trim, shiny red shoes, and she had her hair done up in puppy ears with red ribbons tied around them."

"You're kidding," Bo said, totally absorbed in the image.

Bobby continued. "That's not all. The leash was red with little rhinestones and so was the collar, and the little dog was, well, have you ever seen a West Highland white terrier, those little mop dogs?"

"Yes, I have. I know exactly what you mean. They're so cute."

Bobby said, "Well, this little dog had red ribbons like hers tied around the base of each ear."

"Oh, how precious!" she said.

Then the cop went on. "That is exactly what the little old lady said; she told the little girl how precious she and the puppy were, and the little girl started rocking back and forth and thanked her, and I noticed she even had a tooth or two missing, which made her even cuter.

"The old lady said, 'You are so cute. What is your name, young lady?'

"The little girl said, 'Petals.'

"The woman said, 'How precious. How did you get such a name?'

"This was almost too much," Bobby said. "The girl said, 'When I was in my mommy's tummy, Mommy and Daddy were sitting under a dogwood tree and the wind blew and petals fell down and one landed on Mommy's cheek, so my daddy kissed Mommy's cheek, and said if I was a girl, they would name me Petals.'"

Bo was so touched by the story now, she had tears in her eyes, but the general was more reserved and just grinned.

"The old lady was really amazed and said so.

"Then she said, 'And your puppy is so cute, too. What's his name?'

"I swear I thought I was in a TV commercial," Samuels added. "Then the little girl answered her, and I died. She said, 'Thank you, his name is Porky.'

"The woman got more excited and said, 'Oh how cute. Why do you call him Porky?'"

Bobby paused briefly and said, "The little girl rocked back and forth and said, 'Because he likes to screw pigs.' "

Bo stared at him a second, and then burst out with a laugh, slapped the grinning detective on the arm, and hissed, "Bobby, you son of a bitch! You mean son of a bitch! You really had me going there."

She got embarrassed realizing she had called him Bobby in front of General Perry, but the man wanted them to lighten up. General Perry was now tearing up, but from acute laughter, not sensitivity. He was howling. Taking a long puff and blowing out a big streamer of smoke, he finally stuck his hand out and shook with Bobby.

"That one was hilarious, young man," he said.

10

BACK TO THE SANDBOX

Iraq

Bobby was trying to doze, but the loud laughter once again awakened him. Boom and the general had not shut up since the C141 lifted off.

Bobby had not seen Boom Kittinger in several years, and the man did not age. He looked even younger, Bobby thought, and he could not believe how well Boom and General Perry got along. Then he rethought it and realized Boom was the prototypical Special Forces senior NCO. They were all, to a one, very colorful characters, in the army and after they got out. For hours, all the way to Iraq, Bobby listened to the two tell war stories, some sad, many humorous, all exciting.

It was also funny looking at Boom talking to the general. He had not shaved since hearing he was going to Iraq, and he was dressed in civilian clothes with a black-and-white checkered scarf wrapped several times around his neck. Bobby could also tell Boom had been hitting the tanning booth ever since hearing he was going. Under his loose tunic, Bobby saw he was wearing a stainless-steel Ruger Redhawk .44 magnum.

Boom was telling how he and a fellow martial artist first met an old Oklahoma rodeo cowboy, who had been a Special Forces medic for years, a man whom General Perry knew, and he had rodeoed whenever he was on leave. His name was Chancy, and he was one of those colorful SF characters.

Boom had finished working out, grappling with a friend who owned a karate, judo, and jujitsu school in Fayetteville, North Carolina, outside Fort Bragg. After the workout, they both showered and decided to stop at a local restaurant. Brand was going to have a soda while his friend had a drink, and they would talk. They visited for about an hour in the large and classy bar, and his friend decided to head home to his wife and children.

Unfortunately, there were two men in the bar who looked like they might be bankers, and they both had been drinking for a while. Both men were very large, but it was hard for Boom to judge how much was muscle and how much was body fat. One of them had red hair with a little premature gray at the temples, and the other had lots of black hair and lots of baby fat in his face. Both were white and both were tall. They looked like they were linemen in football years ago in their youth, and had since maybe spent a lot more time on bar stools than on any athletic fields.

The one with black hair stepped in front of Boom and his friend as they were starting to head for the door. Then the other came up and roughly shoved Boom's friend.

The one with black hair said, "We saw you two wrestling when we walked by that karate school. Karate guys ain't nothing against a real street fighter."

Boom said, "You're absolutely right, sir. See you," and he tried to step past, but the redhead blocked his egress.

Boom's friend said, "We agree with you totally and were just wanting to leave. We have no intention of—"

The redhead took a roundhouse swing at Boom's friend, which would have missed anyway if the black belt had not pulled his head back.

The black-haired jerk said, "You boys want out of here, you have to go over us."

Both men chuckled.

That is when Sergeant First Class Chancy Gates came into the picture. As calmly as could be, he got up from his seat at the bar, carrying his bottle of Coors. He stopped a young busboy carrying two plastic buckets of water to the kitchen. Chancy set his beer down and carried the buckets over and set them down between the four men. He then walked over to the pool table and grabbed two pool sticks. All eyes in the place, mainly those of soldiers with white-wall haircuts, were now on Chancy as he walked back over with the cue sticks.

He looked at the drunks and said, "'Scuse me, but I heard you two fellers sayin' how tough you was, and I jest wondered if that was true."

The black-haired one stepped forward menacingly, saying, "Yeah, you think you're gonna stop us with a cue stick?"

Chancy chuckled, and put his hand up. "No, sir. Not me. I'm a lover, not a fighter. I jest wondered if I could put ya to the test, if you ain't chicken?"

"What test?" The redhead exclaimed, "We're not scared of anything."

Chancy said, "This ain't a test about courage, but about how tough you both are."

Boom was totally puzzled, but also thoroughly enjoying

the show. He saw the jump wings tattooed on Chancy's forearm, but didn't know him yet.

The black-haired one said, "Well, what is it?"

Chancy stood up on a chair and held the rim of one bucket up flush against the ceiling.

He looked at the black-haired man and said, "Now stick that one cue stick up under the center of this and see if ya can hold this bucket in place for me."

The drunk did so, holding the bucket against the ceiling by pressing firmly upward with the stick. Chancy simply climbed the chair and placed the second bucket against the ceiling and got the redhead to hold his bucket up, too, with the other stick.

Both drunks were now pushing two sticks against the bottom of two buckets filled with water. They looked helplessly at Chancy, who had climbed down and moved the chair under a table.

"Now what?" the redhead growled.

Chancy grabbed Boom and his friend, heading for the door, and popped over his shoulder, "Now try not ta get wet. See ya, boys."

As the trio, laughing, made it out the door, they heard screaming and cussing from inside, and the whole bar was laughing uproariously.

Outside, Boom's friend said, "We better get going. They're going to drop those things and be madder than hell."

Chancy said, "Nope. Against the nature of the male ego. They'll stand there until they can't hold the buckets no more, then they'll get wet. It's not the water: It's the humiliation."

Boom stuck out his hand and said, "Howdy, Brand Kittinger, You oughta be in SF!"

Chancy said, "I am."

Boom said, "Yes, you sure are. I haven't met you before. Who ya with?"

"The Third Herd," Chancy replied. "You?"

"Training Group right now," Boom said, "but I been around a bit."

"You full qualified SF, I suppose?"

"Yep."

Boom's friend said, "What's he mean by that?"

Boom glanced at Chancy, and they both chuckled.

Chancy said, "Wal, those of us who are in Group have our own unofficial qualifications to wear a Green Beret."

The friend said, "What are they?"

Chancy replied, "You gotta have at least one divorce."

Boom said, "Got that."

"You have to have pissed in the Mekong River."

"Did that," Boom added.

"Have to own at least one fake Rolex watch but a real Gerber knife," Chancy said.

Boom said, "I have those."

"Have to have jumped out of a perfectly good aircraft at night, in high winds, wearing a hunnert pounds of gear, a weapon, and forty pounds of parachute, and missed the whole damned drop zone," Chancy mused. "Anything else is sport jumping."

"Many times." Boom laughed. "How can you even find St. Mere Eglise DZ, it is so small."

Chancy said, "And you had to call Batman a pussy to his face."

Boom laughed. "Scariest thing I ever did."

General Perry and Bobby laughed their heads off when Boom finished the story.

Finally, the general said he was going to nap, and Boom and Bobby parlayed to start discussing the case, and Bobby explained what part he wanted Boom to play.

When they arrived in Baghdad, it was blistering hot. A Blackhawk with an escort of two Apaches lifted off with them and carried them to command headquarters in the Green Zone.

In the lush Presidential Palace, Bobby met privately with General Perry.

He said, "Sir, I checked and found that Sergeant Ajamo is in northern Iraq, embedded with the 173rd Airborne. Can we get him transferred to an A-site up there with the Kurds?"

"Absolutely, son. Which one?"

Bobby replied, "Don't know yet, sir. I have to kind of scout around a little with Boom and find the right spot."

General Perry said, "Take the Blackhawk and escort we rode in on. Go where you need to. I'll give you clearance right now."

The general walked over to the phone and made a call, while Bobby sat back and swigged on a cold Gatorade.

General Perry said, "Arranged. Segeant Major Kittinger said he would need supplies. Either of you need help, get on the horn. Good hunting."

Bobby turned on his heels and walked to the door, his footfalls echoing off marble everywhere.

"Bobby," the general's voice boomed out, "plug the dike."

Bobby smiled and went out the door. When he walked into the hallway, Boom met him and was upset.

"Major, we have a problem already," Boom said. "There is some asshole lieutenant colonel who is some G-4 honcho and is not letting me get some supplies I need. I had it set with the E-8 I was dealing with, but this O-5 butts in. Not only that, he is wearing an SF combat patch on his right sleeve. That's what really pissed me off."

Bobby said, "What was the name?"

"Rodgers."

Bobby said, "It can't be the same guy. He is still around and is still the same rank. No way."

He thought back to an incident at Fort Bragg, North Carolina, when he was a captain. There was a Lieutenant Colonel Edwin Rodgers who commanded one of the companies in the 7th Special Forces Group, where Bobby was brought up from his A detachment in Bravo Company and worked as the acting S-2, the intelligence officer for the group, until they could fill the slot. The colonel was very boisterous and was not very well respected, telling everyone he met that his nickname was "Colonel Hardcore." In actuality, because of his overweight appearance, everyone, behind his back, referred to him as "Colonel Tightskin." In fact, it was a common joke for someone to refer to Colonel Tightskin and for another in the group to draw laughs by simply saying sarcastically, "You mean Colonel Hardcore?"

Bobby had had some childhood experience in Boy Scouts, so he was enlisted to be the scoutmaster of a Boy Scout troop that the group decided to sponsor. On the previous weekend, headed for an overnight camping trip, Bobby had had two Boy Scouts in his car and was driving through an intersection on Yadkin Road, one of the main drags through Fort Bragg. With the light turning yellow as he approached, he had to make one of those split-second decisions about slamming the brakes on or gunning the accelerator to get through the intersection before the light turned red. He chose the latter, and sure enough, he soon heard a siren and saw flashing lights in his rearview. It was a military one-quarter ton truck, never called a Jeep in the army then, which was what everyone else in civilian life called it. It had a big white banner painted on it and the letters "Military Police."

At that time, in the army, if you were an officer, you just did not get traffic tickets, period. As an officer, you were expected to set an example in all areas, and a simple ticket could significantly affect your OER, officer efficiency report, which, in turn, affected promotions and assignments.

Captain Samuels immediately went into the command sergeant major of the 7th Special Forces Group, one of the most powerful men at Fort Bragg, and said, "Top, I need your help."

"You got it, sir," the highly decorated old war horse replied. "What's up?"

Bobby related the events, and the top sergeant of Group asked the young captain to give him a few minutes.

An hour later, the sergeant major called Bobby. "Sir, you need to call the deputy provost marshal of Fort Bragg, who is a Boy Scout executive, in two days. He's TDY [temporary duty] at a training course in Fort Gordon, Georgia. He'll make the ticket go away."

Bobby was very relieved, "Top, thank you so very much. I owe you one."

"Ah bullshit, sir," the command sergeant major responded. "It's my job. Gotta take care of my troops, including our officers."

Bobby hung the phone up and thought to himself, "Were it not for Green Beret sergeants major, the defense of our country would be in major trouble." These were the nonpolitical guys, in real power, who did many things behind the scenes to make commanders and their officers and senior NCOs look good and stay out of trouble.

The problem was that Lieutenant Colonel Rodgers happened to have driven by when Bobby was being issued the ticket, so he later checked with a friend at the PMO (Provost Marshal's Office). He learned about the nature of the ticket, so he could sufficiently backstab Bobby Samuels at the appropriate time.

The time came when he could do just that, when Bobby showed up early for a command and staff meeting in the

Group conference room. The shiny table was constructed around a giant 7th Group red flash. Bobby was outside the conference room and commanding officer's office, actually in the adjutant's office, which was connected to the Old Man's. He was quite a bit early for the meeting. The good Colonel Tightskin showed up early, too, and said hello to the S-1, or adjutant, who was seated there, and he shook hands with Bobby.

Then, speaking loud enough for the Group commander to hear through the open door, he said, "Say, Captain Samuels, I heard you got a ticket for crashing a red light with kids in the car. Did they nail you for reckless operation?"

Bobby didn't respond, but instead stormed out of the room and down the steps to the second floor and his office. He walked past the S-3 sergeant major, whose desk sat at the front of the S-3 office, and he went around the corner into the S-2 office, his office. He slammed the door shut and sat at his desk, closing his eyes.

Seconds later, there was a knock on the door and Samuels growled, "Come in!"

It was Lieutenant Colonel Rodgers, apparently wanting to gloat, and rub salt in the wound. What he forgot about was the fact that Bobby had not been back from Desert Storm that long and was still filled with a lot of rage.

The senior officer said, "Hey, Captain, you didn't answer me."

Bobby smiled and softly said, "Sir, would you please close the door?"

Tightskin closed the door and turned to find himself face-to-face with Bobby Samuels. Bobby's piercing stare was enough to turn most men to Jell-O.

He spoke softly between clenched teeth, "Now it's just you and me, Colonel. If I want, I can just reach out real fast and crush your windpipe. In fact, if you move, I will. Do you believe me?"

The color left the face of the lieutenant colonel.

He meekly whispered, "Yes."

Bobby continued, "This is the U.S. Army Special Forces. We are men here, real men, not backstabbing wusses like you. Now, come with me, and if you ever try to backstab me again, I will visit you at home late at night. I'll sneak into your house and slit your fat throat and watch you bleed all over your wife's nightie. Do you believe me?"

Tightskin meekly nodded and again whispered, "Yes."

Bobby opened the door and said, "Follow me."

Samuels went up the stairs two at a time, and entered the adjutant's office, with Light Colonel Rodgers huffing and puffing trying to catch up.

Bobby said, "Got to talk with the Old Man. Urgent."

Before the S-1 could answer, Bobby was knocking on the colonel's doorjamb. The group CO, a good-looking man with close-cropped silver hair and piercing blue eyes, looked up and smiled.

He motioned. "Come on in, Captain, Colonel."

Rodgers was too shook up now, but simply followed the young captain's lead. Captain Samuels walked up to the colonel's desk, and the double-thick heels of his highly spit-shined Corcoran jump boots clicked together loudly as he snapped to attention and saluted. "Sir, Captain Samuels reports!"

The full bird colonel returned the salute and said, "Relax, gentlemen. Have a seat."

Bobby walked over to the door and closed it, saying, "With your permission, sir?"

The CO nodded, puzzled. Ed Rodgers was sweating bullets.

Bobby sat down in the chair next to the one Tightskin occupied.

The colonel said, "Okay, gentlemen, is someone going to tell me what's up?"

Bobby said, "Sir, earlier when Colonel Rodgers and I were in the S-1's office, he made a comment about me getting a ticket. Did you hear the remark, sir?"

Tightskin's face reddened.

Raising his eyebrows, the CO said, "Yes, I heard the remarks."

Bobby replied, "Colonel, with all due respect, may I request, please, that you call the PMO right away and ask if I have any tickets?"

The colonel leaned over and pushed the intercom.

The familiar voice of the command sergeant major came over the speaker. "Yes, sir?"

"Sergeant major, call PMO ASAP and find out if anybody in Group has any outstanding tickets."

"Wilco, sir," came the reply.

The colonel got up from his desk, walked to the window, and looked out. He already had tons of respect for Bobby Samuels for his actions in Desert Storm when the officer came to Group, and his actions right now were cementing it. He knew he had to be open-minded, though.

A minute later, the intercom buzzed. It was the sergeant major again.

"Yeah, Top?"

"Sir," the NCO said, "as of thirty minutes ago, only those two E-5s that got nailed for DUI last week."

"Thanks, Top," the colonel said, casting a stern eye toward Lieutenant Colonel Ed Rodger.

Bobby looked at Tightskin, saying, "As I told you, Colonel, this is SF. If we have a problem, we handle it eyeball-to-eyeball, man-to-man, sir, not like backstabbing pussies. With all due respect, sir."

The lieutenant colonel jumped to his feet and started to

speak, but he was stopped by the Group CO's sharp words. "He's right, Colonel Rodgers. We have no room in the Group, or in SF for that matter, for backstabbers. Pack your bags."

"Sir?" Rodgers said.

The commander said, "You need to be in a conventional leg unit somewhere, and I am going to arrange it. Unless you want to fight me on this?"

The dejected Colonel Tightskin said, "Yes, sir. I could use some command time in a conventional unit."

The colonel said, "Command time, my ass. I was just thinking it would be better to have some staff time in a basic training unit, or maybe AIT."

Dejectedly, Ed replied, "Whatever you say, sir. I apologize, Captain Samuels. I didn't mean to backstab you."

"Colonel," Bobby responded, "yes, you did. I would recommend, sir, that you not compound the dishonor for yourself and the officer corps by lying, too."

Rodgers looked like he was going to cry. He stormed out the door.

The colonel turned to Bobby. "Young Captain, you took a hell of a chance on how I would handle that situation."

"No, sir, I didn't," Bobby replied. "You and I are both SF. He's not."

The colonel chuckled.

Bobby and Boom went to G-4 [Supply], and sure enough, there he was, but Lieutenant Colonel Ed Rodgers was a little fatter and totally gray now. When he spotted Bobby, he looked like he had seen a ghost, but then he got a smug look on his face.

Bobby walked up to him and said, "So, you decided to spend thirty instead of twenty and screw things up a decade longer."

"Who do you think you are talking to, Major? You don't have a colonel around to protect you now." Rodgers fumed. "Who do you think you're talking to?"

"A lard ass that should have been put out to pasture years ago," Bobby replied. "If you remember our conversation from years ago, everything still applies. Now, Colonel, this sergeant major will be waited on hand and foot and given whatever he needs. Believe that, player, or I'll make you a believer."

Rodgers shook. No, he vibrated like a giant vat of Jell-O surrounding a cement mixer.

"Now see here, Samuels," he replied, red-faced, "I let you get away with that back then, but I am more experienced."

He stopped short as Bobby put his sat phone up to his ear and in seconds said, "General Perry, please. Tell him it is Major Samuels."

Rodgers's eyes opened as wide as saucers, and he put his hands up in a pleading gesture. Bobby hung up.

Fifteen minutes later, he and Boom left with supplies, with more being delivered to the helipad. Boom carried a large cardboard box.

"Major Samuels," Boom said, "you are definitely SF! That was awesome!"

Bobby ignored the compliment.

"Three-layer desert spec combat boots, all used, and in varying sizes?" Bobby said, "What is the deal with that, Boom?"

Boom grinned, hoisting the box up an inch higher. "Major, don't you always say, 'Give a sergeant a job and then don't tell him how to do it?' You'll find out when the time is right."

* * *

Bobby put on a headset and spoke to the Alpha Charlie, the aircraft commander, while they sat on board the Black-hawk waiting for the big rotors to crank up.

"There's a classified Special Forces detachment in a walled compound at the north end of As Sulaymaniyah in northeastern Iraq. That is where we are headed," Bobby said.

"Gotcha, Major," the chief warrant officer said. "You're talking about Det-Echo-Alpha?"

"Roger," Bobby replied. "You know where it is, Chief?"

The pilot said, "Affirmative, sir. We have flown support for those boys. The world's badasses. You two part of them?"

"All SF is one big dysfunctional family." Bobby grinned.

The pilot turned his head, laughing, and looked at Bobby. "Roger that, sir, but what a family. Rather try to jerk off a grizzly than mess with SF."

Bobby laughed. "Wise man. Are the marshes flooded up there?"

The aircraft commander responded, "No, sir, not too bad this time of year."

The top secret operational detachment E-A or Echo-Alpha had been added long after the invasion of Iraq and was under the leadership of one badass general in Washington, DC. It had one job: Find all foreign terrorists living in Iraq, especially al Qaeda, and execute them by the most expedient means. In fact, the letters Echo Alpha stood for quite simply "Eliminate All." The detachment was set up based on the infamous top secret Phoenix Program from Vietnam.

Set up by the CIA but manned by SF personnel, the Phoenix Program had had district coordinators all over the country. The army fought the North Vietnamese Army reg-ular troops, as well as the insurgent guerillas called the

Viet Cong, but the political arm that bossed the VC and told them where to go, who to fight, and so on was called the National Liberation Front. It was a shadow government, with a clandestine NLF hamlet chief for every governmental hamlet chief, as well as village chiefs, district chiefs, province chiefs, and so on.

Al Qaeda was now trying to set up something a little bit similar in Iraq, knowing that the foothold of a democracy there would start the ball rolling around the Middle East. The big difference was there were two types of fighters; the AQ terrorists and the martyrs. The martyrs, to the AQ, were simply fools who were used as effective weapons against the "infidels," the nonbelievers.

Martyrs would blow themselves up thinking they would go to Paradise with a carload of virgins. Using vehicles or body packs, they would simply take as many infidels with them as possible.

The standard AQ terrorist, however, would move around Iraq as much as possible, using the fools who were martyrs to help him fight, but never having a problem running if the fight was not in his favor. On the other hand, AQ terrorists were no pushovers. Most were highly trained, highly motivated warriors.

The men of Det E-A had no problem with making martyrs of as many al Qaeda as possible. Although the Ba'athists and the al Qaeda knew who Det E-A was, the American public did not.

They did not have a need to know. Usama Ibn Ajam-Vash sure knew. He was also excited when he heard Veronica's voice on the sat phone telling him that Bobby Samuels had pinpointed the saboteur, and he was a black soldier with the 101st who was a Muslim, with a deep, abiding hate for the U.S.

Sergeant Ajamo was equally excited because he had just been told by the Public Information Officer at Corps headquarters out of Baghdad that they wanted him to do an exclusive on the highly elusive top secret operational detachment Echo-Alpha headquartered at As Sulaymaniyah. This was like getting the biggest Popsicle in the world. He would take out some of America's absolute elite and would have to plan it carefully. First, he had to sweat out getting orders to travel north to the city close to the border of Iran.

He would meet that night with his al Qaeda contact in the city of Arbil. The streets were very narrow as Sam Ajamo drove them in the military HUMVEE. He wore his army uniform, but had a small white strip of cloth tied to the rearview mirror, which let terrorists know he was a spy and not to stop him, blow him up, or shoot at him.

He went into a small shop and greeted the man within. "*Asalam alukim.*"

With frightened nervous eyes, the man disappeared quickly into the back and was replaced by a narrow-faced AQ fighter with a long scar running the length of his face, starting at the hairline and running down to his chin. He wore a slung folding-stock AK and ammo belt.

"*Asalam alukim,*" he said. "*Maa asmuck?*"

Sam replied, "Usama Ibn Ajam-Vash. *Hal anta whadaka huna?*"

The terrorist said, "*Naam, anaa huna wahdii,* [Yes, I'm here alone.] Ismii Muhammad Abdul-Aziz."

Sam told him about his new assignment and was assured by Muhammad that he personally would courier the message to the head al Queda leadership in Iraq, and they would get word, by personal courier, to the Director himself, who was going back and forth between safe houses in Pakistan and Turkistan.

The sound of the UAV, the unmanned aerial vehicle, was barely audible in the distance, but its onboard digital video camera was on telephoto right now, getting good clear shots of both Usama and Muhammad.

Later, the high-resolution satellite thousands of miles overhead would pick up Usama and follow him as he drove off in his HUMVEE. An analyst for the Advanced Research Projects Agency, ARPA, in DC would watch the vehicle and record the trip, reporting all activity to the locked black ops room in the basement of the Pentagon. The hardcore general who was the commanding general of the overall top secret project that encompassed Det E-A would share his intel with General Perry and the secretary of defense (SECDEF).

The little UAV, meanwhile, would pick up Muhammad as he drove off, as well, but would not take him out with a missile. They wanted to follow him to his higher commander. He would also be watched with satellites.

11

BUCKEYE LAND

Akron, Ohio

Bo Devore looked out the window of the United Airlines jet. Down below, she saw plenty of civilization and many lakes, streams, and patches of woods dotting the countryside outside the urban areas, with large areas of cornfields in between the woods. The aircraft was on final approach into Akron-Canton Airport. She unloaded and picked up her rental car. The first thing she did was head for the Stark County Sheriff's Office to let him know she was in town working on an investigation. He was very accommodating, and she was appreciative of the simple lesson she'd learned at Bobby's elbow about respecting another cop's jurisdiction.

Less than a half hour later, she was driving down the quiet maple- and oak-lined street in Canton where the father of Usama Ibn Ajam-Vash lived. She drove by three times in the next hour, twice from one direction and once from another. She also drove around the surrounding neighborhood to pick out the spots she would use for surveillance the next day. Bo had purposely rented a dark nondescript Ford Taurus, as she knew then most people would not notice her third trip down the street, let alone her first or second.

Unfortunately, she did not know the extreme care, or maybe even paranoia, of the father of Usama Ibn Ajam-Vash, Bahiyy al Din, who went by the name of Barry Ajamo. He was up every time a car drove down his street at night, and he was peeking through a crack in his curtains when Bo drove by each time. He also noticed her looking over at his house when she drove by, so he was ready before her third go-round. Bahiyy al Din was in his car, actually a white Ford Taurus, peeking out the back window. His Smith & Wesson Model 10 was tucked into his waistband. After Bo passed the third time, he followed.

She went around the block and checked side streets, and he could, from a distance, see her always looking toward his house. Bahiyy al Din would take no chances. He would kill her.

He muttered to himself as he followed her back toward her hotel next to I-77 at the Belden Village exit, *"Maa fa'altahu kaana humqan, yaa ahira!"* ("What you did was stupid, you bitch!")

The hotel and a twin cinema movie theater shared the same parking lot, so Barry Ajamo simply pulled into one of the theater spots. Cars zipped back and forth nearby, and slightly above them on Interstate 77. She never had a clue she was followed. He waited patiently and watched as she went to her room.

Bahiyy al Din watched her window with a $1,700 pair of digital Nikon 14×40 StabilEyes binoculars. He watched one thing only, the edges of her room window. After an hour, he spotted what he was watching for, a little mist running along the edge of the window where the curtain had a break. She was in the shower. He opened his trunk and grabbed a roll of duct tape, and ran up the steps two at a time. He walked quickly to her room, placed several strips of duct tape over the edge of the window and hit it with his elbow. It broke, but the tape kept the window from shattering and crashing on the floor. He silently lowered the taped pieces into the room. He stuck his arm through the hole and reached over, unlocking the door. He went in, gun in hand.

Steam poured out of the open bathroom door, and he could hear the shower running as well. Bahiyy al Din moved forward cautiously, gun in hand, ready to fire. He stopped at the foot of the bed and cocked the gun, noticing that the shower had stopped running right then.

As quickly as that, Bo Devore stepped into the room, her right hand wrapped around the polymer plastic grip of a Glock Model 17 nine-millimeter semiautomatic, the magazine loaded with Cor-Bon copper-jacketed hollow-points, the preferred ammo of many FBI agents. She wore a white terry-cloth bathrobe. Everything turned to slow motion. He fired and hit her dead center in the chest. She flew backward, but immediately started yelling, as she put five rounds into his chest that could be covered with a one-dollar bill.

He fell to the floor dead, face-first, after bouncing off the door, with no thought of virgins when he died, only milliseconds of excruciating pain in his chest and sheer panic. He knew he was dying quickly.

Moaning in pain, Bo quickly pulled her robe off and was naked except for the black-and-white Second Chance Kevlar vest with a ceramic heart plate inserted in the center pocket. It was where his bullet had hit dead center and dropped harmlessly to the floor. The impact knocked the wind out of her and really shocked her, but she was alive. And the ceramic plate had prevented her from getting a bruise.

Bo sat on the edge of the bed, as her knees felt like rubber, and she started shaking. The phone rang, and she answered.

A voice said, "This is the front desk. We had a call that someone heard gunshots in your room."

Bo immediately said, "I am sorry. My husband and I had a big fight, and I flew here, and when I called my house, a woman answered. I was ironing and slammed your ironing board against the bathroom door a bunch of times just raging. I'll pay for a new one tomorrow if it's damaged."

"Yes, ma'am," the young man answered. "I'm sure it is okay. Sorry about your husband."

"Don't be. Good night."

"Good night, ma'am."

Bo sat back on the bed grinning at herself for her clever and immediate lie, but she was still shaky all over. She had to think.

She always wore her IIIA-rated Kevlar vest, also thanks to the sage advice of Bobby, and if she did not have time to wash it when traveling, she would do what she had just done. She would hang it in the shower while showering herself so the steam would help clean the stink out of it a little anyway. When she turned off the shower, she heard the unmistakable click of a revolver being cocked, or at least thought she had. She threw her body armor on, followed by her robe, grabbed her weapon, and stepped into the room.

Bo had to do something, so she made a pot of coffee, then pulled the card out for the Stark County sheriff. She called the number and asked the dispatcher to have the sheriff call her immediately, stating that it was an emergency.

A minute later, the phone rang. She told the sheriff what had happened and explained that they were after a saboteur, who was probably this man's son, and the last thing our country needed was for this to get splashed in the press, or anything that would enable Sam Ajamo to find out his father was dead, at least not for a while. Bo explained everything to the sheriff, and he said he and two detectives would be there in an unmarked car. Bo got dressed and then called Bobby and also told him everything that had happened.

Bobby called General Perry, who got word to the SECDEF, and the secretary of Homeland Security was also informed. Bo was the contact officer on the scene and was soon getting calls from FBI officers. One came down from Akron and two from Cleveland. Canton Police were also involved. The sheriff bravely assumed responsibility, but he was very concerned about the county getting sued if Sam was not the bad guy and found out his father had been killed, and that they had withheld the information from him.

Then one of the FBI agents from Cleveland, Pete King, took charge and said he was the ASAC on the case now. This relieved the sheriff, and Bo sat there trying to remember what ASAC meant, while three FBI agents, the sheriff, two detectives, and Bo sat around her room, with a bloody corpse on the floor waiting on the coroner to show up. One of the detectives present was from the Canton PD and the other was from the Stark County Sheriff's Office. They talked about the problems they would have if Sam was not the terrorist that Bobby thought he was.

This is where the hard-core general came in. He was a very devout Christian and even preached sometimes, but he was considered by just about everyone in SF and Specops as the ideal ass-kicking unconventional warfare commander. His exploits were legendary among Green Berets. He was briefed, and immediately put out his own classified report about Usama Ibn Ajam-Vash meeting secretly with Muhammad Abdul-Aziz, the number three man maybe in the country of Iraq for al Qaeda, and the meeting and rendezvous was all recorded by drone camera and satellite. He stated emphatically that it could not possibly be a coincidence. Usama Ibn Ajam-Vash was definitely a bad guy, if not the "bad guy." He personally called the FBI ASAC and briefed him on this, which the ASAC shared with the rest. Bo was very relieved. It even hit her in the middle of that meeting that ASAC stood for assistant special agent in charge.

Further, in a private aside to Bobby Samuels and General Perry, the general suggested that when they gave Usama his permission slip to go to As Sulaymaniyah, he would be allowed to bring one trusted Iraqi apprentice/interpreter, if he would vouch for the man. The three-star, or lieutenant general, wisely reasoned that, with that ground rule, Usama Ibn Ajam-Vash might just try to smuggle a major AQ operative in to help him, maybe even Muhammad Abdul-Aziz. Perry and Samuels loved the idea.

When the coroner arrived, he brought no assistant, and by then, the ASAC had rented the adjoining room, and less than two hours had passed since the shooting. The hotel night manager was indeed suspicious of the seemingly inordinate number of visitors at the south end of the hotel, but she still did not know what was happening. The desk clerk told her about the conversation he had had with Bo about her husband, and they reasoned that Bo might be having her own private party, and chuckled about it.

An assistant DA was called in, one all the local cops liked, and she was briefed on what happened.

She asked Bo to reenact the entire sequence of events, and the male law enforcement officers made several jokes about it, including the obvious about Bo getting in and out of the shower naked, putting on and taking off her robe and the Kevlar vest. On the other hand, when she went though exactly what happened, they all were very respectful and complimentary about the way she handled herself.

The assistant DA called a judge and requested a search warrant for the FBI, so they would not have to even mention the Patriot Act and could take the house keys from Bahiyy al Din's pocket and thoroughly search his house.

Bo asked if she could accompany the FBI officers, and they agreed, but the ASAC would not let the Stark County detective go. Then the coroner said he wanted the detective to represent him as part of his investigation. The ASAC finally relented after fifteen minutes of arguing.

It all ended when Bo Devore said, "Gentlemen, one of you is a city detective, another a county, one a sheriff, several are feds, and I am an army investigator, but we are all cops, and some of you are sounding like Crips and Bloods wearing badges, and only worried about protecting your Hood."

Her words were really directed at the FBI ASAC, but she softened her attack by attacking all. He really backed off then and got much more cooperative.

Afterward, when Bo walked out onto the second-floor outside hallway just to get some air, the sheriff followed her and said, "Captain, you ever want to leave the army, you are most welcome to move here and work in my county."

Bo gave him a handshake and a smile, thanking him.

She and the others, with the house keys from the dead bad guy, headed to his house in the unmarked car of the FBI ASAC. They went inside and started going through his things. Their biggest find seemed to be the IBM computer in his home office. They also found an assortment of weapons and cash.

12

SEND-OFF TO HELL
Iraq

In Iraq, Bobby and Boom had settled in quite well with Det E-A, and Bobby left Boom there with the team, as he had to do some more investigating, scratching his head over what Boom wanted sent right away: three large pigs.

A Chinook arrived the next morning, and Boom drove a small backhoe off the back ramp and into the top secret compound, despite the protestations of the backhoe operator.

The operator said, "Do you know what my MOS [Military Occupational Speciality] is?"

Boom said, "What is your security clearance?"

He puffed out his chest, saying, "Secret."

Boom grinned, "Sorry, this is a Top Secret installation, so you can't even go through our gate. Just stick around the Chinook, Sonny Boy. I won't be long."

The young man said, "I am a 62 Foxtrot, a heavy equipment operator, and I am the one who is authorized to operate that backhoe."

Boom said, "Sonny Boy, I am 01 Kilo Yankee Alpha, and I said to go away."

The angry troop puffed his chest out, replying, "I never heard of any such MOS. 01KYA? What MOS is that?"

Boom grinned, saying, "It means, I am the One who will Kick Your Ass, if you don't get the hell outta here now."

The backhoe operator had almost done an about-face, when he quickly turned, without a word, and headed toward the Chinook, his face bright red and his ears burning.

Boom expertly maneuvered the backhoe around the concrete barriers placed there to prevent suicide bombers from getting in to the gate with any vehicles, through the gate, past the MPs on duty, and on into the compound. He drove it to a building near the right rear of the walled detachment site. Once there, all anybody could hear was the backhoe busy at work for two hours. Then Boom appeared again heading for the gate. He drove it expertly up the cargo ramp extending down from the back of the giant twin-rotor Chinook cargo helicopter.

Next, Boom and the chopper crew chief came down the ramp pushing wheeled cages, three of them. Inside each was a pig.

The Chinook started warming up, with the backhoe operator safely on board, while Boom enlisted the aid of several team members to move the cages inside the high-walled compound.

They took the pigs to the building where Boom had knocked out the back wall and worked inside. Outside, he had driven to the closest wall and dumped many buckets of dirt and sand over the top.

The following day, several pallets of two-by-fours and flooring were brought in, as well as mortar and bricks. By this time, the members of Det E-A knew all about Boom

Kittinger, as Specops and SF is such a small, tight-knit community. Nobody was shocked, as there were, and are, so many colorful characters like him in Special Forces. In fact, several members of that team were young Boom Kittingers in the making.

Boom had the building prepared in just three days' time, and the call was made to Bobby. Bobby called General Perry; and two hours later, Sergeant Samuel Ajamo, AKA Usama Ibn Ajam-Vash, American-born al Qaeda terrorist and jihadist, was told by his 173rd Battalion commanding officer that he was being picked up the following day to go to his new assignment doing a feature story on the top secret Det E-A at As Sulaymaniyah, and he could bring one Iraqi interpreter/intern of his choosing, so long as he would personally vouch for their allegiance.

Bobby flew back into the compound that evening on a Pave Low carrying two team members, six SF-trained hard-core Kurdish Peshmerga fighters, and one handsome dark-skinned man who functioned as an advisor to the Manhunter team. He was in fact, an Israeli commando for the super secret Israeli Mist'aravim, who had been acting as secret advisors to Task Force 121 as well as Det E-A. Known for seeking out and eliminating members of Hamas for years, they now were sharing their secrets with the U.S. Specops. They had been out on a Manhunt mission.

A-Team Echo-Alpha was not a part of Task Force 121 but very similar in scope. Many reporters had heard of Gray Fox and had heard of Task Force 121, comprised of mainly Special Forces personnel and headed by Lieutenant General William Jerry Boykin, a Special Forces legend in his own right. The idea was to locate, target, and kidnap or execute Ba'athist and al Qaeda terrorists in Iraq, and immediately, the press started comparing it to the troubled Phoenix Program in the Vietnam War. The CIA-operated and CIA-backed Phoenix Program in Vietnam had targeted

and executed over forty-one thousand Vietnamese civil-
ians, with many of those being hapless victims of revenge
by someone in the Phoenix Program who had a grudge
against them.

No sooner had Task Force 121 started than the news
media got wind and started attacking it as a new Phoenix
Program with unlimited assassinations. General Jerry
Boykin, as well, was unmercifully attacked by the press,
for, God forbid, being a devout Christian and speaking his
mind.

When Task Force 121 started getting too much press
and, worse yet, congressional political attention, the CINC,
the commander in chief, called in the SECDEF, SEC-
STATE, and the national intelligence director and made a
very straightforward, unambiguous statement: "Create a
new, smaller top secret unit similar to Task Force 121, but I
want this one to be totally out of the eyesight and earshot
of the damned paparazzi. I want it to execute and kidnap
Ba'athist and AQ terrorists, and I want it to conduct cross-
border operations into Iran like MAC-V/SOG did in Vietnam, and locate it not too far from Iran. We need more
humintel there, and we need people ready to go in there
someday if need be with some damned knowledge. We
have to think ahead, gentlemen, and dammit, there better
be a need to know for this unit. The only people that should
know about this unit are the dumbass terrorists. I want the
mention of its name to terrorize them."

This was the reason Usama Ibn Ajam-Vash was so excited about going to As Sulaymaniyah. It was also the reason that Bobby had picked this particular location among
all others to take care of the saboteur. Several things would
be accomplished all at the same time.

When Sergeant Sam Ajamo flew in the next day, Bobby
was one of the team members to greet him.

Bobby was armed with a neat little package, an M4A1,

which was a sawed-off M16 rifle, with a telescoping stock that you squeezed with your hand and pulled out, used frequently by modern-day special operations forces. Replacing the forward stock of the 5.56-millimeter weapon was an M203 40-millimeter grenade launcher and, beyond that, a special vertical handle grip. On top of the deadly little rifle was a Trijicom TAO1NSN 4×32 scope. Not counting adaptions like the M203, this younger brother of the M16 was a full ten inches shorter than the weapon made popular in Vietnam, and over one pound lighter. Also, at Bobby's request, the end of the sawed-off automatic rifle sported a Surefire M4FA silencer and flash suppressor, which would cut the sound of the loud weapon firing to the noise of a man clapping his hands. It would also enable Bobby to fire at night without the big muzzle flash being so prevalent as to give away his position.

He also wore crossed Glock 17 nine-millimeters, each with eighteen-round magazines, but the team weapons genius, an E-9 with twenty-four years of SF experience, had converted both of the high-polymer plastic pistols to full automatic, or to semi, with the flip of a little lever. The Glock only has one safety, which is a tiny trigger depressor that protrudes from the center of the main trigger, so if you have a round in the chamber and catch the trigger on something, it can accidentally fire. The old weapons man did not like this for combat, so he modified Bobby's weapons with the automatic lever as well as a better safety, so he could carry it safely with "one in the pipe" and eighteen in the magazine.

Of all the nine-millimeters in the world, Bobby really preferred the Glock 17, especially for the Mideast, in that there were many less misfires and with its space age technology and high-polymer plastics throughout, it was lighter, felt more balanced than its smaller brother, the 19, and could get banged around more yet still do the job.

The only problem for Sam was that he had no idea he

was meeting Bobby, when he shook hands with the very light gray-haired, gray-bearded man in a head scarf, and dressed like an Iraqi civilian, except for the aviator sunglasses. This was especially reinforced when Bobby spoke with a bit of a French accent, one of his language fluencies, a requirement for all Special Forces personnel. The gray was something that he could easily shampoo out when ready, and he'd started growing the beard when he knew he was going to Det Echo-Alpha.

Bobby, amusing himself, walked along as Boom, who introduced himself simply as Brand K, told Sam he would show him to his new digs.

They went to the building, and Boom explained along the way, "We are eventually going to use this building for a dispensary, but it is large and well built, except we had to do a new floor and some work on the back wall. But you'll have it all to yourself, so you can write in private."

Bobby's phone rang, and he excused himself. He went outside and answered, "This is Major Samuels, sir or ma'am, and is a secure line."

"Bobby," Bo Devore said, "we got the bastards."

"Great," he replied. "What's up?"

Bo said, "We found tons of good stuff on his dad's computer with links to other cells in the U.S. Homeland is planning on hitting several home runs, and all the evidence clearly shows you have got your killer."

Bobby said, "That is super, Bo! What about keeping your shooting quiet? How long can we keep a lid on it?"

Bo said, "I don't think we can. I was talking to a DIA al Qaeda expert, and he said they've found that some of these cells check in with each other. Miss one or two preplanned calls, they split, erase files, move their G-bases, you know. You know how you're going to handle the disposition of this case?"

"Keep an eye on the news, Early Bird Brief [the Pentagon daily unclassified written briefing], the usual sources. Girl, right now, I am 007 and have a license to kill. We are going to do a favor for some of the nine-eleven victims and families who have lost sons and daughters over here," he replied enthusiastically.

Bobby returned to the house for Usama.

Boom was still showing him around and basically giving him a phony briefing on Det Echo-Alpha.

With a French accent, Bobby said, "Monsieur, *pardon-moi,* Sergeant Ajamo, you do not have an interpreter?"

Sam said, "Yes, I do have an outstanding intern and interpreter from Baghdad who is totally reliable and pro-American. He arrives tomorrow afternoon by POV [privately owned vehicle]."

Bobby said, "*Bon!* He can bunk weeth you, Sergeant. There is plenty of room, *n'est ce pas?*"

Sam said, "Yes," and tried to figure out where this old guy was from and how he'd got into SF.

He said, "Are you from Quebec?"

Bobby chuckled. "*Non,* no, Sergeant, I am from zee part of France wheech ees near zee border weeth Germany. It is called Alsace-Lorraine."

"Oh yeah," Usama replied. "I have seen it on maps. Tell me, how did you get to the U.S., and how did you get into Special Forces?"

Bobby decided to have fun lying and showing off for Boom.

He ad-libbed, "You see, may I call you Sam?"

Usama said, "Of course."

Bobby went on. "Een World War II, my papa was zee head of what do you call it, *la Resistance?*"

With his dry wit, Boom said, "The Resistance."

Bobby grinned. "*Bon!* So anyway, Papa was zee commander of all resistance forces een France. He worked closely with zee First Special Service Force."

Usama enthusiastically added, "The Devil's Brigade."

"Exactly, Sergeant," Bobby countered. "I mean, Sam. Zay were zee, um, uh, ancestors to zee Green Berets."

Usama said, "So he sent you to the U.S. to become a Green Beret?"

Bobby was really having fun now showing off for Boom. "*Non, non,* he beat the sheet out of *ma mere,* I mean my mama. Zay finally put heem in jail in Pareee. He was zere many years, because he kept getting een trouble beating zee sheet out of zee other preesoners."

Just being a smart aleck in this private joke with Bobby, Boom said, "Why?"

Bobby did not miss a beat. "Oh, hees papa before heem, my grandpapa, used to beat zee sheet out of heem. He beat the sheet out of everybody."

Boom said, "Why would he do that?"

Bobby responded, "He was just a mean son of a beetch."

Usama said, "So how did you become a Green Beret?"

Bobby said, "Oh, my mama fell in love weeth an American businessman who was een Pareee. My papa died when I was a baby."

Usama said, "Yes? What kind of businessman was he?"

Bobby replied, "He sold condoms."

Boom said, "What?"

Bobby said, "Yes, to drugstore chains. He was zee top rubber salesman for Trojans."

He knew Boom had to be fighting to keep from breaking out laughing right then. He was correct.

"So, zees was when I was much bigger, and we moved to zee United States," Bobby said. "I joined zee army and left home, because all he ever talked about was condoms. He was a very boring man."

"Was?" Boom said. "Is he dead?"

Bobby said, "He died *trois,* I mean, three years ago."

"Sorry."

Usama said, "How did he die?"

Bobby said, "He cheated on my mama, weez zee wife of his sales manager. She choked on a condom wheech came off heem, and zee poor woman died, and he was een trouble weez my mama, he lost hees job, and was so embarrassed. So, after zat he blew out hees brains."

Bobby and Boom left Usama to get settled in and returned to the main team house. The men of Det Echo-Alpha were inside laughing when the two came in, as they had watched and listened to the whole conversation on several screens in the TOC, the Tactical Operations Center, which was fifteen feet under them, and under several varying layers of reinforced concrete, PSP, perforated steel plating, and rocks, to prevent the penetration of large rockets. Boom had equipped the building with several hidden cameras and microphones.

The team looked like a bunch of Iraqi misfits. All wore neck scarves, Iraqi civilian clothing, scruffy beards, and a variety of weapons. In actuality, only one man was a sergeant first class, an E-7, and everyone else on the team was either a warrant officer who had been a senior NCO, a master sergeant, an E-9, a sergeant major, and there was one captain. One was the recipient of the Distinguished Service Cross; many had Silver Stars, Bronze Stars, and every man on the team had been awarded at least one Purple Heart for wounds received.

All but two on the team were HALO-qualified, all were SCUBA-qualified, four had master's degrees, one a Ph.D., and five had bachelor's degrees. One of the sergeant majors was also a full bird colonel in the National Guard, and in a year, when he retired, he would retire as a colonel. One of the men was also a qualified Apache helicopter pilot and could fly fixed wing, as well. Several of the men spoke Farsi, two spoke Pashtun, five spoke French, four spoke Russian, one spoke Thai, six spoke Spanish, three spoke Arabic, one spoke Swahili, one spoke Japanese, one spoke Korean, three spoke Filipino, and two spoke Mandarin Chinese.

Five of the team members were qualified snipers, one was an LPN, and three were certified EMTs. One had been in the National Guard for years and was a corporate CEO of a $710-million-per-year business, but gave it up to become a full-time warrior, after 9/11.

Det Echo-Alpha was a bit different in scope from the stereotypical military unit. But one thing they all had in common was that they were each SF. They were all Green Berets.

Even though they were all in Det Echo-Alpha and had Top Secret clearances, few on the team had a need to know, so they did not really understand what Bobby and Boom were there for, and why Ajamo was there. They would guess among themselves and knew to keep their mouths shut if Sam asked questions, or tell him lies, but they did not know what Bobby's mission was or what he was about.

As darkness settled in, several of the team members sat down to play poker at an octagonal felt-topped poker table, and two sat on bar stools at the makeshift lacquered bar, while another went around the room cleaning the fine layer of dust off everything. It was the month of May and temperatures were climbing back toward and into the hundreds and the winds were blowing a lot. Two of the men went out continually to check around the perimeter. A commo man was on his computer in the TOC commo room and also monitoring the screens from the perimeter cameras and motion sensors around the compound.

Sam Ajamo walked in the door of the team house and

was introduced around the room. Several team members grinned to themselves when they heard Bobby suddenly switch to a French accent when Sam came in.

One of the men looked to Usama, as if he could have come from his own home country, and then he opened his mouth. "Hey, Sonny, why doncha have yerself a seat thar, and pull out yer wallet? Ya play poker, doncha?"

Sam said, "Uh, yes sir, thank you. I like poker." He pulled money out and bought twenty dollars' worth of chips. What are we playing?"

The thick-accented speaker answered, "Nickel ante, no more than three raises per hand, dealer's choice, and they ain't no wild cards, unless you call low hole."

Bobby sat down. "I'll play eef zere ees no progressive ante, progressive cards weeth jacks or better."

The speaker replied, "Naw, we don't like that either. It keeps the next dealer from havin' his own damned choice."

Boom bought in also, and the game became a forum for all kinds of conversation, including many jokes.

After an hour, Bobby decided it was time to make the worm squirm and wiggle on the hook.

Bobby was taking cards and calmly said, "Say, deed you guys hear about zee big-hitter al Qaeda jihadist that just got smoked in Ohio?"

He let his glance go across the crowd, but read volumes as his eyes swept across Usama. The man was red-faced and obviously trying to restrain himself and stay calm.

One of the others said, "No, what happened?"

"Oh," Bobby said, "zere was a terrorist hiding like a sewer rat in zee town of Canton, Ohio, and he got hees cowardly ass waxed by some woman."

Bobby tried to suppress a grin and hide his glances, but he could clearly see that Usama Ibn Ajam-Vash was about ready to come unglued, untied, and undone.

Boom already knew the story, so he said he was heading

to bed, and left immediately for Usama's building. He ran inside, quickly checked the size of Usama's desert combat boots, and ran to the hidden trapdoor he had placed under the bookcase in the corner. He reached inside and pulled out several pairs of boots, finding two pairs that fit Usama, which he swapped for those of the young terrorist.

Boom then got out of there and headed toward his room. He had monitors to watch.

Usama Ibn Ajam-Vash was dying to ask questions, but he knew he had to remain cool. He wanted to jump up and run from the room, but he knew he had to sit there and pretend like he was enjoying the poker game. He was dying for someone to ask another question of the Frenchman, but he could not do it himself.

Another team member broke the ice. "So, Pierre, what was the deal on this raghead?"

Inside, Sergeant Sam Ajamo smoldered. He felt his ears burning and his face felt like he was standing in front of a roaring fire.

Bobby said, "Oh, yes, he had one of zose stupid sounding names zey have. Lessee. Eet was, ah *mais oui,* Bahiyy al Din."

Usama wanted to scream and grab a weapon and kill all these infidels. He used all his self-discipline he had been trained to use over the years. Interacting with Jewish kids in school and pretending like he did not hate them. Acting like he loved America, instead of hating it. He kept his cool.

Finally, he spoke, "How was the terrorist killed?"

Bobby said, "Oh, I guess he went after some female cop, and she smoked him real good. Four nine-millimeter rounds in the upper torso, I heard. Heard her shot group was real tight, and she had excellent placement. She turned that dude into a martyr."

One of the other team members laughed and said, "Wait

till that guy gets to Paradise and runs into Thomas Jefferson, George Washington, and Nathan Hale, and they all start beating the ever-loving shit out of him, and one of them will tell him, 'You misunderstood Mohammed, pal. He said, "forty-two Virginians," not virgins.' "

Everyone laughed uproariously, and Sergeant Ajamo tried to fake it the best he could.

Bobby continued. "I guess zey went to hees home and found *beaucoup* intelligence on hees computer about other cells in zee U.S. I sink I read he has a son somewhere. Zey want to find heem badly, I understand."

The Southerner said, "Wal, I reckon when they do, thet ole boy is gonna have his little balls in a vice."

Usama Ibn Ajam-Vash could stand it no longer.

He stood, let out a fake yawn, and said, "I am really tired and want to interview some of you tomorrow. I'm going to hit the hay. Good night."

When he put his hand on the doorknob and turned it, he was stopped by a shout from Bobby, "Hey, Ajamo!"

He turned, wondering what would be next.

Bobby was pointing and smiling, saying, "You forgot your cheeps, my friend."

Usama forced a smile and walked back to the table. He checked in his chips and forced smiles with the men, faking yawns several times.

He waved good night to all and left, and was stopped again by Bobby's yell, "Ajamo!"

He turned again, totally shook up and nerves fried beyond imagination.

Bobby smiled broadly. "Brand and I weel bring you breakfast in zee morning, and brief you on a top secret mission you can go on, if you want. We got you pairmeession to go along."

Usama thought to himself, "I will kill them on that mission, and leave a bomb here, too."

He said, "Oh, thank you very much. See you in the morning."

He left the team house and walked to his building. Bobby watched through a firing port in the door, then turned, saying, "The traitor is in his building."

One of the team members said, "Traitor?" then added, "Whoops! Never mind. Need to know."

Bobby said, "Night, guys. Big day tomorrow." He looked at the man who'd said "Whoops" and added, "The AQ terrorist in Canton, Ohio. That was his father."

He heard cries of "Oh shit! Whoa!" and similar remarks as he closed the door.

Bobby and his dad, side-by-side, dug graves, their own graves. They were so worn out when they finished, each gave the other that look that he would not give in. The Vietnamese commander, who wore traditional Arab dress, had two firing squads come out, side by side, gave them commands, while father and son stood at the foot of each grave, and they all fired, but their weapons were not loaded.

They then were in a building, and their upper arms were tied up behind their backs and they were raised up with ropes.

Bobby and his dad then slept on a concrete floor and the guards came in, in the middle of the night, and took them outside. Bobby didn't know what the hell was going, but that was the way it always was. Honey, his father, was against a large post and his arms were tied behind it. He had been beaten up a little. The commander stood there grinning, with a gold tooth shining at Bobby. He had a dog on a leash with him, and he had been drinking.

He spoke in English and said, "Honey, Bobby, you ready speak, make recording, confess you are Yankee spy?"

Bobby shook his head no. The commander grinned and walked over to Honey, and there was a pleading look Honey gave his son. Then the commander produced a straight razor from somewhere and very quickly made an incision across Honey's stomach and his intestines started to fall out. Then the commander tied a piece of parachute suspension line to the dog's tail and tied one end of Honey's intestines to it.

He fired a gun behind the dog, and it took off running, taking Honey's intestines with him, while the old Green Beret gritted his teeth.

Bobby sat up screaming, "No!"

Chest heaving, he looked all around the darkened room, eyes opened wide. He realized he had just had a nightmare. Bobby looked at his watch. It was the middle of the night, and he could not sleep. Lying there for a while, he realized that what he was going to do would send a very strong message to al Qaeda. It was very necessary. It would also protect U.S. troops and their image worldwide. Bobby decided he needed a drink and got out of bed. Wearing flip-flops, he headed toward the team house. He got there and poured out a shot of bourbon from the hidden cache. He got it almost to his lips, and a chill went down his spine. Bobby had been too busy to think about drinking much lately, but he thought about how he could not guarantee he would stop. He set it down, grabbed a pop from the refrigerator, and headed back to his building, which was shared with Boom and two others team members.

Bobby lay down and called Bo Devore. He really missed her company, and thought about how solid she was in comparison to Veronica. He told Bo to wait two hours, then have Veronica call Usama and tell him she got a heavy-duty scoop. She was to tell him that Bobby found out who the saboteur was and he was going to be killed.

He still could not sleep, and it was still a couple hours to daylight, so Bobby grabbed his toilet kit and headed to the shower room. He was surprised that the mirrors were steamed when he walked inside, then Boom emerged, a towel wrapped around his waist.

He winked at Bobby and said, "It's normal, Major. We are taking out a combatant, but he isn't shooting at us. We are warriors not murderers, so this will feel strange, but we must be SF about it."

Bobby set his jaw, saying, "We will, Boom. We will. This is a lot bigger than us."

"Aye, Lad," Boom said, "that she is."

The word "she" suddenly made Bobby think of Bo, his partner, and her classic beauty. He missed her, he realized, and wondered why he had not told her. Then he thought of Arianna and understood why.

"War sure ain't like the movies, is it?" Bobby said, walking into the shower and removing his towel.

"Sure as hell, sir," Boom replied. "I think we are stauncher peace lovers than the hippies, because we go through shit like this. I hate it."

"There's a big difference," Bobby said.

Brushing his teeth, Boom mumbled, "Watsh that?"

Bobby said, "We know, not think, that some of this has to be done to actually have peace, but we have the balls to do it."

Boom swished water in his mouth, spit it out, and said, "I know. Those love-grubbers still think we can go up to an al Qaeda fighter and hug him and give him lots of love, and he will just see the light and love us back."

Bobby said, "It pisses me off that the news will not show the nine-eleven attacks anymore. Sometimes we need reminders, so we do not get lulled back into denial."

He walked into the shower. The hot water felt good on his neck and back muscles.

* * *

Usama got out of bed when his sat phone rang, not knowing Bobby, Boom, and Sparks, the team medic, were just outside his building. Sparks held two SOFTTs, and Bobby and Boom held one each.

SOFTTs were Special Operations Force tactical tourniquets, designed for use by the Specops community. The manufacturer wanted to provide every soldier the ability to apply a tourniquet to him or herself with one hand in a matter of seconds. And they developed the most effective and reliable device of its type.

The lightweight first aid device became popular with Specops types in both Afghanistan and Iraq. The primary tightening device (windlass) was constructed of aircraft aluminum. Unlike other materials, aircraft aluminum is essentially indestructible. The zinc and black chromate steel locking buckle wouldn't rust. The catch rings were made of acetyl, an extremely durable material that withstands great temperature ranges and would not become brittle. Then the bulk of the tourniquet was made of heavyweight polypro and nylon webbing. It was made by Tactical Medical Solutions, LLC, in Raeford, North Carolina, just down the road from Fort Bragg—Highway 401, in fact, one of the main routes running through Fatalburg, as SF called Fayettteville.

Sparks said, "Boom, you sure this plan a yours'll work?"

Bobby gave him an exasperated look. He said, "Doc, how can you ask that? He is the best in the world."

Inside, Usama Ibn Ajam-Vash had no color in his face. He felt like someone had stepped on his grave. He felt sick to his stomach. In the TOC, several men were watching the monitors for the cameras Boom had emplaced around the room. The computer was recording it all.

Veronica hung up after telling him the news, and looked over at Bo Devore.

"Now what?"

Bo replied, "We'll get ahold of you when he returns from Iraq, and he will give you an exclusive interview."

She said, "About Sam Ajamo."

Bo said, "No, Bobby will tell you what you will say."

"That's not journalism." Ronnie sneered, getting arrogant again.

Bo laughed and replied, "How in the hell would you know? Wonder which network would like to cover a firing squad?"

The color drained from Veronica's face, and she began crying again, running out of the coffee shop where they had met.

Bo chuckled, as she saw Ronnie heading down the street in a hurry, and said to herself, "You hollow spineless phony bitch."

Bobby whispered, "Well, we heard the phone ring, so now he knows, and he is either preparing to blow himself and some of the guys here up, or he is making preparations to get the hell out of Dodge."

Sparks said, "Blow some of us up! What the hell, Major?"

Boom grinned. "Relax, Doc. He isn't going anywhere. Just have your tourniquets ready."

Bobby had washed the color out of his hair and shaved off his beard. He now wore desert BDUs.

Boom!

They could hear much screaming inside, and Bobby went through the door first, a Glock 17 in each hand.

Usama Ibn Ajam-Vash lay in the middle of the room screaming. Both of his feet were gone and his hands were shredded bloody flesh. The three men immediately applied the SOFTTs, and Sparks treated him to keep him from going into shock. He started to give him a morphine syrette, by plunging it into the man's thigh, but Bobby stopped him, grabbing his wrist.

He said, "No, Doc, I want him clearheaded, and I do not want him fainting on me."

The medic reached into a bag, grabbed a bottle, and poured some liquid from it onto a large nose swab.

Boom said, "What's that, Doc?"

Sparks replied, "Adrenalin 1-1000. He'll stay alert. Keep his feet elevated, Major."

Usama looked at Bobby, and did not know what to do.

"Thank God, you showed up, Major Samuels. I got attacked," he said, breathing heavily, between sobs.

Bobby smiled, saying, "Oh, I have been here all along."

Sam Ajamo said, "You have?"

Bobby grinned and switched to his Pierre voice, saying, "*Bonjour*, Sergeant Ajamo, *comment allez vous*?" He continued. "Shit, Usama Ibn Ajam-Vash, guess things aren't going too smooth for you right now."

Usama shouted, "I want an attorney!"

Boom laughed, "First of all, you won't need one, boy, where you're going. Second of all, you weren't attacked. Don't you know what happened?"

Usama said, "What?"

Boom said, "Well, those weren't exactly your boots. Your size, but the boots were modified. I had a battery inside each heel and wires running up to the top eyelet, actually the positive wire. The negative wire ran up the laces, which were made out of slightly modified det cord, so when you touched the top eyelet lacing your boots, either one, Boom. Bye-bye, hands and feet. The det cord blowing up one boot detonated the other."

"I am an American citizen! I am an American citizen!" Usama screamed in panic. "I have rights."

Bobby said, "So did all those screaming passengers in

the jets on September 11, 2001, Usama. How does it feel to be helpless and know you're going to die shortly?"

Usama's eyes opened wide in panic, and Bobby smiled, saying, "Careful, your al Qaeda brothers are going to be watching you die on tape. Don't want to be a coward, do you?"

Usama started screaming and crying.

Bobby said, "You know, Traitor, I was watching that video of Nick Berg being decapitated, and your old buddy Zarqawi literally started sawing on the back right side of the neck first, through the shoulder muscles, so he would live a few seconds longer and scream in terror knowing what was happening to him. Now, your AQ buddies can watch you die screaming."

Bobby and Boom walked over and sat in two chairs, leaving Usama lying in the middle of the room sobbing "Please?" over and over.

Boom walked over to a spot in the corner and pulled a wedge out, and the floor slowly started moving. Usama heard grunting noises immediately and smelled a foul odor.

He yelled, "What is going on?"

Boom said, "Well, you know that tower outside. Inside, I have water counterweights with fifty-five-gallon drums hanging from steel cable. It runs along a pulley system through the top of the tower, back down here, and hooks into the floor. When I want the floor to slide back into place, I just drain some water from one of the drums and it moves back. Kinda like Saddam Hussein's hidden rooms, tunnels, caves, even his little spiderhole."

"What are you doing? What are you doing to me?" Usama screamed in terror.

He could now see down into the pit below and was looking at one of the large pigs.

Bobby said, "Now you know how those people way up in the World Trade Center must have felt, the flames getting closer. Don't you boys consider pigs unclean animals? Huh? Cat got your tongue? Pretty soon it will be hogs getting your tongue."

Boom laughed, adding, "And your balls, your pecker, your guts, your arms and legs, your head. You see, boy, you decided to use explosives to murder innocent red-blooded American soldiers, and explosives did you in."

Usama voided his bowels and bladder and cried profusely as the floor kept moving sideways, disappearing under the back wall.

Bobby said, "Don't worry, Usama. We'll kill the pigs before they eat you all the way, and you'll be buried with them, dead pigs, underneath this building in this top secret compound that nobody can enter."

Usama screamed and screamed and screamed, as the floor kept moving under the far wall. He could now see all three of the hogs, as they licked his blood now dripping into the pit. He fainted.

Usama did not know how much time had elapsed, but he looked up and saw the back wall of the building looming over him. He was going to be swept into the pit. He screamed as he felt his body fall, and he saw the hogs rushing toward him. He heard grunts and felt teeth tearing into his flesh. He was being dragged through their excrement as they tugged at his flesh back and forth.

This was not how it was supposed to be. The floor was slowly sliding back closed above him. He tried to scream, but something had a ferocious grip on his mouth and nose. He was helpless, and he pictured those screaming Americans in the planes and towers and he thought of their helplessness. Suddenly there was a final snap, and he thought no more.

An hour later, Sparks, who was Hispanic and spoke very fluent Arabic, met with Muhammad Abdul-Aziz. He handed him a videotape in a clear plastic container.

Sparks said, *"Uzur ila haadha! Zurnii laahiqan! Ila al-liqaa. Yushaahid ma'a Mudiir."*

Muhammad wondered what could be so important that this man wanted him to watch it with the Director. He took off fast, though knowing something was up. He did not see the UAV several hundred feet above his car as he sped along, unaware that all Americans he got near were being told "Do not detain."

He could not take it personally to the Director, but he could take it to the head of al Qaeda for all of Iraq, his boss.

13

FINALE

The next day, in fact, they sat in front of a large screen TV in the mansion of a former Ba'athist leader who was hosting the Boss. One American had recently had his head sawed off in this man's garage. It was there that they scanned the tape and had an electric smell tester check it for explosive residue. It was clean.

Muhammad Abdul-Aziz took the tape out of the clear jacket and handed it to his boss. He put it in the machine and sat down. The first thing they saw was a slow-motion shot of Usama Ibn Ajam-Vash's hands and feet being blown off.

While they watched the tape in shock, Muhammad and his superior, the head of the al Qaeda for all of Iraq, each wondered separately why he suddenly had the strong taste of garlic in his mouths. They both wished they could get rid of their headache, and wondered why they were starting to feel queasy.

Around the world, in Washington, DC, Bobby walked up to Bo Devore, and they hugged, lingering a few extra seconds. The general's limousine waited for him, and the driver opened the back door. Veronica sat there next to General Perry. Bobby looked at her and, smiling, shook hands with the general.

Bobby said to Veronica, "Sergeant Samuel Ajamo was killed by insurgents with an IED in northern Iraq. This was all we could recover. Bobby handed her the piece of twisted coin and one of Sam's dog tags. "My investigation concluded there was no saboteur, just coincidence. That is what you will report, without using my name or any of ours. I will do a short interview with you with my face in shadow and my voice distorted."

"Yes, sir," Veronica said meekly.

Bobby put his hand on the limo door, saying, "You have your own limo, Superstar. I'll call."

She walked away, and Bobby winked at General Perry, and Bobby looked at Bo, who grabbed his upper arm.

The general pulled out three cigars, saying, "They're Cuban. You know, sometimes the good guy wins."

"With our C.I.D. unit, sir," Bobby said, "we will always win."

ABOUT THE AUTHOR

Don Bendell is the author of twenty books with over 1.5 million copies in print. He is also a former Green Beret captain and Vietnam veteran, a 1995 inductee into the International Karate Hall of Fame, former president of the Rocky Mountain chapter of the Special Forces Association, and is a member of the Special Operations Association. As an enlisted man, Don was an MP at Fort Dix, New Jersey, and in Vietnam. He was also in the top secret Phoenix Program. A cowboy, he lives on a mountain ranch with his black belt master wife, Shirley, and has four grown sons, two grown daughters, and four grandchildren.

MICHAEL HAWKE

Night Stalkers
They left no man behind at Mogadishu.
They chased the Taliban out of Afghanistan.
Now the Black Hawk pilots of the 160th
Special Operation Aviation Regiment must
locate and destroy weapons of mass
destruction smuggled into Lebanon.
And failure is not an option.
0-425-19992-4

Night Stalkers #2: Coercion
The Night Stalkers have taken prisoner one
of Al Qaeda's most prominent leaders—and
his capture sparks a bloody string of attacks
in Europe and Asia. Now, the Night Stalkers
must finish the fight they began, and stop
the devastation before it takes aim at home.
0-425-20392-1

Available wherever books are sold or at
penguin.com